A Place To Call Home

More Fiction By Amy...
Novels
A Place to Call Home
Picture Me
Whispering Vines
The Good Wine
Summer's Squall
The Devil's Fortune
Chincoteague Island Trilogy
Island of Miracles
Island of Promise
Island of Hope
Chincoteague Sunsets Trilogy
Seeking Tranquility
Seeking Sugar and Spice
Seeking Space and Time
Buffalo River Series
Desert Fire, Mountain Rain
Under the Summer Moon
Sapphires in Snow
Rescuing the Rain Man
Children's Books
Crabbing With Granddad
The Greatest Gift
A Very Loud Christmas

A Place To Call Home

By Amy Schisler

To my parents, Richard and Judy MacWilliams.
I love you.

CHAPTER ONE

After

The sun slowly rose over the horizon as Ellie watched Cassie pull a squishy banana out of the garbage and brush bits of white rice from the darkened peel.

"Look, Ellie, here's a whole banana," Cassie whispered. She tore away a torn piece of newspaper clinging to the peel, showing the previous day's date—April 13, 2013.

"It has just one bad spot on it, and I can break that off," her sister said, holding out the fruit.

A hedge enclosed the back yard, and a tall white gate separated the area from the side and front of the property, hiding the little girls as they sifted through the plastic trash cans near the rear garage door.

Ellie looked skeptically at her older sister but took the half banana she offered. She stared at it for just a second before mashing it into her mouth, almost swallowing it whole. She greedily licked her dirty fingers, gulping down the first bite of food she'd had since the afternoon before. Her golden ringlets stuck to her fingers as she tried to push the strands away from her face.

"Slow down, Ellie," Cassie told her. "If you choke, I can't go for help. And remember what Mrs. Moore used to say about eating too fast and getting a tummy ache."

Ellie nodded, wiping her mouth with her sleeve as she watched Cassie dig through the sticky rice and slimy, sauce-covered chicken and vegetables that spilled from the take-out container. Cassie sucked in her breath and held it as she once again lifted the lid off the trash can. Ellie wrinkled her nose at the stench of the trash and watched Cassie dig for their breakfast. Cassie found two pieces of pizza still wrapped in aluminum foil and set them aside. She pulled out a few more things for later before she stopped pawing through the can. Cassie looked at the pizza slices and smiled apologetically at her sister. Ellie tried not to think about where they came from.

"I'm so glad Miss Susan left early this morning, so we didn't have to wait too long to eat. I don't think she's working at home today."

Ellie listened to Cassie talk, accepting a slice of pizza but waiting for Cassie to take the first brave bite. Following her sister's lead, Ellie bit into her slice. Her mouth hurt as she chewed the hard crust, but at least the foil had kept the slice clean.

"We were lucky to find her house. I know Miss Susan will help us once we know it's okay to talk to her, and I don't think he knows we're here. How could he, right?"

Ellie frowned. Was Cassie right?

I'm scared, she thought, still unable to find her voice

"Ellie, I'm tired of doing all the talking. Why aren't you answering me?"

Ellie's eyes filled with tears, and she squeezed them shut, wishing she could answer. She wanted to talk, but her words wouldn't come.

Cassie put her arm around her sister's back. "It's okay, Ellie. Everything's going to be okay."

Ellie just nodded. She hoped Cassie was right.

Cassie looked around the yard and squinted. Ellie wondered if her sister had developed x-ray vision, like Superman in the movies, that would let her see anyone coming close to their hiding place. Ellie knew exactly who Cassie was looking for.

"If he did know, he would've been here by now. If he doesn't show up today, we'll talk to Miss Susan tomorrow."

The younger girl nodded. If Cassie said it was okay to trust this lady, then Ellie trusted her, too. Cassie always knew what to do.

***

"We have to clean up before that builder man comes to work on Miss Susan's house." Cassie rambled as she cleaned up the pieces of trash. She amazed herself at how well she was able to keep up the one-sided conversation, but she desperately wanted Ellie to talk.

"I only wish Miss Susan wasn't locking her door now." She frowned, looking through the glass windows of the cozy but inaccessible house. She talked incessantly, trying to distract her sister from their circumstances and the unappetizing food. She secured the take-out carton and set it aside. "We're going to space out the food we found this morning since we can't sneak inside for more later. Okay?"

Cassie sighed. "I guess it was my fault. I probably shouldn't have been sneaking into her house anyway. Mommy would be very disappointed in me."

Cassie wiped a tear from her eye as she looked down at her dirty hands and the grime under her once meticulously trimmed and painted fingernails. Ellie placed her own grubby little hand in Cassie's lap and intertwined her dirt-streaked fingers with her sister's. Cassie looked back toward the crawl space where they were now living, silently praying she was doing the right thing. Cassie saw Ellie glance at the crawl space and felt a tug at her conscience. She knew how much Ellie hated the dark. Cassie understood all too well her sister's thoughts of despair.

She pointed to the garden in the back corner of the yard, hoping to distract her sister from thoughts of the impending darkness. "The flowers are coming up in the garden, Ellie. See them?" Small green shoots were just starting to peek through the soil in anticipation of the coming spring. "It'll be warmer soon, you know."

Ellie only nodded.

⚬

When the sun was almost over the treetops, Ellie knew it was time to go back to their hiding place. She gazed at the yard as she took the plastic bag her sister held out to her with the few shriveled grapes laying loose in the bottom. Ellie wished she could sit on the garden bench next to the statue of Mary. Her foster mother taught her about Mary, about how she was called the 'Blessed Mother,' which made Ellie think of her own mother.

Ellie longed for Mommy. The only memories she had of her now were flashes of her mother's face in fuzzy dreams. But those images seemed to be gone, too, since she no longer had dreams. For the past few nights, she'd only had nightmares.

"Finish up, Ellie," Cassie said. Ellie knew her sister was watching the rise of the morning sun, too. "We need to get back under the house before that man gets here."

Cassie carefully re-tied the trash bag and covered the can before they wiped their hands on a used paper towel and crawled back under the house. She was careful not to drop the mostly empty jar of applesauce and plastic bag holding rejected heels of bread. She felt a chill run down her spine as she looked around the dark, cramped space. True to the nursery rhyme, April had been a wet month, and the ground in the crawl space smelled like the stinky, damp laundry their mommy sometimes used to forget about in the dryer. Sleeping on that cold, smelly, soggy ground was almost unbearable.

They were able to sneak into the unfinished room one time when Miss Susan forgot to lock the back door. Cassie looked guiltily at the blanket she 'borrowed' from the house. The girls were able to take a few apples and drink some water, and how refreshing that was. Cassie had never imagined she would be so grateful for a glass of water. Sneaking into the house that night had given them a little ray of hope, but that was gone now.

"Wipe your feet, Ellie," Cassie gently reminded her sister. "We don't want to get mud on our blanket." The little girl nodded and wiped her feet on a patch of grass before crawling into the hole. She lay down, wrapped herself in the blanket and closed her eyes.

Cassie so wished she had a toy or book or anything to help them pass the hours, and she wished they could have a real conversation. The days seemed so long with nothing to listen to but the buzz of the saw and banging of the hammer above them. And how she missed the sound of Ellie's voice, a thought she'd never had before that day a week ago.

"Let me fix your hair, Ellie. We don't want it to get too messy." Cassie crawled into the space and settled behind her sister. Ellie sat up and let her sister comb her hair with her fingers.

Cassie tried to keep Ellie's curls from getting too tangled. She knew they couldn't stay under the house for much longer. Ellie needed a mother, and Cassie wasn't sure how long she could keep being one. And though she'd never admit it to her baby sister, Cassie yearned for a mother, too. Not Mommy, of course—that was impossible now—but someone to help them out of this mess.

"I've been thinking," she told her sister hesitantly. "If Miss Susan doesn't want to help us, maybe we should try to go back home." Ellie pulled away from Cassie and looked at her in horror.

"No, Ellie, no! Not that home!" Cassie assured her, pulling her close. "Our real home, I mean. Maybe it's still there. Maybe we could figure out how to get back there and live there and have Mrs. Johnson take care of us. Remember her, Ellie? She was so nice. You liked her, didn't you?"

Ellie nodded, and Cassie pictured the elderly woman who used to watch them when Mommy was out.

Later, the sound of the power tools lulled the girls to sleep. Cassie's mind took her back to a few days before...

The Day the Nightmare Began

Cassie counted, her eyes closed.

"One hundred. Ready or not, here I come," she opened her eyes and called.

Cassie looked in all Ellie's usual hiding places—behind the living room curtains (no, they were called draperies in this house), in the hallway powder room (she had no idea why it was called that), inside the foyer closet amid fur and cashmere coats. Ellie was in none of those places. Cassie nervously swallowed and peered into her foster father's office.

"Ellie, Ellie, where are you?" She called to her sister in a hushed voice. "I saw you go downstairs, and I've looked everywhere. You'd better not be in Mr. Moore's office."

"Cassie," the housekeeper hollered. "Señor Moore es home. I am leaving."

"Si, Señora. We're just playing. Hasta mañana."

Cassie ran into the office as soon as she heard the servant's door close. She spied her sister under the desk, and Ellie giggled.

"What are you doing in here, Ellie? Do you wanna get us in trouble? We have to get out of here. You know we're not allowed..." The front door opened, causing Cassie to jump. She squeezed under the desk with Ellie.

"Do you think he'll know we're here?" Ellie whispered.

"You better hope not, Ellie. Now, shush!"

Beneath the front panel of the desk, they watched as the door to the office swung open and Mr. Moore's highly polished shoes moved nearer. They held their breath when he stopped just inches from their hiding place, their wide eyes staring at the tips of his shoes. They heard a click and then...

"Alex, we've got problems," said a familiar voice. "Reynolds just called me, and he's gone nuts. He's on his way over to your place. His wife is leaving him, and he's blaming us. He says he's not covering for us anymore. Says he's going to the press with what he knows about Cassie and Ellie and about the company. All the money in the world won't keep them from running with this story, Alex. If he talks, nobody can stop this, not even your people." Another click, and the room was quiet.

Cassie and Ellie looked at each other in alarm. Mr. Moore started to come around the desk but was stopped by a loud pounding on the front door.

"Open up, Mr. Moore," someone yelled. "If you don't let me in, I'll blow the door handle off."

Mr. Moore hesitated for a moment then started across the room toward the front hall. The girls huddled down and peeked out from under the desk. They watched him go into the foyer and both jumped when they heard a loud bang and the sound of the front door flying open. They saw shards of wood rain down in the office doorway.

Ellie started to cry, but Cassie put her arms around her and clamped one hand over Ellie's mouth.

"Don't cry, Ellie, please don't cry," she whispered to her frightened sister.

A strange voice echoed through the house. "Don't move, Mr. Moore, or I'll blow your head off."

"Okay, Eddie, take it easy. We can talk about this."

The man yelled at Mr. Moore. He was using words they weren't allowed to say or hear, and he was crying. He said his wife found out something he should've told her. He said he ripped up some checks. Cassie was confused by what he said and meant, but she tried hard to concentrate so she could remember what he was saying. He said his wife and boys were gone. What did that mean?

Mr. Moore tried to get the man to calm down, but he only got angrier. The man threatened to go to the police, but Mr. Moore said the man would be the one in jail, and his wife would be more determined than ever to leave him.

"Shut up," the man yelled. "Don't you ever talk about my wife."

Suddenly the girls saw a quick movement in the foyer. Both men were out of their line of sight through the partially open door. The girls grabbed their ears as the sound of another bang echoed through the house. Ellie started to scream, but Cassie slapped her hand back over her sister's mouth.

There was a loud scuffle in the entrance hall, another bang, and a loud thump. A rush of air blew the office door all the way open. They listened as something was dragged across the floor, and they sat frozen as the room filled with an eerie silence after the front door slammed shut. Outside, a car started, and they heard the familiar crunching sound as it rolled down the gravel driveway, but Mr. Moore never came back inside.

Cassie and Ellie waited under the desk for what seemed like hours. When they ventured out, Ellie was still shaking.

"Come on, Ellie. Let's get out of this room before he comes back." Cassie led her sister to the front hall.

When they reached the doorway, Ellie screamed at the sight of blood fanning out across the floor, running in dozens of little streams through the grooves in the marble. Ellie fainted, just missing the red sea and its many tributaries.

"Ellie, no," Cassie screamed as she lunged but failed to catch her.

CHAPTER TWO

After

Susan O'Neil hurried to the gate for the early morning flight. Her mother's voice drifted through the phone.

"You know I hate that you fly so much. Why can't you hire someone else to do all this traveling?"

"Mom," Susan started, rushing past other sleepy-eyed flyers. "I'm not getting into this again. I run a one-woman show. I can't afford to hire anyone right now, and I don't have the time to train anyone to do things the way I want them done. It's 2013, and technology consultants are crawling out of the woodwork these days. I need to make sure my clients get the specialized care they're used to, or they'll find someone else."

"I know, I know. I won't say any more, for now." Her tone, as well as her wording, implied she wasn't through with the topic. "Will Mannie be at the house today?"

"Yes, he's hoping to get the insulation started so he can move on to the sheetrock. He thinks the sunroom will be ready by summer."

"Good. Did you remember to ask him about the missing food?"

"No," Susan said, spying the gate ahead. "I don't want him to feel like I'm accusing him of anything."

"Of course not, but maybe he should be keeping an eye out for anyone suspicious."

"Mom, if someone did take the blanket and food from my house, they didn't do it when Mannie was there. But just in case, I've been double checking the doors the past couple nights."

"You should've been doing that all along. For heaven's sake, Susan, you live alone! You can't just leave the door unlocked all hours of the day and night these days. You have to be careful. Whoever took them knows you live alone."

"Mom, I'm not convinced someone was in the house. You know me, I probably shoved the blanket in a closet somewhere. But I *am* being more careful. I promise. Look, I'm at the gate. Go back to bed, and I'll call you later, okay?" Susan pushed the annoyance away. She knew her mother was right. The thought of someone in her house while she slept upstairs was alarming, but she didn't want to upset her mother. She was even thinking about installing a security system as soon as she could afford one.

"Okay," her mother responded. "Just stay safe. I love you, you know."

"I know, Mom. I love you, too." Susan sighed as she disconnected. She knew she should not have answered the phone.

<hr>

"Please turn off all electronic devices and stow them under your seat."

Susan powered down her cell phone and put it away, grateful she had time to send a few emails before the flight took off.

"Welcome aboard for our non-stop flight to Seattle. We should reach Seattle Tacoma International Airport at 10:17 AM, Pacific Time." Susan listened half-heartedly to the flight attendant as she demonstrated safety procedures. Once the flight was in the air, Susan retrieved papers from her briefcase and began going over notes for her meeting. She knew the company inside and out but wanted to refresh herself on what she was to go over with the new tech. She hadn't slept well the night before and needed to be at the top of her game.

Every so often, the Channing Tatum movie on the tiny monitor over the seat in front of her caught her attention. *If only I were a few years younger, or he were a few years older.* She smiled. The movie playing was one she'd seen before, and she was able to block it out while she worked. She'd read somewhere that some airlines were beginning to offer private screens at each seat with a selection of movies. Even in her line of work, technology always impressed her.

Six hours later, between going over her work for the week, watching the hero save the day, and even getting in a nap, Susan felt rejuvenated. Her worries about an intruder were gone. She was being ridiculous, she told herself. She was so tired the other night, she simply misplaced the blanket. Mannie—who was more than welcome to anything in her kitchen—probably forgot to tell her about eating the apples, and nobody was sneaking into her house at night. Since when had she become so paranoid anyway? Still, maybe she should get that security system. She could probably build it herself, save some money, she mused, and would please her mother.

Susan hailed a taxi and headed for her client's office, a thirty-minute ride from the airport. It was an unseasonably clear day, and Susan enjoyed the rare opportunity to see the beautiful skyline of the city as the taxi headed north on Interstate 5. Seattle was just starting to get busy as the taxi zoomed toward Blue Sky Communications at the Columbia Center downtown.

She picked up her phone and tapped on her parents' number in her Favorites list. Her father picked up the phone.

"Hi, Dad." She smiled at the sound of his voice.

"I take it you landed safely?"

"I did, and I'll be at Ed's in about ten minutes." The CEO of Blue Sky, Ed Tyler, was a dear friend of her father from his short stint in the Air Force. An older man with no children, Ed treated his Goddaughter as his own flesh and blood.

"Please give him my best," her father told her, "and have a good meeting."

"Thanks, Dad. Could you tell mom I've landed? She was in one of her worrying moods again today."

"She can't help it, Susan. You're still a little girl in her eyes."

"I know, Dad. Thanks." They said goodbye as the taxi turned onto 4th Avenue.

It was Ed who had given Susan her first big break on the West Coast when he hired her five years ago, and he had referred many new clients to her over the years. Susan always looked forward to seeing him.

She entered the building and headed for her favorite deli, which specialized in a vast variety of delectable wraps. It was still early in Seattle, but Susan's stomach told her it was time for lunch on the East Coast. She loved the deli's spinach wraps and took the time to eat one before heading to one of the building's forty-six elevators. She took another sip of water and slipped the rest of the bottle into her shoulder bag as the door opened to the Blue Sky lobby.

"Miss O'Neil is here, Mr. Tyler." Ed's secretary spoke into the phone when Susan exited the elevator.

Within a minute, Ed, still looking like he was in the military with his well-cut body and barely thinning gray hair, was coming into the lobby with his arms outstretched. "It's so good to see you, Susan," he said as all six-foot-four of him bent down to give her a kiss on her cheek. "Come in and tell me how life has been lately. How are your parents?"

"They're just fine and send their love," Susan told him. "As for my life, I've been working as hard as always."

"That doesn't surprise me at all. All work and no play. That existence must suit you, though. You look fantastic."

"Thanks, Ed. You're looking good yourself." Susan followed Ed into his office.

"I think you're going to like our new tech," Ed told her, closing the door behind him. "His name is Seth, and he's close to your age. He's a nice, grounded guy, a hard-worker."

Susan smiled. "That's great, Ed. Does he have a good tech background?"

"Depends upon how you classify 'good'." Ed chuckled. "He's more than good at tech. Had some, er, problems in high school, but that was a while ago. I think you'll find him quite capable of maintaining the network." Ed sat behind his desk.

"Problems?"

Ed sighed. "Caught hacking into the school's grading system. Got into trouble and was almost expelled, but he was completely up front with me about it. No troubles since then."

Susan sighed. "Well, he's not the first tech-savvy kid to do that."

"True. On another note, as your Godfather, I have to ask you—"

"Don't." She held up her hand.

"Is there anyone new in your life?" he continued.

"Stop, please. I'm here on real business, not personal business."

"Susan, I'd be doing your parents a disservice if I didn't keep an eye out for you. You're far too smart, too pretty, and too nice to be alone." Ed gazed at her sympathetically.

"Ed, I love you, but I'm not going to discuss this with you. At least not here, not now." Susan tried to keep the annoyance from her voice. This was a familiar topic of conversation between Ed and her parents.

Thankfully, Ed backed down.

"Okay. Okay. It's none of my business. Just go on down to the computer room and talk to Seth. I promise, you'll be pleased with him as a colleague. He's very good with computers, maybe even as good as you." Ed looked down at the papers on his desk. "I'll be in here if you need me." He waved her off and went back to work. Susan left the office and started down the hall.

Walking into the server room, she spotted Seth bent over a computer monitor.

Susan noted that Seth, as Ed said, was close to her age, minus a year or two. He was not too tall or too thin. He had auburn hair, cut short but with bangs that were combed across his forehead. With glasses perched on his nose, and he reminded Susan of Tobey Maguire's Peter Parker in the *Spider-Man* movies.

"Seth, I presume." Susan held out her hand.

"Hi. Seth Winfield." Seth took her hand with a smile. "It's nice to meet you, Susan. I'm very impressed with your work."

She appreciated his compliment. So many men acted like women couldn't possibly understand the technical aspects of computers.

"Thanks. I've heard good things about your work as well."

"I really like what you've done with the website," Seth continued, "and I think you've done a tremendous job getting these old guys into the 21st century. I know from experience that's hard to do with some of these companies that've been operating the same way for thirty-plus years."

"You're right," Susan agreed. "But, as you know, Ed is very interested in competing in today's global market."

The conversation continued as they worked. Susan liked Seth, and she admitted he was charming and showed signs of what her mother would call good breeding. From the looks of his Ralph Lauren shirt, Gucci jeans, and Prada shoes, he must have money as well, or come from money. Or maybe Ed was paying him a lot more than Susan imagined.

As they got down to work, she decided Seth not only had the same look but also the same traits as Peter Parker—smart, nerdy, and probably hiding an alter ego of his own.

A couple hours later, Seth was up to speed on the network configuration, various routers and connections, and administrative settings. They finished by updating several network drivers.

"How about a bite to eat?" Seth asked.

"Thanks," Susan said. "But I really need to tell Ed good-bye and get back to the airport. I have a 3:25 flight back to Baltimore."

"Wow. That's quite a long day. At least let me take you to the airport. I'd be happy to drive you instead of having you take a cab."

Susan took him up on his offer, but she didn't dare tell Ed, thinking back to his inappropriate question and remarks. She knew he loved her like she was his own, but still, they had to have boundaries.

The trip to the airport was nice. The sun was now hidden behind the clouds, the typical Seattle rain having moved in sometime during the day. Susan and Seth chatted on the way to the airport, conversation coming as easily as the raindrops bouncing off the car.

Seth got out of the car and walked around to open her door. "Got your boarding pass?"

"Right here." She held up her smart phone. "What did people do before airline apps?"

They laughed as he handed her the briefcase from the back seat. Seth shook her hand to tell her good-bye, a true gentleman.

Susan went through security in no time and bought a salad at an airport deli to take on the plane. She ate it after the plane took off, wishing she had bought something sweet to go with it. She looked up at the in-flight movie—a Reese Witherspoon romantic comedy. Without WIFI, there wasn't much work she could do, and she was exhausted.

Ignoring the bit of work in her briefcase she could look over without the Internet, she settled in and watched the movie. She made a promise to herself that tomorrow morning she would work twice as hard.

CHAPTER THREE

After

The next day, Susan overslept. She had gotten home close to midnight, but her internal clock usually woke her no later than seven. After hastily showering and getting dressed, she went to the kitchen to make herself a cup of tea. She filled a cup with hot water from the instant-hot faucet Mannie had installed and dropped in the tea bag. While it steeped, she stood at the counter and looked around the kitchen. The blue paint she picked out was just the right shade—it really brought out the hues in the countertop. She couldn't wait for the sunroom to be finished and was so pleased with how the house was becoming her home. She was throwing away her tea bag when she remembered what day of the week it was.

"Oh shoot," she said to herself. "I didn't put out the trash. Now I'll be even later getting started."

Mannie's wife had a doctor's appointment that morning, so there was no hope he might have knowingly put the can on the curb. Mannie was usually the one who looked out for stuff like that even though it wasn't his job. Despite Susan's meticulous work habits, she was terrible at keeping up with housework or remembering to take out the trash.

She knew she needed to develop a system for her home life that meshed with her work life.

Susan threw on her jacket and headed out the back door, hoping to get the can to the end of the driveway before the garbage truck pulled up. What she saw when she stepped outside made Susan stop in her tracks. Two small children, very dirty and unkempt, were digging through her trashcan. They stopped and stared at Susan when they saw her watching them. The older girl, looking surprised but defiant, spoke up, hiding the candy bar wrapper she held in her hand—Mannie's favorite brand.

"We were just looking for something we thought we threw in here by accident. We're real sorry if we bothered you. We'll just be leaving now."

The older child took the hand of the younger girl and started to back away. The little girl looked confused by the older child's reaction. Her blue eyes pleaded with the other's green ones.

Susan looked around for an adult. "Are you alone? Where are your parents? And don't tell me you threw something away in there. What are you really looking for?"

The children stopped, and Susan watched as the younger one yanked the other's arm as if to command her to stay. She realized what they'd been doing.

"Are you looking for food? Have you eaten anything this morning? Would you like some real breakfast?" She tried to keep her voice calm and soothing, but the questions came in a rush. Again she wondered, *Where are your parents?*

The girls didn't reply, but they looked past Susan and peered into the open door behind her.

"There's nobody else here," Susan said instinctively. "You can come in and eat. But I need to know where your parents are."

"We don't have any," the older girl said matter-of-factly, waiting for a reaction. Susan noted the defiance and realized she knew this girl somehow.

Where do I know you from? What am I missing here?

"Come on in," she told them, still at a loss as to how she could possibly know them and wondering if the girl told the truth about their parents or if they were runaways with a frantic mother looking for them. "I'll get you something to eat."

The girls hesitantly followed her through the almost-complete sunroom into the house.

"Before you eat, we need to get you cleaned up, and I have a hunch you might like to use the bathroom." The defiant one blushed and gave a slight nod.

Susan led them to the small half bath off the family room.

"I'll start breakfast while you girls wash your hands and faces and go to the bathroom," she told them as she closed the door.

Susan kept an eye on the bathroom door as she quickly straightened the throw she'd haphazardly tossed on the back of the couch and took a dirty glass—no telling how long it had been sitting on the end table—to the kitchen. There, she pulled out everything she could think of that would make a healthy breakfast—fresh fruit, pancake mix, eggs, milk, and orange juice. If Mannie hadn't been a juice drinker, she never would've had that in the house. Heck, she was lucky she had fresh food of any kind. She rarely took the time—when she had it—to cook for herself. She examined the grapes and decided they were passable.

As she gathered the ingredients, she tried to place the face and voice of the older girl. She was taking a bowl from the cabinet when she heard the bathroom door open followed by their light footsteps.

"You actually look like humans now." She smiled when they walked into the room. They still needed their hair and clothes washed, but they looked cleaner. Susan motioned to the table, and they walked toward it, clutching each other's hands. As they sat, realization dawned on her, and Susan tried to hide her recognition.

"Why don't you two have a seat?" She held up the milk and juice, watching Cassie carefully—she remembered her name and how smart she was at the camp Susan helped with the past summer. "Which would you like?" Susan wasn't sure how to handle this situation.

"Juice, please," Cassie said as she sat in the chair.

Did she seek me out, or does she not recognize me?

"What would you like?" Susan asked the little blonde-haired girl. Ellie pointed to the milk.

She seems very shy, not at all like her sister.

Susan took out two small juice glasses and filled them. "Would you like pancakes or eggs?"

"Pancakes, please," Cassie replied, using perfect manners. Susan was not surprised. She remembered who Cassie's foster parents were. She also knew a lack of manners was not tolerated at the elite private school they attended and where Susan had volunteered to teach computer classes at the school's educational camp.

The younger girl looked around the kitchen at the white cabinets, marble counters, and blue walls. Susan watched as she got up and walked over to the hutch, lightly fingering some of the teacups that hung from tiny hooks in neat rows on the underside of the shelves. She walked back to the table and ran her hand across the tablecloth with its bright yellow daisies and blue trim. Sitting back down, she took a sip from her glass. Susan wondered what she was thinking.

After flipping the pancakes, Susan placed a bowl of grapes on the table. She gave each girl a pancake and helped them with the butter and syrup. She poured a bowl of her usual cereal, added a sliced, almost too-soft banana, and sat at the table. She ate her own breakfast and watched the girls gobble down every bite of theirs.

Susan wondered what on earth they were doing there. Cassie's light brown hair looked like it hadn't been combed for days. Her green eyes, which Susan remembered as bright and inquisitive, were lifeless and wary. She used her best table manners, but she appeared to be starving.

Cassie's sister—*Do I know her name?*—had blonde curls that fell around her face hiding her pale blue eyes. Her chubby cheeks reminded Susan of those pictures of little cherubs. Susan compared their features. They had the same mouth and chin and looked very much alike except for the hair and eye coloring. Susan remembered seeing them both at the school, but only Cassie was in her program.

She waited until they were finished eating to say anything.

"Now, how about you tell me what you're doing here, *Cassie.*" Susan watched for a reaction. She casually ran her fingers around the rim of her teacup, one of many she had started collecting as a teenager.

The girls looked at each other before the older one spoke. "I wasn't sure you remembered me," Cassie said quietly.

"Well, I'll admit, it took a little while." Susan leaned back in her chair. "You look different without your school uniform."

Cassie didn't react.

"Well?" Susan continued after a moment of silence. "Are you going to tell me what's going on?"

Cassie shook her head and slouched in her chair while letting out a defeated sigh. "I can't do that, Miss Susan. I'm sorry. I can only tell you we ran away and we're never going back. We were going to come to tell you, but you saw us before we were ready." Tears threatened, but she wiped the back of her hand across her eyes.

"Cassie, sweetie, whatever happened at home can't be that bad. Why don't you let me call your mom and—"

"We don't have a mom," she cried. "Our mom's gone."

"I'm sorry, Cassie, I wasn't thinking. Let me call your foster mother."

"No!" Tears cascaded down Cassie's cheek as she pleaded with Susan. "Please don't call her, Miss Susan. Please. Nobody can know we're here."

Susan wasn't sure what to say. She waited a few minutes before asking another question.

"Refresh my memory. How old are you girls?"

"I'm eight, and Ellie is five," Cassie answered. She did all the talking.

Had Cassie ever mentioned her sister was deaf or didn't speak?

Susan didn't remember hearing anything to that effect, but perhaps that was because it was natural to Cassie and didn't come into normal conversation.

"How long have you been hiding out there?" She pointed to the back yard. Cassie shrugged but wrinkled her brow in thought.

"A few days," she said, still looking unsure. "What day is today?"

"It's Tuesday."

Cassie thought again. "Um, I think we left the Moores' on Wednesday, or maybe Thursday. I'm not sure. I can't remember. Are there any more grapes?" She grabbed the bowl and nervously started scraping bits of fruit from the bottom.

Susan stood up and took a fresh apple from a basket. She silently washed it, handed it to Cassie, and sat.

Wednesday or Thursday? They've been out there for almost a week in this cold?

Susan was horrified but tried not to show it. What were they hiding, and more importantly, *why* were they hiding?

Susan looked at the girls, trying to get a sense of what they were thinking. They seemed frightened, but she wasn't sure if they feared her reaction or something at home.

"Are either of you hurt or has someone done something to you? Did anyone ever hit you or touch you in a way that made you uncomfortable?"

Cassie didn't answer right away. She swallowed and slowly shook her head. "No, nothing like that."

Susan wondered how she could get her to talk.

"Where did you sleep when you were out back?"

Cassie looked down and didn't say anything. Ellie looked away, but Susan saw a small tear roll down her cheek. After a moment, Cassie spoke up.

"We've been hiding under the house in that little space where the pipes are. The man working out there uses lots of things that make noise, so he never hears us. It's not as cold now that the snow is gone, and we stay smushed together to keep warm."

Cassie turned bright red as she rushed on. "And one night when you went to bed without locking the door, I sneaked in and took some apples and a blanket you left on the couch." Cassie's words tumbled from her mouth. "We were really hungry, and we were gonna put the blanket back, we promise. But it helps us stay warm at night, and the ground is awfully cold and hard under there..." She lifted her eyes toward Susan as her story hung in the air between them, then shifted her gaze.

The mystery of the missing blanket and apples was now solved.

Susan followed Cassie's gaze as she watched a hummingbird hover at the feeder hanging just outside the window.

"Do you like birds?" She motioned to the hovering bird. Cassie shrugged.

"When I was little, I loved to go to the park near the post office and feed the birds. Have you ever done that?"

Cassie shook her head. "I've never fed the birds," she said after a minute, "but I've seen other people do it. I like to play on the swings."

"Me, too," Susan said, hoping she might be getting somewhere. "Do you like sliding boards, too?"

She nodded. "I like the red curvy one, but it scares Ellie." Ellie's curls bounced as she bobbed her head. "She likes the yellow one."

"I'm with Ellie." Susan smiled. "Did you go there a lot?"

"Sometimes," Cassie replied.

"It sounds like you had fun with Mr. and Mrs. Moore," Susan said cautiously.

Cassie shrugged. "Mrs. Moore was all right, I guess. We mostly went with Señora."

"Señora?"

Cassie shrugged. "She works for Mrs. Moore."

Susan gave a quick nod. "Are you finished with your apple?"

Cassie looked down at the half-eaten fruit, brow furrowed, as if she'd forgotten she had it. "Yes, ma'am," she said, handing the apple to Susan and wiping her face with the napkin she took from her lap.

"Okay," Susan said after stacking the girls' plates and her own bowl. "If you won't tell me why you ran away or what you're doing here, I have no choice but to call Mrs. Moore and take you home." She started to stand.

"No!" Cassie yelled and jumped from her seat. She grabbed Ellie, pulling her out of the chair and toward the door. "You can't do that! Don't you understand? We can't go back there. Can't we just stay here? You don't have to tell anybody. I trusted you, Miss Susan." Cassie begged, her voice in agony, tears welling in her eyes.

"Cassie, calm down." Susan moved quickly toward the door and blocked their exit. She tried to think of a way to convince Cassie everything would be okay. "I really think we need to let someone know you're both okay. There must be somebody I can call."

"There isn't. Don't you understand? They can't find out where we are." Cassie's imploring eyes never wavered from Susan's.

Susan thought about it for a moment. She didn't know what to do, but maybe her mother would have an idea. She should probably call the police or social services, but her gut told her to wait for now. Something terrified Cassie, and Susan suspected it had something to do with their foster parents.

"Okay, you can stay for a today, but just so I can figure out what to do."

Cassie nodded.

"So, who wants to take a nice, warm bath?"

Once the girls were in the bathtub, Susan threw their clothes into the washer and debated whether she should leave them alone. She didn't know anything about children. Were they safe in the bath alone?

Well, they have been living alone under my house for almost a week.

She went to her office in the next room and turned on the computer. There were no Amber Alerts issued for Cassie and Ellie, nor was there anything about their disappearance in the news. She performed a few searches but saw no headlines about the girls or their foster parents, at least not in relation to anything that seemed pertinent.

One search did give her a picture from the community events page from the previous summer. The caption read:

Alex Moore, Chief of Staff to the Mayor of Baltimore, and his wife, Penny, attended the dedication of the new Harbor Playground with their foster children.

They look like a happy family. Why on earth would the girls run away? Cassie was always cheerful in class. What changed?

After checking on the girls, who were smiling and washing each other's hair, Susan called her mother. She told her about the unbelievable events of the morning.

"What are you going to do?"

"I don't know what to do. I guess I should find a way to contact the Moores. The thing is, the girls seem genuinely terrified to go back there." Susan talked as she tossed her clothes from day before into the hamper.

"Maybe you should look into the situation first," her mother suggested. "If there's one thing I've learned over the years, things are not always what they seem in many families, particularly foster families."

"I wonder..." Susan began. "If I went to the police, do you think they'd just take the girls away, or would they investigate the family first? What would you have done if this happened at school when you were the principal?"

"Well, that was some time ago, and we were required to call the authorities. I've seen many cases where the law wasn't always on the side of the children, but things are different these days." She seemed lost in thought for a moment and then said, "Why don't you ask Jim?"

"Jim?"

"Yes, Jim. You know, he's the department's lead detective now."

"Yeah, but, um, do you think he'd be willing to help?"

"I would guess so. It's worth a try. He could at least advise you as to what to do with the girls." Her mother paused. "Are you going to take them with you?"

"Could I bring them to you, Mom? I'm afraid they'll freak out when I pull up in front of the police station."

"Well…" Her mother hesitated. "Oh, all right. Go ahead and bring them here if you like. I'll look after them for a bit." She couldn't hide the disapproval in her voice.

"Thanks, Mom." Susan put the phone on speaker so she could pull her hair into a ponytail. She lowered her voice and leaned toward the phone. "One other thing. Ellie has yet to talk. I don't know why. Maybe you can get something out of her."

"I'll try," her mother said, her voice a blend of emotions.

Susan quickly tapped the audio button on the phone and held it to her ear. "I hear them getting out of the tub. Let me go put their clothes in the dryer so I can get them ready. We'll be there as soon as the clothes are dry."

She disconnected the call and said a quick prayer she was doing the right thing.

⊰⊱

Ninety minutes later, they arrived at her mother's house. The girls seemed mesmerized by the house as soon as they pulled into the driveway. The treehouse and swing set in the backyard were visible from the car, and Susan couldn't remember a time they hadn't been there. Her parents, Ida and Patrick, refused to get rid of them even though she hadn't used them in twenty years. Her father continued to keep them up, and Mannie's kids used them on occasion when Susan's mother watched them.

A white picket fence surrounded the yard. Susan's mother stood on the front porch, ready to greet them with a wide smile and open arms. Susan could read the girls' thoughts. This was every child's dream of the perfect arrival at Grandmother's house.

"She looks nice," Cassie said approvingly.

"She is nice." Susan smiled at the girls in the rearview mirror. "I promise, you'll like her, and you'll have fun."

She turned off the car and turned around. "Are you ready?" They nodded without a word, and Susan opened the back door for them and led them up the walkway. Cassie looked around, eyes wide, as if expecting someone to jump out and grab them.

"Come on in." Susan's mom welcomed them with a smile and open arms as Cassie and Ellie hesitated in the doorway.

Susan coaxed them through the foyer and into the living room. Cassie looked at the pictures of Susan at every age on the walls and bookshelves. The pictures told the story of a family who loved each other very much. Susan and her dad surf fishing, she and her mother at Susan's college graduation, an eight-year-old Susan in her First Communion dress and veil. Pictures of all of them with friends or relatives were displayed around the room.

"Where are their shoes?" her mother whispered as they watched the girls looking around.

"They didn't have any," Susan told her. "They must have left the house without them. I checked under the house before we left, but they don't have anything other than the clothes on their backs. It's a miracle they don't have frostbite or pneumonia."

Ida shook her head. "I wonder what happened."

"Maybe you can get more out of them," Susan said.

"Is this you?" Cassie pointed to a picture of Susan when she was the same age as Cassie. She had long, dark braids and glasses and was sitting on the swing set next to Jim, his curly hair blowing in the breeze.

Susan walked over and picked up the picture. "Yes, it is." She looked at Jim rather than herself and hoped her mother was right about going to him for help.

"You were so close," Ida said, coming up behind her. "I'm sure he will help."

"How do you always know what I'm thinking?" Susan asked.

"Not always," her mother said.

Susan knew her mother still wondered why she and Jim suddenly stopped being friends. Susan couldn't tell her because she didn't know the answer herself.

CHAPTER FOUR

After

Susan was directed to an office down the hall from the registration desk at the town police office. She could hear expletives as she neared the office of the lead detective. She rolled her eyes. Obviously Jim's computer abilities, or lack thereof, hadn't changed since high school.

Neither had his looks, Susan thought as she stood in the doorway. He jabbed buttons on his computer and continued to curse the 'machine.'

Her gaze swept the office. It was cluttered with paperwork, but somehow didn't look messy. What was the phrase? Organized chaos? Above Jim's desk was a picture of him with his father. Jim was holding a certificate or award of some sort. Susan couldn't see what it said, but he smiled broadly, and his father wore a proud grin. Susan had never seen Jim's hair short as in the photo, and she liked it, but she was happy to see he'd grown back his curls. The picture showed someone very different from the boy Susan knew, and she wondered about the man behind the desk. Who was he now?

She scanned the room for clues about Jim's life. They lived in a small town, so she knew he wasn't married.

He dated, but like Susan's own dating life, nothing ever seemed serious. She didn't see any photos on his desk. In fact, other than the picture of his father, there were no personal touches in the office at all.

"Susan? Is that you?"

Susan lowered her gaze and caught her breath. He was even better looking than he used to be, and she couldn't help but notice his blue eyes were just as beautiful as she remembered. She pulled herself together and smiled.

"Hi, Jim."

When he stood, Susan took him in. Unlike the picture on the wall, and more like the boy she knew, Jim wore his dark blonde hair beneath his collar, the curls framing his handsome, sun-kissed face. He was still tall and lean, but not skinny. He'd filled out nicely with muscled arms and a broad chest, and she pictured the high school quarterback he'd been when she'd known him, just beginning to develop a man's body. He wasn't wearing a uniform, and he looked just right in his buttoned-down shirt and jeans. She could still see him in similar clothes, a little dirtier maybe, sitting on a tractor, wearing an Orioles ball cap. But that was years ago when he worked at a local farm on weekends. Susan thought back to how some of the girls from school would drive by the farm just to see him sitting there, his biceps bulging out from his sleeves. Secretly, Susan was one of them.

"Are you okay? Your parents?"

"Yes, thank you. I'm fine, and they're fine. But I need your help with something."

"Sure, anything," Jim said, gesturing to a chair loaded with files. "Just let me get these things out of your way and find something to write with. Gosh, it's been years. What have you been up to?" Jim moved the pile of papers and went back around the desk. He rooted through his drawer and triumphantly yanked out a pen.

"I have my own computer consulting company, O'Neil Technology. I do a lot of traveling." Susan tried to keep her voice steady as she took a seat.

"I'm not surprised. You were always a real computer whiz."

She frowned. *You mean, 'computer nerd.' Isn't that what your friends called me behind my back?*

Susan shook the frown away and gestured toward his monitor. "I see you're quite the computer whiz yourself." Her eyes twinkled as her mouth twitched into a grin.

Jim laughed. "I'm getting there, slowly. Every darn thing is done on the computer these days whether I like it or not." He took a seat at his desk, shaking his head and chuckling. "Now, what can I do for you? Please say you aren't here to sell me one of those fancy iPad things. I can only handle one machine at a time."

They both laughed, but Jim's expression turned serious as Susan relayed the amazing events of the morning. She watched his eyes widen when she told him the girls had been sleeping under her house and eating out of the garbage.

"So, you just found these kids picking through your trash?" he asked her incredulously.

"Mm-hmm," she said, "and they won't tell me anything except they ran away from their foster parents and can never go back."

"They won't tell you why?" He squinted with a look of disbelief.

"No, they won't." Susan answered with defiance although she knew Jim's disbelief wasn't directed at her. Even she knew the story sounded ludicrous.

"I don't have much experience with kids," he began, "but I do know they're prone to lie when it suits their purposes. Are you sure they're not putting you on?"

"Why would they be eating out of the trashcan if they didn't have to?"

Jim considered her question for a moment. "I don't know. It just seems so unreal." He blinked as he leaned back in his seat.

"I know, and that's why I came to you. I'm not sure what to do. Should I call their foster parents and let them know the girls are okay? Or should you look into whether something may have happened with them?"

"Since they're foster children, we need to call Social Services." He put his pen down and reached for the phone. "I have some contacts there. I can call—"

"Wait," Susan snapped, leaning across the desk, putting her hand on his. "Are you sure that's the right thing to do? I mean, they really don't want to go back to the foster parents. Will Social Services find out why, or will they just send them back? What if these girls are being abused in some way?"

The implication hung in the air between them.

⸺◆⸺

Jim slowly moved his arm away from Susan's grasp and sat back. He looked at her for a moment. She'd always been able to take control of any situation. Obviously, that hadn't changed.

She was just as beautiful as he remembered. Her long, dark hair was pulled back behind her head, and Jim tried to recall if there was ever a time she just let it hang down. Not to his memory, and they'd known each other their whole lives. He used to wonder what it would feel like to run his fingers through it.

He shifted his focus to her face. Susan's hazel eyes, without glasses these days, changed colors with each passing minute. He always liked how they reflected whatever emotion she felt.

He blinked and forced himself to concentrate on Susan's words rather than her modestly beautiful features. He used to have the same problem when they had class together.

"So, do you know who their foster parents are?" He picked up his pen again, ready to take more notes.

"Yes, although we've never actually met. A servant, or maybe a nanny, always picked them up from camp."

Jim raised his brow. "Really? Who are these people?"

"Get this," she said, lowering her voice. "Cassie and Ellie's foster parents are Penny and Alex Moore, Mayor Simpson's chief of staff."

Jim blinked in genuine surprise. "Alex Moore?" He, too, kept his voice low as he leaned conspiratorially across the desk toward Susan.

"Yes. Do you think we should contact them?"

"Not yet," Jim said, keeping his voice steady. "First, I want to check into missing persons reports and see if anything is officially documented. If so, I'll have to let Social Services know they're okay. They're going to want to move them into an approved home or facility if there's evidence they're not safe at the house."

Susan held up her hand. "Absolutely not. They trust me. I can't just hand them over to someone else."

Jim shook his head. "It doesn't work that way, Susan."

"It has to. I don't care what strings you have to pull. They need to stay with me."

Jim sighed. "I can try, but I don't think it will happen."

"Then you can't tell Social Services. I mean it, Jim. I won't do that to Cassie and Ellie."

Nothing about her had changed. She was just as stubborn as always, trying to talk him into some crazy scheme that brilliant mind of hers had concocted.

He relented, but he had his own reasons for doing so. "Okay. Let's see what we can find out about the Moores and go from there."

Susan nodded. "I already checked online, and there's no mention of the girls being missing."

Jim smiled. "I should've known you would've already looked into that."

She smiled back, but it was forced. "You know me," she shrugged.

Jim forced a smile, his mind going haywire. *More than you know.*

———— ⋄ ————

Susan reached down to retrieve her purse and stood. "When should I expect to hear back from you?"

"Soon," he replied. "We can't sit on this for long. We need to follow the law, even if you don't like what it says." He gave her a leveled stare that told her that he would be following the book on this one. Her heart started to sink. Then he winked at her. Nothing else, just a wink, then back to business. The meaning was not lost on Susan. It had been their signal for years—*I've got your back*, he was telling her.

"Thank you, Jim. Thank you so much." She reached across the desk to shake his hand. He stood and reached for hers. It felt awkward to be shaking hands when they had once been best friends. They held each other's hands for a moment longer than necessary, and Susan felt a strange need to hold on.

"Well, thank you again," she said nervously as she let go and turned to leave. Something stopped her, and she turned back to Jim. "Can I ask you a question?"

"Sure, what is it?"

She grinned and nodded toward the picture. "Did your dad finally catch you with his razor?"

Jim laughed. "I guess you could say that. I had to cut it for the academy."

"And now?"

"One of the perks of being a detective." His dimples caved on each side of his mouth the way she remembered. "I get to look however I want."

Susan laughed and shook her head. Jim hadn't changed a bit.

"I'll let you get back to work," she told him, not quite ready to leave but knowing they each had many other responsibilities to attend to.

"I'll be in touch as soon as I know something." Jim walked back around the desk and led her to the door. "Just get back to those girls and take care of them while I see what I can dig up."

Susan impulsively pulled him into a friendly hug. "Thanks, Jim." Awkwardness gone, she released him, smiled, and left.

As Jim watched her go, a knot formed in the pit of his stomach. He wasn't sure if the feeling had something to do with Susan or the information she'd just given him. He hadn't seen her in years except in passing, and he often looked the other way, pretending he hadn't seen her at all. She hadn't changed. She was the same girl whose braids he used to tie in knots, who fell off his skateboard in fifth grade, who he kissed on her front porch swing at the tender age of fourteen and never had the guts to look in the eye again.

Now she had come to him for help and to ask him to investigate Alex Moore. He could hardly believe that *her* Alex Moore was *his* Alex Moore, the Chief of Staff to the Mayor of Baltimore, but he knew there was no other. What she didn't know was that she and those girls could be in much more danger than she ever imagined.

"I'm calling Social Services today," Penny warned her husband. "Cassie and Ellie have been gone for a week, and I'm not waiting another minute."

"You can't call them, Penny," said Alex, visibly fighting to keep his anger under control. "I've told you, if they find out the girls aren't here, they'll have the police out looking for them. They'll issue an Amber Alert, and their faces will be plastered all over the country. They'll be scared to death."

"Alex, that's a good thing! We need an Amber Alert! If you won't let me go directly to the police, I'll go to Social Services myself." She pleaded as tears formed in the corners of her eyes. What was wrong with him? "Don't you understand? They could be kidnapped, lost, or dead!"

"No!" Alex roared, displaying disgust at her despair. He pushed her away vigorously, sending her flying to the living room floor. "I told you, we're not reporting them missing! I have all the resources I need to find them. I'll keep looking. Do you want Social Services to take away your precious little children? Do you want to be left with no children at all? Let me find them and bring them back myself. And stop that sniveling. What happened to the strong, confident woman I married?"

Penny glared at Alex as he marched to his office and slammed the door. She pulled herself up from the Oriental rug and wiped her tears.

You happened, she thought to herself. *You stripped away every bit of strength and confidence I ever had, but that ends now.*

She sat on the expensive leather sofa, trying to think of what to do.

I'm going to find a way to get my life back, starting with getting my children back.

She was afraid of her husband, and with good cause, but she was still strong and would use that strength to get herself out of this situation. She had a plan, and she was ready to put it into action. Alex was a powerful man, and there was no end to what he would do to keep it that way. To everyone who knew him, he was God's gift to Maryland, or at least to the city of Baltimore. She looked around at the pictures of Alex with the mayor, with former presidents and dignitaries, as well as local businessmen.

She was aware Alex was involved in illegal doings, but she never questioned him or let on that she knew. She didn't want him to think she had any interest in what he did. She wouldn't give him a reason to 'dispose' of her, as they always did in the old movies she watched at night when she couldn't sleep.

Penny realized she'd been blinded by his charm and often wondered why he married her. Had he really been a friend of her late husband, or had Alex just used Joe like he had everyone else? Joe, her first husband, had introduced Penny and Alex years earlier at a political fundraiser, but she'd never had any personal dealings with Alex until after Joe's death.

Well, this time Alex had gone too far. What was he afraid of? Why couldn't they go to the police? Why wouldn't he talk to Social Services? What was he not telling her about Cassie and Ellie? She needed to get into his files again. The truth had to be there somewhere, and maybe a clue as to where the girls had gone.

Penny married Alex so she could have children. When she realized it wasn't going to happen, it took years for her to convince him to adopt. Now, her very reason for existing was gone. She was going to get her girls back on her own. She was going to go to Social Services whether Alex liked it or not. After that, she would find a way to expose everything he was involved in. All those nights watching Bogart as Philip Marlow, Jack Nicholson as J.J. Gittes, and William Powell and Myrna Loy as Nick and Nora

Charles were about to pay off. She had been doing some detective work of her own, and it was almost time to use the information she had.

Susan headed back home, grateful to her mother for sending her to Jim. She commanded her phone to call her mother, and the sound of the her voice flowed from the car speakers.

"Hi, Mom, it's me. How are Cassie and Ellie?"

"They're fine. We're really having a great day, and you're right. They are wonderful children."

"Has Ellie talked yet?" Susan asked hopefully.

"No, and I don't think she will," Ida said. "I think she should see a psychologist. I can contact someone if you want."

"Thanks, Mom. Let's wait and see what happens, okay?"

"Sure. How did it go on your end? Did you see Jim? What did he suggest?"

"There's not much to tell. Jim's going to try to find out more and call me back."

"Okay. Are you on your way here?"

"Actually, I was hoping you could watch the girls for the rest of the day. I've got work to get done, and I thought I'd get them some clothes and shoes."

"Sure, they can stay as long as you need them to. Oh, Susan, I had a thought. Ellie is very small, and she's only five. She should be in a car seat. I know they aren't cheap, but you really shouldn't be driving her around without one."

"You're right, Mom. I'll figure something out."

Susan thanked her mother and hung up, grateful she would have time to take care of some things. In addition to catching up on her business, Susan was anxious to do some research.

She drove through the town toward her house. Lakespring was a small town, but large enough to have everything its citizens needed. Susan passed the town office, the library, and the park, complete with two baseball diamonds and a regulation soccer field. Susan smiled at the group of people being led down the sidewalk on a walking tour conducted by the town's historical society. Having been established just before the Revolutionary War, there was a lot of history in this old town.

Susan drove past the elementary school where her mother worked for many years. The high school was on the other side of town, close to her parents' house. Many old, Colonial era houses and shops filled the narrow streets of the little town. While close to metropolitan Baltimore but surrounded by family-owned farms, Lakespring had managed to keep its small-town flavor, a trait being stripped away from many towns in the Old Line State.

As Susan pulled into her driveway, she thought again about how lucky she was to live here. Sometimes, she still couldn't believe her good fortune in getting this quaint Cape Cod in one of the loveliest parts of town.

When her accountant suggested it was time to purchase a home and set up a home office for tax purposes, Susan dreaded the thought of time lost looking for a house. During one of her daily conversations with her mom, Susan asked her to keep an ear out for anyone wanting to sell. Susan was shocked to hear back from her mother the very next day regarding this potential buy. Ida's best friend, Mattie, was moving to Florida and loved the idea of Susan purchasing her home.

Susan walked into the house and recalled hiring Mannie Hernandez, at Mattie's recommendation, to update the house. Mannie was a hard worker, and Susan was thrilled with all the work he had done. She and her parents became close to Mannie and his wife, Gina. When Gina was diagnosed with cancer, Susan and Ida pitched in to help. Ida cooked meals for their family and drove Gina to many appointments. Thanks to Susan's project, Mannie was able to work and provide for his family. If they were out of school for some reason, Susan's mom insisted Mannie bring the smaller ones to her house so Gina could rest and Mannie could work.

When she wasn't traveling or sitting behind her computer, Susan spent every spare moment painting, wallpapering, and working from her kitchen table. After just a couple months, she now had the existing first floor rooms just the way she wanted them, and the new sunroom was well underway.

She went to the under-construction room and smiled. The addition was completely walled and under roof, and the sheetrock was going up this week with the help of Mannie's nephew, José.

How had Cassie and Ellie managed to stay hidden under the house all day when Mannie was here?

Susan walked outside and peered under the house, wondering what it must have been like for Cassie and Ellie. She shivered, knowing it was freezing in the dark, damp space.

She went back inside and made a cup of tea. She sent a quick text to her best friend, asking about a car seat, then settled down with her laptop. She needed to take care of business, but after that, she planned to find out as much as she could about Mr. and Mrs. Alex Moore and their foster children.

After Susan left, Detective Jim Russell looked through his files. He'd been working on a case for a couple years that had him puzzled, astonished, and outraged at various times. It was a case few others knew about because it was not only explosive, but potentially dangerous.

Money from nearby Baltimore City was disappearing from the coffers each year. Yes, there was always an excuse, a reason why so much money had been displaced or redirected, but Jim knew there was more to it than what was on the official books. He had been working hard, in secret, to discover where the money was going.

To most people, Jim was a small-town detective like his dad, working to keep the streets of his neighborhood safe. Only his handler at the FBI knew why Jim stayed in the small precinct all these years rather than moving up to bigger and more prestigious departments. And now, without knowing it, without even suspecting she had handed him what might be the gift of a lifetime, Susan O'Neil walked into his office with potential, new evidence against Alexander Moore.

Jim had been investigating Moore since the previous August when a man named Anthony Morelli showed up at the precinct and requested a meeting with the son of his old friend, Officer Mike Russell.

CHAPTER FIVE

Before

Morelli told Jim he wanted to talk about a possible break-in at his business. Once inside Jim's office, though, the agent quietly closed the door, revealed his badge, and made his proposition.

"You want me to do what?" Jim asked the man sitting in front of him.

"Investigate the goings on in Mayor Dennis Simpson's office," Agent Morelli replied.

Jim eyed Morelli intently. His hair was clean cut, his black necktie tight beneath the collar of his crisp, white shirt. His black suit was perfectly creased. He was the epitome of an FBI agent. All he needed was a pair of black Ray-Bans. Jim was sure the designer sunglasses were in the agent's suit pocket.

"I don't understand," Jim said. "Why me? I have no special training, no affiliation with the FBI, and more importantly, no affiliation with the mayor's office or even the Baltimore City Police Department."

"Exactly," Morelli said. "You have no ties to corruption, no skeletons to keep hidden in your closet, and you're not a city cop on the take. You're the perfect picture of a small-town cop, hoping to make an easy living and retire at a nice old age. More importantly, you live in Lakespring. You're neighbors with Alexander Moore."

"Moore, Mayor Simpson's chief advisor, best friend, and confidante."

"Precisely. We may need to monitor his activities at times to see who visits the house, how long they stay, where he goes when he's not at the office, that sort of thing. You never know who might be out to get you these days. He should welcome the extra surveillance. Of course, he won't know about it, but he should be grateful, just the same." True to the stereotype, the agent's sense of humor was dry and not funny.

"Doesn't the FBI have more sophisticated ways of doing surveillance these days than run-of-the-mill stakeouts?"

"There is nothing about this that is run-of-the-mill," Morelli replied. "But for now, we're off the record, so you're just the low-key kind of guy we need to help us up the stakes."

"It's the mayor you want, isn't it?" Realization dawned on him that this operation was perhaps more 'off the record' than implied. "How is he related to this?"

Morelli cleared his throat. "I didn't say they were related."

Jim raised his brow and sat silently, waiting for more.

"We believe Moore, Simpson, and perhaps others in the office, may be embezzling money," Morelli said casually. "Both men come from the same type of middle-class families. They make good money in their current jobs, but their lifestyles suggest they have more money coming in than the IRS can account for. There doesn't seem to be anything on paper that warrants an audit, but there is money coming in from somewhere."

Morelli paused for a moment. "We don't have confirmation of anything yet, but the city's accounting office seems to be paying higher prices on merchandise than even the regular government-inflated prices. There may be a connection there. We've contacted a guy on the inside, name's Reynolds. He's about your age and comes from a good, solid family, but he's skittish about helping. He seems to be afraid of Moore."

"So, am I supposed to be doing something or just looking into things?"

"Just keep an eye on Moore, what he does, where he goes, who he meets with. We've got a cop in the city trying to figure out the crime connection. He has to stay pretty deep undercover, though, because everyone on the force seems to be on the take. That's why we need someone who isn't affiliated with the city."

"So, I just keep doing my job like always," Jim said. "But I watch Moore and keep track of his activities, whereabouts, visitors, etc. Find out who they are and what their story is. See what their connection is to his job or illegal money-making schemes. I'm basically to try to figure out where the extra income is coming from, right?"

"And whatever else your surveillance might lead to. We all know the mayor is no more than a figurehead. He's serving his second term with an eye toward the White House. He's in good health for a man his age. But from what we can tell, he's merely a yes man. We believe Moore and his people are the ones running the city. We're trying to get someone into Moore's company, but it hasn't been easy. The mayor may not even know all of what's going on there.

"And if this thing has political implications, well, you know what party runs the State of Maryland and what party runs the White House. This investigation would be cut off at the knees. We need to look into other options, so to speak."

"You think the business is a front?"

"Could be. It gets a lot of government contracts." He held up his hand. "Yeah, don't get me started on the conflicts of interest there. The council approves them, so they're probably all in Moore's back pocket, too."

"Contracts for what?"

"Harbor Supply and Distribution supplies local hotels with towels and linens, toiletries, paper products, in-room bar stock. But it also supplies similar things to the city as well. They provide towels for gyms in government buildings at exorbitant prices and linens, dishes, and paper products for government receptions at extraordinary costs." He shrugged. "Could be legitimate, could be fraud. We'll take what we can get if it brings them down."

"Hmph, okay," Jim said. "So, what happens if I get caught in a sticky situation? Will the FBI back me up?"

"We'll be there for you, Jim," Morelli honestly replied, "but as we've said, this is an off-the-record investigation. We're not sure how far Moore's reach extends, and we don't want word getting out that we're investigating. If it becomes known that we're on to whatever is happening in the city, everyone involved will hide their tracks or go underground."

"So, nobody will know that I'm working for you," Jim said quietly. "Will I be going at it alone?"

"Not exactly," Morelli answered. "I'll be your only contact, but you can bring in someone if you need to. Give me his or her name first so I can run a background check. And be assured, I will be there for you if you need me. You won't get a badge, but you'll receive FBI clearance, and I can supply you with whatever you need as far as sophisticated surveillance equipment. And you will be compensated, but I'll be the only one watching your back. If something happens to you, your father will be well taken care of. We're not sure how far Moore will go to protect himself if he thinks someone is on to him."

"I see," Jim said, turning to look out the window and letting that thought sink in. Here he was, being presented with the job opportunity of a lifetime, a dream come true. But he couldn't tell anyone, may not be able to trust anyone, and could be putting his life in jeopardy, or worse. Agent Morelli remained silent while Jim thought about the proposition. After several minutes, Jim turned back to him.

"Okay, I'll do it," Jim said. "Under one condition: if anything ever happens to me, I want my dad looked after, not just 'taken care of' monetarily. A ride home at night when necessary, a good place to take care of him if and when the time ever comes. I'm all he's got, and I can't afford to not be there for him."

"We can certainly arrange that," replied Morelli. "Now, here's a copy of my file on Moore, what we know about him so far." Morelli handed over the folder, rose, and shook Jim's hand. "Good luck, Jim."

After

For the past nine months, Jim had been working to find out as much as he could about Moore, but the man kept his hands clean. Jim couldn't find anything even remotely shady about him until recently. He had more than one lead and many hunches, but Moore covered his tracks well.

So far, Jim had discovered several large payments to the corporation, Harbor Supply and Distribution, by the City of Baltimore and hundreds of checks from the same corporation to Moore. He wondered how far they were on tracing those.

Jim picked up his phone and dialed. "Lank, checking in."

"I was on my way to your office. Hold on."

In less than a minute, Jim's door opened, and his young protégé walked in.

"Hey," Officer Abe Lankton said, taking a seat across from his boss. "This computer program your guy sent over is incredible. I was able to break into Moore's private accounts, and I think we can tie him and Simpson to a human trafficking ring in Baltimore City that's operating under the auspices of Harbor Supply."

"Keep going," Jim encouraged him.

"Well, I said I think we can. The problem is, no human trafficking cases trace back directly to Harbor Supply. The Crimes Against Children Squad in Baltimore's FBI office has rescued almost two-dozen juveniles forced into prostitution since its inception, but none of them have any connection to Moore, Simpson, or the company."

"So, if the business is involved, Moore is able to find ways to hide it."

"Yeah. His warehouse is always clean and doesn't have any of the giveaways that people are being held there—barbed wire fences, nailed windows, guard dogs, and the like."

Jim shook his head and sighed. "And Moore's chummy with local politicians and shovels all kinds of money into their campaigns, so if they know anything, they aren't going to talk."

"Right, boss. The authorities broke up some prostitution rings involved in trafficking but don't seem to see anything fishy with the city's hotel and convention business. If Moore is trafficking people through his business, it's the perfect racket because the city either doesn't know or is looking the other way."

Jim stood and paced as his brain erupted with questions.

How did the foster children fit in? What happened at that house over the past few days? Was Moore trying to use his own foster children to lure in victims? Were their parents trafficked? Was their presence just a ruse? Or worse, was he planning on using them, and they figured it out? Unlikely at their ages, but who knows. What if Moore's wife stumbled onto something? Would she have told anyone?

He shook his head, squelching the volcano in his mind before turning back to Lank.

"Okay. We've been monitoring Moore's activities, but we haven't done actual surveillance at the house lately, and I learned something troubling earlier today that makes me think we should go back to watching the house. The Fed's inside man, Eddie Reynolds, has disappeared. We need to find him before Moore does."

"Unless it's already too late," Lank said.

Jim didn't want to think about that. Worse were the other thoughts bouncing around in his head.

Did the girls hear or witness something related to Reynold's disappearance? Is their presence in Susan's house putting her in danger?

Alex dreaded having to share this information with Denny Simpon. He walked into the mayor's office and closed the door behind him.

"Denny, I have some bad news," he said as he took a seat.

"Are we down in the polls? Is there a problem with the Harbor project?"

Alex shook his head.

The mayor walked around to the front of the desk. "You're not quitting, are you?" Denny laughed, and Alex wanted to deck him.

"Let me talk, will you?" Alex said, not even trying to tamp down his disgust for the mayor, which had begun festering when he learned of the man's secrets. "I've put this off for several days, and I need to tell you before word somehow gets out."

"What is it, Alex?" he asked with an air of boredom. Denny sat on top of the desk, and his casualness further irritated Alex.

"Cassie and Ellie are missing. They have been since the day Eddie showed up at my house."

"What? Alex, what do you mean 'missing'?" Simpson exploded, the causal demeanor gone. He stood up and leaned down toward Alex. "What the hell happened?"

"I don't know, Denny," Alex said honestly. "They may have heard, or even seen, what went on with Eddie."

"You idiot! That was days ago, and you're just telling me now? Didn't you think I had a right to know? Have you gone to the police?"

"Of course not. Are you crazy?"

A sudden wave of rage washed across the mayor's face. "If you have touched a single hair on either of their—"

"You know I haven't. Get a grip." Alex spat the words at his 'boss.' "I'm sick and tired of having to care for those brats, but I wouldn't hurt a kid."

While that wasn't entirely true, Alex knew better than to hurt the girls. He never intended to harm any kids, and never planned for any of their 'supplies' to be teens, but over time, he'd become more involved in Denny's politics and less involved in his business. Without his oversight, the girls had gotten younger. Still, he told himself, none of them were technically children.

"And you haven't gone to the police."

"I already told you I haven't," Alex said through gritted teeth.

"What am I supposed to say when this gets out? My right-hand man has two foster children disappear while in his care, and he hasn't even gone to the police?"

"Come on, Denny," Alex shouted, jumping up from the chair. "What am I supposed to tell them? You know what they'll find if they start digging into Cassie and Ellie's past. I can't go to the police."

"Then what are we going to do?" The mayor jabbed his finger into Alex's chest with each word. "What are *you* doing to find them and keep this under wraps?"

Anger exploded in Alex's brain, but he remained in control as always. "Nothing you need to worry about. I know how to do my job. You just keep doing yours." Alex's lips barely moved as he clenched his teeth.

"A lot is at stake if their past is discovered." Denny leaned in so close to Alex, he could smell the mayor's breath. "Just fix this. Find them, and fix this."

Denny turned and walked behind his desk. He stood and stared out the window at the streets of Baltimore below.

"You were such a fool," Alex sneered at him. "A fool, and this may be the beginning of the end. I hope you know that."

Alex turned and walked from the office, slamming the door behind him.

Alex thought back to the day he met Denny Simpson in college, and they quickly became best friends. Alex grew up in Baltimore County, the son of a prominent businessman. He graduated with a business degree and spent many years searching for just the right type of business—a big moneymaker with little government oversight. He opened Harbor Supply and Distribution with Daddy's money after getting his MBA, but it was in 2003 that he struck gold with an idea that would change everything—human trafficking in the hospitality business. That was before human trafficking was a regular news item and became a common topic on shows like *Law and Order: SVU*. Still, most operations and laws focused on prostitution and kidnapping of minors with little thought to the hospitality businesses. With Denny Simpson on his side, and under his thumb, Alex had felt untouchable. Until now.

Before

"It's a no brainer," Alex told Denny. "The Fed and that local group, Safe House of Hope, concern themselves with children and prostitution. Girls disappear all over the world and end up in big cities like New York and Las Vegas, but our girls won't be prostitutes and won't even be on the city streets. The Feds won't suspect a thing."

The mayor listened, intrigued by his friend's idea.

"You know Harbor Supply and Distribution is a legitimate business. We supply everything local hotels need, but the biggest cash cow could be housekeeping staff. Everyone needs them, and Americans don't want the jobs. I've given a lot of thought as to how we do this." Alex explained his plan.

"And how would we get the girls?" Denny asked, now invested in the idea.

"Cargo comes in and out of the Baltimore Harbor every day and is unloaded and taken to my warehouse. There, all the items are inventoried and distributed as ordered to the hotels. My plan is, once a week, an extra cargo shipment would come in at night with cargo smuggled out from Cuba, Haiti, or the Latin American coastline. We'll make sure they're all adults. I don't want any kids involved."

CHAPTER SIX

After

Alex had come to resent being the one who did all the work while Denny reaped the rewards. Alex was Denny's biggest campaign donor, and he provided jobs for the sons and daughters of Simpson's supporters in the hotels—high-paying positions in the human resources departments of course—and found them other jobs around town. It was good, old-fashioned political patronage at its finest, and all the donors took a kickback.

Alex was forced to give away a larger share of his profits than he would have liked to maintain his ties with the city, but his alliance with Denny opened doors he wouldn't have had access to under different circumstances. Much of the money also ended up in Alex's and Denny's personal bank accounts as legitimate stock dividends. Eventually, they began using excess funds to pay off charges for trips, goods, services, and any other expenses they wanted to hide from the public or from their wives.

The only thing his business had never given Alex was a satisfying love life. He'd had many love interests but was never happy with any of them. He always had the feeling, true or not, that the women were interested in his money and power—both growing steadily. Alex had tried marriage on more than one occasion but easily became bored with his gold-digging wives until he met his match in Penny. She was the one thing in life, other than power and money, Alex truly loved, though after five years of marriage, his affection for her was wearing thin.

He was smart enough to have had each of his wives sign pre-nuptial agreements that let him get out of paying alimony. There was never any child support. None of his wives could ever figure out why they had so much trouble conceiving, but Alex knew he'd taken care of that problem after a pregnancy scare in college. He didn't want kids and never regretted having the surgery, despite the doctor's misgivings about rendering a healthy young man sterile. He told Penny it was out of love for her that he agreed to take in the foster children.

What a mistake that had been.

⸺◦⬦◦⸺

Jim was able to finish paperwork on a couple minor cases, then left the police department and went to see his contact at Social Services.

"Hello Lynette," Jim said, pushing open the door to her office.

"Well, look what the cat dragged in." Lynette greeted Jim with an easy smile. She sat back in her reclining desk chair and motioned for him to enter. "How have you been?

"Just great, and yourself?" Jim noted the new picture on her desk of Lynette and a local attorney. *Good for her.*

Lynette was a beautiful woman, blonde and curvy, in her late twenties. Often hit on by guys blind to her inner beauty but drooling over her bombshell looks, Lynette was careful about her relationships. Jim should've been thankful for her when they dated a few years back, but it just never completely clicked for him, and he knew why.

"As good as can be expected for someone who had her heart broken," Lynette said with a shrug. "But I'm over that guy now."

"That's good because he needs a favor, a big one." Jim flashed her a smile.

"Anything for you, Jim," Lynette said, and he knew she meant it. But as he made his request, her smile faltered.

"Are you familiar with two little girls named Cassie and Ellie, last name unknown, who were placed with Alex and Penny Moore?"

She went pale but held his gaze.

"I am," she replied slowly. "Why do you ask?"

"They've apparently run away but haven't been reported missing, at least not to the police. Have the Moores contacted you about their disappearance?"

Lynette fiddled with some papers on her desk, her fingers restless.

She glanced at the phone as if wishing it would ring and save her from this conversation.

"Well, I don't seem to have anything about that here..." Jim watched her closely, noticing how she tried to steady her hands while looking through the papers. "I'm sure if that were true, Mr. Moore would have notified me."

Jim knew Lynette was lying. They'd known each other for years, and he'd never seen her lose her cool. Her trembling hands and nervous demeanor spoke volumes. Jim leaned over the desk.

"What's going on, Lynette?"

"What do you mean?" She tried to hide her unease, but Jim wasn't fooled. "Nothing is wrong, except someone is sending you on a wild goose chase. Where did you hear that anyway? I mean, if there isn't a report on it." She jutted her chin in defiance.

"I can't tell you that."

"Then I'm sure it's a mistake." She dismissed him, picking up a file and waving him off. Jim remained seated.

"Lynette, it's me you're talking to. I know you. I know something is going on. Is something happening that I should know about?"

She clenched her jaw, and her hands became still as they clasped a folder. "I don't know what you're talking about, Jim. And you're dangerously close to crossing the line legally. Do you have a warrant for their file? It's confidential, you know." She tried to sound tough, but she refused to make eye contact with him.

"No, I don't." He kept his voice calm, his anger starting to surface. He hadn't expected things to go like this, and his instincts told him there was more going on than meets the eye. "I hoped a warrant wouldn't be necessary. I must ask you not to contact the Moores. This is official police business, and you will not tell anyone I was asking about the girls. Do you understand?"

"Jim, I'm bound—"

"You said they're not missing, so you aren't bound to do anything but keep quiet, or I'll arrest you for interfering in an official investigation. Am I making myself clear?" Jim's hands were splayed on the desk, and his face was close to hers.

"Crystal," Lynette snapped, looking away.

"I *will* be back with a warrant," he told her. "And I *will* find out whatever it is you don't want me to know." Jim stood and started to turn. "Call if you decide to be honest with me before then."

He tossed his card onto her desk as if they were strangers. Then he stormed out of the office, slamming the door hard enough to make it bounce back open.

Lynette sank back into her chair, her heart beating so fast she felt it might push itself out of her chest. She still felt Jim's breath, hot with anger as it ricocheted off the desk and onto her cheeks.

Were the girls really missing? And what did Jim know about them?

Lynette tried to think of what she should do. She would not call Alex Moore, but not because of Jim.

The truth was, she never wanted to see or talk to that man ever again. She was scared to death of him and wished she hadn't been the one in the office on the day he came in. Moore insisted the file he created on the girls be added to the foster children registry. He wouldn't take no for an answer even though he provided no paperwork and gave no explanations about their circumstance. Lynette knew that was a day she would always regret.

Susan was determined to have a productive afternoon. It was quiet in the house since Mannie was off for Gina's doctor's appointment.

Susan worked her way through her messages, making calls when necessary and answering emails needing attention. She took a short break when her best friend, Daisy, dropped off a car seat for Susan's 'cousin's child.' Her youngest, Camille, had just outgrown it, and Daisy was happy to let Susan's mother borrow it for a few days.

Susan needed to travel to Denver the following week for a consultation with a company wanting to do their own networking, and she pondered moving it back but decided not to postpone just yet. She was sure the girls would be taken care of by then.

With that thought in mind, she took a break from work and searched the Internet for more information about Cassie and Ellie's foster parents. After a few minutes, Susan sat back and began reading about Alex and Penny Moore.

Alex Moore, chief of staff to the Mayor of Baltimore, and his wife lived on Locust Street. The picture she'd seen earlier of the family in the park was the only mention she could find of Cassie and Ellie. However, there were several articles in the society news about events chaired or hosted by Penny. Nowhere could Susan find any articles about or inquiries into the girls' disappearance even though another whole day had nearly gone by since they supposedly fled the house.

After finding hundreds of hits about the mayor's office and about Moore's own business, Harbor Supply and Distribution, Susan realized it was late afternoon. She left her office to inspect the little room across the hall. Both spare bedrooms in the house had dormer windows with built-in window seats. Thanks to Mannie, the office had recently been painted in blues and greens, and the spare room in white and yellow. She knew, with a little work, this second room could work as a children's room.

She opened the curtains to let in the sun and cleared out the few boxes she had yet to go through—routers, Ethernet cords, VGA cables, things she often needed to have on hand if a client had a need for it—and stashed them in her office closet. She put fresh sheets on the bed, dug out an afghan her grandmother made her, and laid the blanket at the foot of the bed. Good enough, she thought. It's only temporary anyway.

Thirty minutes later, Susan was headed to the mall. She pulled into a space in the newly added parking garage near Macy's. Once inside the store, she piled clothes onto the counter as fast as she spotted them on the racks—blue jeans with cute tops, dresses, pajamas, underwear and socks, and lightweight jackets. Cassie and Ellie needed shoes, but Susan had no idea what sizes.

The cashier helped her as best she could, but Susan ended up buying several pairs of shoes in various sizes, making sure she could return the ones that didn't fit. When she finished buying clothes, she went into the mall. She bought each girl a doll as well as coloring books and crayons, books for her to read to them at night, a Candy Land game, and a little plastic tea set. Susan knew she was going overboard since, even if Jim found a way for them to stay, it wouldn't be for long, but her maternal instincts took over. She wanted to make their stay as nice as possible.

Susan called her mom on the way out and let her know she was heading to the house.

"Thanks, Mom," Susan said as she walked to her car. Although it was still light outside, the parking garage was eerily dark. "I'll be there in about 30 minutes."

"Be careful," was becoming her mother's standard good-bye.

"I will, Mom." Susan gave her usual reply, as a sudden chill slithered down her back. She turned her key in the lock and looked around. The feeling that someone was watching her would not go away. Susan looked around the dim garage. Was it her imagination that all the cars were dark, and the other shoppers were sinister looking?

Susan got into the car and turned the key to start the car. She backed out of the space and, looking in her mirror, noticed a car one row over backing out, too. Susan drove out of the garage and headed in the direction of her mother's house. Night was beginning to fall, and the setting sun cast shadows over the street, which seemed longer and darker than she'd ever noticed before.

In the rearview mirror, Susan noticed the car she had seen backing out was just a few vehicles behind. When she made a right at the next light, the car made a right as well. As her paranoia grew, Susan made another turn, heading in the wrong direction. The car turned, too. It was still a short distance behind her, but there was no doubt it was following her.

What if Moore had somehow tracked the girls to her house? Was someone following her to get them back, or was somebody following her to find them and stop them from talking about whatever they were hiding? Susan sped up, frantically racing through the town, turning right or left at every light. The car was going faster now, keeping up with her every move.

Susan had an idea and headed toward the nearby Target. The lot was big and might be a good place to lose the car. She turned in and quickly pulled into a spot before the other car would have a chance to see her park. She turned off the engine and crouched down under the steering wheel, making sure the doors were locked. Using her phone as a mirror, she angled it so she could see clearly in the passenger side mirror and watched until she saw the other car go by. Once it passed, she peeked out the window and watched it turn down another aisle.

Quickly, Susan started the car and backed out. She sped out of the parking lot, cringing at the slight squeal her tires made as she turned onto the street. She headed toward her mother's, checking the rearview mirror the entire way. She didn't see anyone behind her the rest of the drive.

Susan didn't know the number of the police department, and was too rattled to think of asking Siri to find it for her. She just wanted to concentrate on getting to her mother's house. She'd call Jim as soon as she made it there safely.

***

Back in the parking lot, the driver continued to go up and down the rows until he was sure he had checked and re-checked every one. Cursing to himself, he picked up the phone and called his boss.

"Jim," he said, "I lost her."

CHAPTER SEVEN

After

"Where on earth have you been?" Ida asked as Susan ran into the house. The words tumbled from her mouth, mixed with exasperation and relief.

"I had car trouble," Susan said, looking her mother in the eye, her tone indicating, *Don't ask.*

"Come on girls, let's get going. I have surprises for you when we get back to the house."

"But Grandma Ida has dinner ready," Cassie said. "And we waited for you, so we're really hungry."

Susan turned to her mother, who looked away with flushed cheeks. "Grandma Ida?" she said, trying to hide the smile on her lips.

"Well, they told me they've never had a grandma, and I've never had grandchildren, so we thought it would be fun to pretend." Ida's voice trailed off. "I hope I haven't done anything that will make things harder for them." Ida's head snapped back up, and she looked at Susan with wide eyes. "Wait a minute. Did you just say you're taking them back to your house? You're able to keep them? Did you talk to Jim again?"

"Slow down, Mom. No, I didn't hear from Jim yet, so I'm taking them back to my house under the assumption that it's okay." She looked at Cassie. "I don't know how long you'll be there, but you can stay for now." The girls smiled, more relaxed than they were that morning.

"As for you, Mother..." Susan turned to her and smiled. "You're the expert on children. If you think it's okay for them to call you Grandma Ida, then who am I to argue?" Susan's tone implied otherwise, and her mother's face reddened.

"What about dinner?" Cassie spoke up. "I'm starving."

Susan laughed and was relieved Cassie was becoming comfortable with them. "Well, I guess it's all right. Let's just close the curtains so we have some privacy. Mom, can I park in the garage for a while in case it rains?"

Ida's face paled, but she gave a sharp nod. "Were you—?"

Susan held up her hand and turned toward the girls. "Why don't you go tell my dad dinner's ready." Susan waited for them to run to the family room. "I'm pretty sure I was being followed when I left the mall, but I was able to lose him. And don't say anything, I'm being careful."

"Why would someone be following you?"

"I honestly have no idea."

Ida didn't say another word, but Susan knew that look. Her mother was worried Susan might have gotten herself into something she'd regret. Susan was beginning to have the same concern.

"Tell me again how you lost her." Jim clenched his teeth and glared at Lank as the young office took a seat.

"I told you exactly what happened," Lank said with a sigh. "I followed her into the mall where she bought enough clothes and toys for ten kids. Then she left the mall and headed east. After a few minutes, she turned north, and then headed west. At first, I thought she must have missed her turn. Then she started driving faster and turning at every light. The next thing I knew, she made a quick turn into the Target lot. All I could think of was, it's a good thing she doesn't have one of those big SUVs because those things could never have made that ninety degree turn without flipping over and—"

"Lank!" Jim shouted at the rookie. "What did she do next?"

"Oh, sorry. She disappeared after that." Lank answered with a shrug.

"Lank," Jim said, rolling his eyes, "what do you mean *disappeared*? We're talking about a thirty-two-year-old woman, not Harry Houdini."

"Actually boss, I don't think Harry ever disappeared. He was able to get out of chains and things, but I don't think he ever—"

"Lank," Jim said as calmly as he could, trying not to lose his temper with the kid. Lank tended to ramble when he was nervous, and he was still a rookie. "What happened to Susan?"

"Oh, sorry again. I'm a little nervous. I've never done anything like this before."

"Remind me not to let you do it again," Jim said dryly.

"Sorry boss," Lank said remorsefully. "Um, boss?"

"Spit it out, Lank."

"I think we have a bigger problem than me losing her."

Jim's jaw tightened, and the vein in his forehead began to pulse. "What is it?" he hissed.

"I think she might've known I was following her."

"What? How? What did you do?"

"Well, like I was saying, I was following her, and she turned into the parking lot, so I turned in, too. But she was gone. I didn't see her driving down the row or turning at the end of it. It was like she vanished into thin air."

"Not that again," said Jim. "Did you think to look at the cars *parked* in the row?"

"Of course, I did," said Lank defensively. Then he added quietly, "Just not until I turned down the next row and started slowly looking around. I guess she could have pulled into the first spot she saw and then backed out and got away when I was turning the corner."

"You think?" spat Jim sarcastically. "Lank, if you were texting or listening to music, I'll have your—"

"No sir, I really wasn't," Lank assured Jim. "I promise."

Jim looked Lank in the eye and surveyed his expression for a moment. "All right, I believe you." Jim sighed. "I know you wouldn't fool around while watching over Coach O'Neil's daughter."

———⊙———

Susan and her parents delighted in the attention they were able to give the girls who were craving love and affection after several nights on their own. The girls begged to see all their new clothes immediately, so they put on a fash-ion show after dinner. Susan knew parents were already attached to Cassie and Ellie, and she hoped they wouldn't all end up with broken hearts.

They arrived home around nine that night and headed upstairs. Cassie and Ellie were so excited about their room they practically knocked each other over running up the stairs. Upon entering the bedroom, the girls gasped at the window seat and the yellow curtains and bedspread.

"You bought these for us?" Cassie's eyes were wide in amazement.

"Not exactly," Susan said. "I had them already, but I thought you might like the colors."

"We do. We really do." Cassie beamed. Ellie smiled her quiet acceptance of the room.

"I'm glad you do. Now, take these." She handed them the toothbrushes her mother had packed in a little bag along with a sample of bubble-gum-flavored toothpaste she saved from somewhere. Susan, with her lack of experience, hadn't even thought to buy those. "You need to change and brush your teeth before bed. I'll bring up your clothes while you brush and wash up."

She retrieved the clothes and toys she'd bought and laid out the pajamas. She put a doll on Cassie's bed and a teddy bear on Ellie's, the game and coloring things on the window seat, and the books on the nightstand. She arranged the tea set on a little wooden table with two chairs from her own childhood. Her father had recently brought over the set when he was cleaning out the attic. At the time, Susan had laughed, telling her father it would be years before she had children to use them. Now, she shook her head at her father's foresight.

When Cassie and Ellie returned to the room, it looked like a fairy princess had cast a magical spell over it. Ellie went right to the bear, picked it up, and hugged it fiercely. With tears in her eyes, she ran to Susan and hugged her.

"Miss Susan," Cassie said, looking up at her. "Ellie left her bear in Mr. Moore's, uh, house. I know she's been missing it a lot." Cassie looked around the room. "This is almost like our own bedroom at Mommy's house. Where did you get all these things?"

"I picked up the toys earlier. The table and chairs were mine when I was your age. Do you like everything?" Susan sat on the edge of the bed and looked around the room, surveying it as if through their eyes.

"We love them. Now, you can read to us before bed and have tea parties with us like Miss Pen—" Cassie stopped herself and looked at Susan, her eyes glistening. "Thank you, Miss Susan, thank you!" She ran over and hugged her. "When we left Miss Penny's, I didn't know if we'd ever have anyone to take care of us again."

Susan was speechless. Her heart was soaring and breaking at the same time. What precious children they were. From the way Cassie talked, Penny Moore knew that.

What had gone wrong in that house?

Trying not to dwell on the thought, Susan switched on a lamp and turned off the overhead light. She gestured toward the books. "Pick out a book, Ellie. Let's read a story before bed." She kicked off her shoes and settled into the middle of the bed, not wanting to spoil the mood by reminding the girls, or herself, this stay was only temporary.

Ellie, clutching the bear tightly, looked through the books and chose a *Little House on the Prairie* picture book. Until she saw them in the bookstore, Susan didn't know there were picture books adapted from her favorite childhood book series.

Cassie and Ellie snuggled up to Susan, one on each side of her, and listened to the story of Laura Ingalls' fifth birthday. By the time Susan finished reading the short adaptation, both girls were yawning with droopy eyes.

Susan tucked them into their beds and gave each a hug and kiss on the cheek. She stood in the doorway and watched the girls drift off to sleep before heading downstairs. Her mother told her Ellie never said a word the entire day. Even Patrick couldn't get her to talk, and no female, child or adult, could ever resist his teddy-bear-like charm. Susan had get Cassie to tell her if Ellie had ever spoken.

After Susan and the girls left, Ida said to Patrick, "Get your coat on. We're going out."

"What? Where in the world are we going this time of night?"

"Just come on. You'll see."

They drove to the part of town with which they'd become familiar over the past year. When Ida knocked on the door, a surprised carpenter greeted them.

"Susan needs your help," Ida began. "She may have gotten herself into some trouble, and we'd like you to keep an eye on her."

With a quick nod, Mannie led them into the house and closed the door.

CHAPTER EIGHT

After

Susan sat on the sofa, barely able to keep her eyes open, as she gazed into the back yard. She tried to imagine what it must have been like for an eight- and five-year-old to sleep out there, huddled together underground with nothing but a thin blanket. Her heart broke thinking about it. Although spring had officially arrived a little over a week ago, it was still cold at night, and hadn't it rained a few days ago? Were the girls under the house then? Susan closed her eyes as if not looking out into the cold, dark night would erase what Cassie and Ellie must have been going through.

Just then, her phone played her favorite Kenny Chesney song. Susan didn't recognize the number and wondered who would be calling this late. She found herself hoping it was Jim. She was looking forward to talking to him again, and the thought occurred to her that she'd forgotten to call him about the car that had followed her earlier. She would tell him right now.

"Hello," she said into the phone, fully expecting Jim on the other end.

"Hi. Susan?"

She vaguely recognized the voice and tried to place it. It certainly wasn't Jim.

"Yes, this is Susan," she said hesitantly.

"Hi, Susan. It's Seth."

"Seth? Seth wh...Oh! Seth, yes. Hello." It took her a moment before she remembered the young tech from Blue Sky Communications. She was unable to hide the surprise in her voice. "How are you?"

"I'm fine. I just wanted to make sure you made it home okay yesterday. I figured the number on your card may be a cell and thought I'd give it a try."

Was that just yesterday? It seems like a million days ago. No wonder I'm so exhausted.

"Did everything go okay with the server?" Susan sat up and tried to think clearly. It didn't seem possible she was on a plane only twenty-four hours ago.

"Oh, yeah, everything is fine. I just thought I'd give you a call to say, well...thanks for taking the time to walk me through everything yesterday." Susan could hear the embarrassment in his tone. "It sounds like I called at a bad time. I wasn't thinking about the time difference there."

"No, it's okay," Susan assured him. "I don't mind at all. I'm just preoccupied with something. But now I have the chance to thank you again for taking me to the airport yesterday."

"Not a problem, Susan," his voice lifted. "I was happy to do it. In fact, I'll be in the area next week on some personal business. Do you think we could get together? I might have some questions for you by then. About the server, I mean."

"Um, Seth, I don't know." Susan wasn't sure how she felt about seeing Seth outside of work. Other than with her Godfather, she tried hard to keep her business and her personal life separate.

Seth broke into her thoughts. "Oh, I see. I'm sorry, I just thought we might be able to get together, as colleagues, of course."

"Oh. Um, I'm sorry. It's just been a hectic and bizarre day."

"Anything you'd like to talk about? Something technical? I don't mind if you pick my brain."

"No, but thanks." Susan knew better than to say anything about her situation. "I think I just need to get some sleep. Give me a call next week, and I'll see what my schedule looks like. Maybe we can get together and go over any questions you have."

"Great. I'll call you in a few days when I get to town."

"Sure, Seth. That's fine." They said goodbye, and she disconnected the call.

She didn't give the call another thought. She had too many other things on her mind. The girls, Ellie's silence, the mystery of it all. Not to mention reconnecting with Jim after all these years.

Susan's faith taught her to believe all things happened for a reason. Seeing Jim today stirred feelings in her she hadn't had since high school when the two of them would pass in the hall or be seated near each other in class. She knew Jim never had the same feelings for her. He dropped her like a hot potato as soon as other girls started looking his way, and he never looked back. He dated every pretty girl in high school while she hid behind braces, glasses, and a computer monitor. No, Susan decided, even with straight teeth and contacts, she was not the type of person

Jim would have his eye on. The reconnection was simply for the sake of the girls, nothing else.

⸺◦⸺

Jim watched Susan move through the house from the front seat of his car.

"When are you going to tell me why we're watching Susan O'Neil?" Lank asked after they'd been sitting in front of the house for almost an hour. "I thought you wanted to watch Moore."

"I told you, she's an old friend who may be in trouble."

"Any chance these surveillances are connected? Susan and Moore?"

Jim sighed. Lank had a lot to learn, but he was smarter than Jim often gave him credit for.

"To be honest, I'm not sure, but I have a hunch they are. For now, we're just making sure Susan is safe and sound."

Lank rolled his eyes. "That's a bunch of bull if I ever heard it. Why is she in trouble? What do you mean 'old friend'? Is this some kind of unrequited love thing? If so, I didn't sign up to be a peeping Tom."

Jim looked hard at Lank. "Since when have you ever known me to even have a lover or engage in the acts of a peeping Tom?"

"Well, it could happen. You did date some social worker for a while from what I hear."

"That was three years ago, and I'd hardly say we were 'lovers.' What am I, the subject of the department gossip hounds?"

"Nah. Just some guy talk. And you did say we were watching an old friend; one I know you used to be fond of. I spent a lot of time with her dad back in the day, remember. How much of a friend was she?"

"A good one," Jim snapped, then rolled his eyes. "Back in the day, huh? What are you, twenty-five?"

"Almost."

"Uh-huh. I told you I'd fill you in later, and I intend to." Jim was irritated. He ran his hand through his hair, wanting to concentrate only on the fact that Susan was back in his life. "For now, let's just focus our attention on Miss O'Neil."

Lank turned back toward the house, and his eyes widened. "I couldn't agree with you more."

Jim looked up. Susan was in the kitchen rinsing out a glass. She was wearing a nightshirt in a purplish shade, something Jim thought had a flowery name, like lavender or lilac. She had glasses on, and they enhanced her face, making her look both intelligent and feminine.

Her hair was flowing onto her shoulders, and Jim was struck by the beauty of it. For the first time in about fifteen years, he wondered what it would feel like to run his fingers through it. Was this really the same person he had played with on the playground every day of his childhood? Even in his teenage fantasies, he never remembered her looking so good. Despite looking like she hadn't slept in days, she was the most beautiful woman Jim had ever seen. He looked over at Lank.

"Close your mouth, Lank." Jim felt a bit possessive. "What's the story with you and her dad anyway? You said something about him being your coach."

"When I was sixteen, I was a promising cornerback. They called me Long-legs Lank."

Jim laughed but Lank nodded.

"I'm not kidding. I was pretty good. Scholarship material, the NFL in my future. I was going places." He looked out the window, a melancholy look on his face.

"That's when you broke your back."

Lank turned back to Jim. "Yeah. And Coach O'Neil helped me recover. I don't know if I would've survived without his support. I'd do anything to repay him."

Both men turned back toward the house. Susan looked out the window, and for a minute, Jim thought they'd been spotted. She reached up and closed the blind, blocking their view.

"Do you think she saw us?" Lank asked.

Jim didn't answer. He was thinking about how beautiful she looked in the soft light of the kitchen at night. He swallowed and shook away the image. It had been a long time since Jim had thoughts like that about any woman, but not the first time in his life he'd had them about Susan.

❖

Susan placed the glass in the drying rack and went back into the family room to turn out the light. She headed toward the master bedroom where she slept alone. As she closed the blinds in her room, she recalled the sudden chill she'd had in the kitchen, that feeling she was being watched. It was the same eerie feeling she had in the parking garage, and she was sure she'd been right about being watched and followed.

But who would be watching her now? Only her parents and Jim knew Cassie and Ellie were there. And she was quite certain, if whomever had been following her knew the girls were there, they would have done something by now.

That guilty feeling about not calling Jim returned. She meant to, but they were having such a good time at her parents' house, she simply forgot. She didn't think of it again until Seth called, and now it felt too late to call. She would call Jim first thing in the morning. After all, he was probably sound asleep right now.

As Jim watched the house, he thought back to the first day of kindergarten when he and Susan met. She was quiet and shy, and he was loud and wild. Despite their differences, the two children became friends and remained friends, the best of friends, until high school.

"You're a million miles away. What are you thinking about?" Lank asked.

Jim shrugged. "Someone I knew in another life."

In their early teens, Susan began to develop in ways he never expected. He also never expected his body and mind to react to her the way they did. He couldn't look her in the eye for fear she'd see what he was thinking.

Jim had been embarrassed by the thoughts in his mind, and he couldn't imagine why he suddenly had them about his best friend. Sure, she was pretty, even with a retainer and glasses. Heck, he even thought she was pretty when she still had the braces on, but she was like a sister to him. He didn't want that to change.

"Spill," Lank pressed. "I know you're thinking about Susan. What happened between you two?"

Jim smirked. "Like I'd tell you." Jim shook his head and sighed. "Let's wrap this up."

"No more surveillance tonight?" Lank asked.

"No, let's get some sleep. We'll figure out our next move in the morning. I think I was just being paranoid. I'm sure Susan and the kids are safe."

"Might be the old feelings are stirring a bit of nostalgia. Maybe you just wanted an excuse to spend the evening watching Susan, maybe checking to see if a boyfriend stopped by."

"Shut up, Lank."

Lank's words hit too close to home, but in truth, Jim had never stopped watching out for Susan. He never stopped kicking himself for the way he treated her. After years of denial, Jim still had a thing for his best friend.

Before

The year Jim and Susan turned fourteen, they began hanging out with different friends at school. But at home, they were still inseparable. They did their homework together after school, and Jim ate dinner with Susan and her parents every Sunday. But the end of the school year met them with unexpected changes.

Jim made the varsity football team even though he was just a freshman, and while Susan acted happy for him, their relationship became strained. By August, between his summer job on the Mitchell farm and the start of football practice, Jim had little time for Susan. When they were together, it was like he didn't know what to say to her anymore.

The summer before ninth grade, Susan noticed the difference in Jim's attitude, but she couldn't figure out what had caused the change. He had little to say to her anymore, and he refused to look her in the eye. They were drifting apart, and she didn't know why.

That day was oppressively hot and steamy, as if the whole town had been dunked into a pot of steamed crabs. Jim was done working for the summer, football practice was taking up most of his time, but practice had been cut short due to the heat. Susan worked as a page at the local library a couple days each week, which kept her busy and gave her access to all the latest books. The job was over now that school was getting ready to begin, and she wondered if she and Jim would be in the same classes this year. They hadn't even talked about it.

Deciding it was even too hot to go for a swim, Jim and Susan went to an afternoon matinee before heading back to Susan's for a lazy evening with her parents. They were sitting on the front porch swing, talking about the summer flings of their classmates.

A thunderstorm, during the matinee, had ushered in a breeze, unusual for Maryland that time of year. The air was filled with the perfumed smell of Ida's roses, the color of the setting sun, which grew on giant bushes in front of the house. Patrick's steaks were on the grill out back, and their aroma mingled with the rose fragrance, creating an almost romantic feeling like the scent of a special dinner being cooked for a rose-bearing suitor.

Susan was watching the kids across the street, running through their sprinkler, when she felt Jim's stare. She turned to look at him, and without warning, Jim leaned in and kissed her. It had taken Susan by such surprise, she jumped away from him. Jim looked stunned and hurt. His face turned blood red.

"I, I don't know why I did that, Susan," he stammered. "I'm sorry."

Susan didn't know what to say, how to react. Why, after all these years, would he suddenly kiss her? They were friends, just friends. Right? Her mind raced, but still, she said nothing.

"I'm sorry," Jim said again. He stood up to leave, the look on his face as unbelieving as Susan's.

"Wait, Jim," Susan finally spoke. She didn't know what she should say, but something told her their friendship had just changed. Was it for better or worse?

"I have to get home," Jim mumbled as he turned, without looking at her, though they both knew there was nobody waiting for him at home. He hurled himself down the steps and across the yard to his bike parked in the driveway and raced down the street toward his house.

Susan felt nothing would be the same again, and for the first time, she admitted to herself that she'd been waiting for that kiss for a long time.

Susan watched Jim ride away and hoped they'd get the chance to talk after his practice the following day. She lost sleep that night thinking about what she should say. She decided to let Jim take the lead.

She watched for him the next evening and even left her bedroom light on later than usual that night so he would know she was still up. But Jim never came over that night or any other night after that. Her parents must have wondered why the close bond between the two teenagers suddenly ended after all those years, but they didn't pry.

When school started the following week, Jim moved on with his other friends, and Susan did the same. She watched as he grew into a tall, handsome young man, constantly followed by a group of giggling girls. He dated almost every cheerleader while Susan joined the computer club and competed with the academic organization known as MENSA. In time, Susan stopped looking for Jim in the hallways and ceased wondering what he was doing.

Maybe it was a mistake not to seek him out and let him know how she felt about him. She wondered if this feeling of loss and heartbreak would ever go away.

CHAPTER NINE

After

Jim's phone rang early the next morning. When Susan finished telling him about being followed, Jim took a deep breath. He was furious with her. When Lank told him he suspected Susan knew she was being followed, Jim thought she would call him, but she didn't. He gave her the benefit of the doubt as there was a possibility she hadn't known Lank was tailing her.

Now, she confirmed that she knew, and his blood boiled. She knew she was being followed but had no idea it was his man tailing her, and she hadn't called him to let him know about it. What if it hadn't been Lank pursuing her? What if it had been an expert, and she hadn't eluded him? Jim could only imagine what might have happened.

"Why didn't you call me last night?" he asked between clenched teeth, his white-knuckled hand gripping the phone.

"I'm sorry." Susan's voice trembled with regret. "I know I should've called you right away. I really meant to call as soon as I got to my mother's, but the girls had such a great day, and they were so excited. They couldn't wait to see their new clothes, and—"

"Did you say your mother's?" Jim said. "You were at your mother's house?" He was kicking himself for not thinking of that. If only he'd stopped by to check on his dad, he might have seen her. He should've known that was where the girls were, and he should've been waiting for her there. If anything had happened to her in those few hours, he couldn't have forgiven himself. To lose someone he was trying to protect would have been a nightmare. To lose Susan would have been worse than facing Freddy Kruger himself.

"Yes, I was," Susan said quietly. "I didn't want anyone to know my parents were involved, but I guess I should've told you."

"Yes, you should have," Jim replied, the regret in her voice calming his anger. "You need to be honest with me, Susan. Don't try to handle this alone. You don't know what you're getting yourself into."

"I know, Jim. You're right. I promise to tell you everything right away from now on. I won't put anything off."

"Look, forget about it for now." Jim was still angry, but he also felt guilty letting Susan believe she may have been in danger. "Why don't you just give me a description of the car and anything you can remember about it?"

Susan told Jim everything she could recall. He was amazed by how much she remembered and found himself smiling. Maybe she was better at this than he gave her credit for.

"Okay, I've got it," he told her. "Now I've got some news for you."

"Is it about their foster parents?"

"Not directly. I talked to Social Services and found out they know nothing about the girls being missing. I convinced the social worker, an old friend of mine, a relative had come forward claiming them, and I would handle things from here." The lie came easily and made Jim feel guiltier still. "I told her I would check out the relative's story, and if her claim panned out, I would let the Moores know myself."

I know Lynette is hiding something, but I don't want to worry Susan any more than she already is.

"At any rate, the girls can stay with you for the time being."

"Oh, thank you, thank you," Susan said through tears. "I can't thank you enough. But does this mean that Social Services knows where they are?"

"Not yet, but I'm going back tomorrow to tell them I've verified the story of the relative. I'll have them take the girls off their records."

There, that's not a total lie. I do intend to go back and question Lynette again tomorrow.

"Hmm," Susan said after a moment. "That's strange."

"What's strange?" Jim acted nonchalant.

"I wonder why the social worker never questioned the story about the relative and didn't wonder why they would go to the police before Social Services. And you think they'll just let the girls go with someone they haven't checked out? It sounds totally implausible to me. Is Lynette the social worker? Didn't you date? Is that why she's not checking up on your story? This isn't settling right with me, Jim."

Darn, why did she have to be so smart, so logical all the time? And how did she know I dated Lynette? Has she been keeping up with my life the same way I've kept up with her?

"Susan, whose side are you on?" Jim's tone was harsher than he intended, but his emotions were running high. "Do you want to keep the girls or not?"

"Of course, but none of this makes any sense. She didn't even want to have a meeting with me, or—"

Jim cut her off. "It's not at all unusual for relatives to come to the police station first, especially if they don't know how to find the person they're looking for. Most people automatically assume they should go to the local police when they need help. Most people call the police when they think there's a problem, or they're being followed..."

Susan didn't seem to pick up on Jim's attempt to turn the discussion back to her and end her questioning.

"And you don't think the foster parents would have called Social Services before just letting some stranger take away the children in their care?"

"Susan, stop!" Jim growled. "I don't know why she didn't ask questions. That's why I'm going back there, okay? Just let me do some more digging so we can find out more about their time with the Moores and their life before they came here." Jim let out a loud sigh. He had to get Susan to stop thinking about the inconsistencies in his story, for her own protection.

Nothing has changed. She still over-analyzes everything.
Susan was silent.

Jim shook his head and took a deep breath, exhaling loudly. "Maybe I'll find out something from Lynette later today. In the meantime, I'd like to talk to the girls. Can I come by this morning?"

"Okay. I'll get them ready." Susan paused. "Do you need to know where I live?"

"No, I've got it. I heard you bought the old Harris house. Is that right?"

"That's right. What time will you be here?"

He checked his watch. "How about ten o'clock?"

"That's fine. We'll be ready."

He hung up the phone and thought back to his visit with Lynette. He got to know her pretty well when they dated. He had the feeling she was afraid of something or someone. He needed her to tell him everything about the girls' situation with Alex and Penny Moore.

⸺◆⸺

Penny stood in the doorway with tears in her eyes. She moved her gaze from the queen-sized bed with its pink and white canopy to the bookcase filled with picture books and classic tales. She closed her eyes and allowed her mind to conjure an image of Cassie and Ellie playing with their dolls, the sound of their laughter filling her senses. She elicited a desperate cry.

"Why, Alex?" she cried. "Why won't you let me find my babies?"

Penny went to the bed and stretched out on the frilly Laura Ashley bedspread, one of the many things she had allowed herself to indulge in for the sake of the girls. She wept as she thought back over the past five years.

Recently widowed, Penny was a lonely woman when Alex entered her life. She was a stunningly beautiful woman, inside and out, and her dear husband, Joe, loved making her happy. Their marriage had been as happy as a fairy tale.

In her youth, Penny had the perfect figure and knew how to carry and present herself. She'd been a contender and winner in several hometown beauty pageants. The product of elite private schools, her wealthy parents spared no expense in giving her the best education and the finest start in life. However, once she met Joe Adams, she wanted nothing more than to be his wife and the mother of his children.

Lying on the bed, she stared at the carousel mural she'd hired a professional to paint on the girls' wall. She recalled the pain she and Joe suffered when, after a series of miscarriages, Penny underwent a radical hysterectomy in her late twenties. Her desire for children never waned, and one day she surprised Joe by asking if they could adopt. Joe, knowing Penny's longing to be a mother and always wanting to please her, said yes.

If only Joe were still alive, Penny thought bitterly.

She forced herself to rise from the bed and walked down the stairs to her private library. Penny opened the closet and reached in to retrieve the box of photo albums she kept hidden away. Alex didn't like it when Penny talked about the past, so she learned, over the years, to only think about Joe and their lost children when Alex wasn't home.

Penny ran her fingers along one of the albums before opening the cover. She sighed at Joe's smiling face as he looked at the camera with love and affection. Penny and Joe were in the final stages of adopting a child when he was diagnosed with a serious heart condition. The ailment forced him to take disability and begin several operations to reverse what a lifetime of smoking had brought upon him. In the end, the treatments didn't work, and Joe died at the young age of forty-five.

Penny carefully flipped through the album, noting how little she had changed over the years. At forty-four, she was still an attractive woman. She always kept her weight in check, took care of her skin and auburn hair, and managed to find the money and time to keep herself looking young. With the help of her hairdresser, Penny's hair never veered from its natural color, and she paid good money to keep it that way. Joe had been quite a good-looking man, and after he died, Penny decided she would not let herself fall into the role of self-pitying widow.

She wasn't blind to the way men looked at her, but she never strayed from either of her husbands. She enjoyed the company of handsome men even though she did nothing consciously to encourage their attention. Joe always appreciated his wife's looks and the way his friends complimented her on her beauty. Alex, on the other hand, did not. He wanted her to look like a beauty queen, but he became insanely jealous when other men glanced her way.

Penny looked at her watch, sighed, and closed the album. Though it was early in the day, she was always on the lookout for Alex. He often came home during the day, seeking her out for a romantic daytime dalliance. Penny grudgingly performed her wifely duties, all too aware that any romantic feelings she had for her husband were long gone.

———◆———

Alex sat at his desk and stared at the framed photograph, taken at a political fundraiser a few years back. Penny was stunning in the Oscar de la Renta he'd had custom made for her to wear to the event. Standing next to her, he looked like he'd just won the lottery.

Alex scoffed with disgust as he thought about the sacrifices he'd made for his wife. He stopped taking weekend trips to Little St. James in the Caribbean to party with supporters and their underage escorts. He gave up smoking cigars, not an easy thing to do by any means. And he gave in to her desire to have children. Now, look where that had gotten him. He had a mess to clean up, and it was all her fault.

Alex turned away from the photograph. The muscle in his jaw twitched as his irritation grew. Ironically, it was those connections that led to them finally getting the children Penny wanted. She was overjoyed the day Alex surprised her with the girls, but Alex regretted ever bringing those brats into their house.

What choice did I have?

He shook his head as he answered his own internal question. He'd had no choice. Not only did it provide a way to keep his wife happy, it gave him a place to stash the girls where he could keep an eye on them. His career depended upon keeping them and their secrets within his control.

Control. Alex wondered if he still had things under control. After what happened with Reynolds, he'd begun to wonder who else knew the truth about the company. And what about the girls? Reynolds claimed he knew who they were. Did he? Did anyone else?

As though in answer to his thoughts, his cell phone rang. The voice on the other end relayed bad news.

"How much does she know?" Alex rubbed his temple as he listened.

"Too much, but I'll take care of her."

Alex disconnected the call and looked back at the photograph. He reached for the glass and bottle of gin he kept in his desk drawer. Those girls had brought him more trouble than they were worth. Now, they had caused another problem that had to be taken care of.

As he downed the fragrant liquid, he thought about how to handle the situation. Too many people knew. Eddie had been eliminated. The woman would have to be next. One way or another, he had to end this, even if it meant losing the only woman he ever loved.

Before

Alex never intended to settle down with one woman despite his many marriages. That all changed when he became infatuated with the wife of a Baltimore businessman when the couple attended a political event held by the mayor. Alex knew Joe Adams in college and had a few minor business dealings with him after Denny won a seat on the city council, but he had no idea Joe was married to one of the most intriguing and beautiful women Alex had ever seen.

Four years after meeting Penny, Joe passed away, and Alex made sure he was there to pick up the pieces.

"Let me know if there is ever any way I can help you, Mrs. Adams. Joe was a good friend of mine," Alex said as he took hold of her hand after the funeral service.

Penny contacted Alex several months later, and they met for dinner. She took his breath away when she entered the posh restaurant. Others turned to look at this woman who knew how to make an entrance. Standing in the light of the doorway, as if waiting to walk down the pageant runway, Penny arrived. She wore a two-piece coral suit and heels. She was a petite size eight, and her figure was perfect.

Over dinner, she asked Alex for his help. "Mr. Moore, as I said on the phone, I'm in need of your assistance." Penny tilted her head down and looked up at Alex through her eyelashes, a look that drove him mad.

"Please, call me Alex," he said, unable to take his eyes away from her.

"Alex," she purred, taking his hand in hers and running her fingers along his palm. "I know you have some connections with local and state government, and I can't get anyone to take me seriously. You see, Joe and I always wanted children, but it wasn't meant to be. Now, I'm trying to adopt, but I'm having some difficulties." Penny pouted slightly, a look that made her appear vulnerable and made Alex want to jump through hoops for her.

"Now, Mrs. Adams, may I call you Penny?"

"Yes, that's fine."

"Thank you. I'll do whatever I can to help you out. I have connections, as you know. I might know someone who can pull strings."

"Oh, Alex, that would be wonderful. I don't know how I would ever be able to thank you." Penny laid her hand on Alex's arm and batted her eyes.

Alex had been keeping tabs on Penny ever since the funeral. It was finally time to reap the rewards of his patience.

CHAPTER TEN

After

Susan let Cassie and Ellie sleep until 8:30. She would've loved to let them sleep longer, especially since it had been days since they last had a good night's sleep, but she needed to prepare them for Jim's visit, and she still had questions of her own. Once the girls were dressed and fed, Susan sat them down on the couch. First, she called Mannie in and introduced him to the girls. His nephew continued to work on the sheetrock in the sunroom.

"Mr. Hernandez and his nephew, José, are working on the new room out back, as you know. Mr. Hernandez hasn't had the pleasure of meeting you yet. Mannie, these are my cousin's daughters, Cassie and Ellie. They're going to be staying with me for a short time."

Mannie smiled and shook their hands, treating them as if they were important guests.

"Hola, señoritas. Es nice to meet you."

"Hola, Señor Hernandez," Cassie replied. "Como estas?"

Mannie and Susan looked at each other with equal amounts of shock.

"Soy muy bueno, mi niña bonita." Mannie grinned. Cassie giggled at being called a beautiful girl, and Susan raised her brow quizzically as she realized Cassie understood what Mannie said.

"You speak Spanish," she said. Susan assumed Cassie's elite private school started language lessons at a young age but was surprised just the same.

"Sí," Cassie responded with a laugh. "I mean, yes. Teresa always speaks to us in Spanish."

"Teresa?" Mannie looked at the little girl with surprise, and Susan wondered what he was thinking. "You know a woman named Teresa? Is she Cuban?"

Cassie looked at Susan and knew she had said too much. "Um, I don't know. I didn't see her very much." Cassie looked away, twisting her hair around her fingers.

"Thanks, Mannie," Susan said quickly. "I guess you want to get back to work."

Mannie held Susan's eyes as if waiting for her to say more. When she didn't, he nodded and returned to the sunroom. Susan felt guilty for the second time that day. It was bad enough when Jim fussed at her for not calling him, but this was worse. Mannie was more than her employee. He was one of her closest friends. It was obvious he knew more was going on than she was telling him, but what was she to do? Until she knew what kind of danger Cassie and Ellie were in, she couldn't tell anyone else about their situation. She wouldn't endanger Mannie and Gina.

She took a deep breath, sat on the love seat, and faced the girls.

"I'm sorry," Cassie whispered. "I didn't mean to say anything about Teresa."

Susan shook her head and took Cassie's hand. "It's okay, Sweetie. You can trust Mr. Hernandez."

Cassie nodded and waited for Susan to continue.

"Okay, first, you should know I've gotten permission for you to stay for a little while."

Cassie looked panicked, but Susan continued. "Don't worry. Mr. and Mrs. Moore don't know you're here." She hoped.

"I talked to a friend of mine yesterday, and he'd like to come over and ask you some questions. He's not going to tell Mr. and Mrs. Moore you're here, but he does want to make sure you're okay."

"Do we have to talk to him?" Cassie looked alarmed.

"Well, I'd like you to. He's only trying to help you. That's what we're both trying to do. You don't want to go back home, and we're hoping you'll let us know why."

"No," Cassie pleaded as her eyes went wide.

"Cassie, we can't just let you run away. There must be a good reason for you not to go back. Are you going to tell me what it is?" Susan kept her voice steady. She was growing impatient with Cassie's unwillingness to talk about what may have happened but didn't want to scare her.

"Mr. Moore doesn't like us." Cassie stuck her chin out defiantly.

"Cassie," Susan said sternly. "That is not a reason. Look, I want you to trust me, but I need to trust you, too. I need to know I'm not going to get into trouble if I listen to you. Do you understand that?"

Cassie nodded and looked away, still not giving any explanations. Susan took a deep breath and let it out slowly as she took another route.

"Fine, I'll give you some more time to think about telling me what happened. But remember, Cassie, I can't help you if you don't tell me the truth. Now, I know you can speak Spanish," she said with a smile, "so what else are you willing to share?"

Ellie looked over at Cassie, but Cassie shook her head without saying anything. Susan closed her eyes for a moment and then re-opened them. The girls were staring at her, their expressions a mix of concern and fear.

"Do you remember anything about your life before going to live with Mr. and Mrs. Moore?"

Again, Cassie shook her head, but her eyes told a different story. Susan let it go for the time being.

"Okay, next question, do you go to the Bentley School where you attended my computer camp?"

Cassie replied in one long stream of words without taking a breath.

"Yes, we go to the Bentley School. I'm in second grade, and Ellie is in pre-k. I miss my friends there, and I really like my teacher, Mrs. Keller, but I know if we try to go to school, he'll find us."

Susan contemplated the implications of what Cassie had confirmed. The Bentley School, named after a former state senator, was the only private school in the area, and Susan knew they had a long waiting list.

Families pay a fortune to send their kids there.

Susan knew the school carefully guarded the students' identities and personal lives and attempted not to seek notoriety of any kind. She had to sign a myriad of privacy agreements just to help with the camp.

Moore wasn't sparing any expense for their education. They were well taken care of, taught proper manners, given nice toys and books, and sent to the best and most private school in the area. Why on earth would they have run away?

Susan asked her next question in the hopes of gaining more insight. "Where did you go to school before you moved in with Mr. and Mrs. Moore?"

Cassie shrugged and remained silent.

Susan exhaled. "Okay, I'll be honest with you about something. My friend, Jim, is a detective. Do you know what that means?"

Cassie's eyes widened, and Susan knew she understood. "Like *Nate the Great* and *Cam Jansen*? Does he solve mysteries?"

"Kind of, yeah. I guess he does." Evidently, Cassie did not see the further implications of Jim's career.

"Cassie, Jim's going to ask you questions so we can figure out if it's okay for you to go back home or if you should be sent to live somewhere else."

The panic returned, and Cassie's eyes darted toward the door.

"Cassie, Jim's not going to make you do anything you don't want to." *Within reason.* "He'll be here soon to talk to you. He won't make you answer anything you don't want to, but just as I said earlier, the more you tell him, the more he can help you."

Cassie and Ellie didn't answer but looked worried.

"Don't worry. He's a very nice man, and he just wants to help us. I've known him my entire life, and we can trust him." She paused and took a breath. "Why don't you girls color until he gets here? I have some calls to make for work while we wait." They agreed and went upstairs to get their coloring books and crayons.

While the girls colored at the kitchen table, Susan sat nearby and checked her email. She returned calls but never took her eyes off the girls. She was afraid they would sneak out of the house if she let them out of her sight.

"Señora Moore, it has been five days since you say the girls are with friends." Teresa Muñez spoke to her employer as she refilled Penny's coffee. "Now you walking around this house looking like es Dia de los Muertos."

"Do I look that bad?" Penny looked into the mirror hanging over the buffet in the dining room. Yes, she did, like it was the Day of the Dead. She leaned her elbows onto the table for support.

"I not know what is going on, and is not my business, but I think something bad happened to them and you not tell. I not know why." She began clearing away the dishes without looking at Penny.

Penny put down her coffee without taking a sip and stood. She left the room, walked back to her bedroom, and closed the door. She was sick with worry but didn't know what to do. She stretched out on the bed and closed her eyes. Maybe Alex would find them today.

Penny wanted to go to Social Services as soon as Alex left after their argument the day before, but she had suspected, for some time, he was having her followed. Every so often she was unable to shake the feeling she was being watched. Regardless, she made up her mind she was not going to let Alex control her any longer. She had to know if her suspicions about the girls were true.

Penny stood and went to her closet. She opened the door and looked for something that would make her look livelier, or at least not pale and worried. She changed her clothes, fixed her hair, and put on her jewelry. When she was done, Penny inspected herself in the mirror.

"The makeup doesn't do much to cover the circles under my eyes, but it will do." She turned and headed out the door before she changed her mind.

⚬

When the doorbell rang precisely at ten o'clock, Cassie and Ellie stopped coloring and looked up at Susan.

"It's going to be okay. I told you I've known Jim forever. He's very nice, and he won't bite," she added with a smile.

Susan opened the door, and Jim entered, wearing plain clothes just as he had the day before. She was glad he wasn't in uniform. That might have scared the girls.

She wasn't at all surprised to see that he wore cowboy boots.

Jim always was a small-town, country boy. It's one of the things I liked best about him.

"Come in," she said to him. "Cassie and Ellie are in the kitchen coloring. They're a little nervous, but I told them you won't bite."

"Yeah." He grinned. "There are some things I've outgrown since we were kids."

Susan rolled her eyes and led him to the kitchen.

⚬

Once Susan introduced Cassie and Ellie to Jim, they moved to the living room so the girls could feel more comfortable. Jim sat in the chair facing them. The man in the unfinished room seemed to be hard at work, and the glass door between them was closed, but Jim worried about the guy's trustworthiness. How well did Susan know him?

"Don't worry," Susan said as if reading his thoughts. "He's one of my most trusted friends." Jim was skeptical but turned to address the girls, trusting Susan's judgement.

"First of all," Jim began. "You can call me Jim. I want to be your friend. I have some questions to ask you, and I want you to try to answer as many of them as you can. Okay?" They nodded and waited for him to begin.

Jim asked Cassie and Ellie some easy questions—how old they were, where they went to school, what their favorite shows and movies were. He moved on to more personal questions—how long had they been with Mr. and Mrs. Moore, had they met any of their foster parents' friends, did something happen that frightened them? He let them color when they weren't comfortable talking, which was most of the second half of the conversation. Other than a few shrugs from Cassie and several pleading glances from Ellie, the girls acted as if he wasn't talking to them at all.

Thirty minutes later, Jim knew no more than he had before he arrived. Based on their body language, Jim couldn't help but believe they'd seen or heard something that scared them, but they weren't sharing the information. He was more determined than ever to find out just what Moore had done to or in front of these innocent children.

When Jim was through asking questions, he and Susan went into the kitchen to talk. Susan made herself a cup of tea and poured Jim a mug of black coffee.

"Well, what do you think?" Susan asked as she sat across from Jim.

"I think they've definitely been traumatized by something, but I'm not sure what." He shook his head. "I'm no expert in this kind of thing, and it's hard to tell anything with the little bit they're willing to say." Jim ran his hand through his hair, something Susan remembered him doing when they were younger and he was deep in thought.

"And? What are you thinking?"

Jim took a drink of coffee and looked out the kitchen window. After a moment, he turned to Susan and spoke.

"I'm baffled. I didn't want to tell you this over the phone because I wanted to think it through some more, but you need to know this. Lynette was nervous as soon as I brought up the girls. She was hiding something, but I couldn't get anything out of her. She did seem surprised, though, that the girls may be missing. I didn't tell her anything about you or where the girls were staying. But if she goes to Moore, or someone starts poking around and asking questions about their whereabouts, I don't know how long it will be before I get fingered. It's only a matter of time before someone figures out the girls are here."

Jim looked Susan in the eyes and covered her hand with his. A jolt of electricity shot through her, but she didn't acknowledge it. She looked down at their hands, and it felt as natural as when they were kids.

"I'm concerned about your safety as much as theirs."

"My safety?" Susan looked up from their hands to Jim's face. "What exactly do you think is going on?"

"I don't know, but I've never believed Moore is on the up and up. That's why I was cautious with Social Services."

"Why didn't you level with me about your visit there or your suspicions about him?"

"I didn't want to alarm you."

"Well, you did," she said with annoyance. "I've been waiting all morning for someone to show up at my door and start asking questions about my relationship with Cassie and Ellie. There's no way Lynette would turn a blind eye to someone suddenly claiming to be a long-lost relative of two foster children. So, what did she really say about me finding them?"

"She didn't say anything because I didn't tell her." Jim let go of Susan's hand and took another swig of his coffee. He sighed. "I just told her that I'd been informed Cassie and Ellie were missing and asked if she knew about it or about their whereabouts. She told me there was no way they were missing because she would've been notified. She seemed truly surprised they weren't with the Moores, but she wouldn't give me anything."

Susan knew he hadn't told her the truth and was glad he owned up to it. She moved on with her own update.

"Well, I found a little information, but I don't know how much it will help. I did some research online while Cassie and Ellie were at Mom's house." Susan stood and retrieved printouts from a kitchen drawer and handed them to Jim as she sat back down.

"Here's what I came up with." She watched as Jim leafed through the papers. "Alex and Penny have been married for almost five years. She's very active in the community, and you know about his political ties." Jim gave a quick nod without looking up.

"Cassie and Ellie were with them last summer, according to that picture." She gestured to the paper in his hand. "I couldn't find out exactly when the girls went to live there." She took a sip of her tea. "We already know, in addition to working for Simpson, Moore owns Harbor Supply and Distribution. What I didn't know was that the company has several contracts with the state." She looked at Jim with a raised brow.

"Yes, that's true," he admitted.

"So, you knew that."

He only nodded.

Susan sighed and asked, "So, a dead end there, huh? What about you? What have you found?"

"You're the computer expert. I'm sure you've found more than I could."

Susan frowned. Why did that sound evasive? "You have the department's techs behind you. I know they have resources I can only hack into."

Now it was Jim's turn to raise a brow.

"I didn't, if that's what you're wondering. I could, but I'm leaving that to your people."

Susan caught his wince, but he quickly covered it with a grin. "Good thing. I wouldn't want to have to haul you in." When she only stared at him, he sighed and continued. "I can't tell you much. What I will tell you is that one of the guys who works for Moore was recently reported missing."

"Do you think it has something to do with Cassie and Ellie taking off?"

"I really don't know."

"Has Moore been involved in illegal dealings in the past? Is he above board?"

"Those are good questions that I'd like to know the answers to, and I think there are two people who may be able to help us figure them out." Jim turned and looked at Cassie and Ellie who were still coloring. He and Susan sat in silence for several moments.

Susan had a thought. "Jim, you won't believe this. Cassie speaks and understands Spanish. She learned it from someone named Teresa. I don't think she's a student at their school, but where else would Cassie encounter someone who speaks Spanish?"

"I can answer that question, and I'm surprised you didn't think of the answer yourself. The Moores have a Latina housekeeper. It's not at all uncommon."

Susan mulled over the news for a moment before Jim spoke again.

"I'm going to make a visit to the school and see what they know about Cassie and Ellie's past."

"I doubt it will do any good. They have very strict privacy rules. I had to sign all kinds of confidentiality agreements when I ran the computer camp. I know they won't tell you anything without court orders."

"I'm sure you're right, but I'll try anyway. I doubt they'll tell me much, but maybe I can learn something."

Susan was at a loss as to what to do next. "I just want to help them, Jim." She looked up at him, and his eyes held hers. Her fingers nervously played with the tea saucer in front of her. He reached across the table and took her hand again. Her heart took a leap in her chest.

"You're in way over your head, Susan. Moore has the means to find out where the girls are. Don't do anything stupid or take any more risks. Keep in touch with me throughout the day. Don't go anywhere without your phone. Also, I'd like to stop by every evening and check on you all, if that's okay."

Susan swallowed. She wasn't sure if her heart was racing out of alarm or because Jim was still holding her hand. "You said you're worried about my safety, but you conveniently side-stepped me when I asked why. What's going on, Jim?"

"I don't know, Susan. I just have a gut feeling you all may be in danger, and I'm not going to let anything happen to you." His eyes blazed, and his voice was hard.

Susan squeezed his hand. "Thanks, Jim. I promise to be careful and keep in touch with you. Please come by in the evenings. How about starting tonight? We'll have dinner at six."

"I'll be here."

CHAPTER ELEVEN

After

Just before noon, a woman wearing dark sunglasses and a long cape walked into the Lakespring Department of Social Services. Lynette observed her through the open office door and felt a chill run down her back when the woman introduced herself as Cassie and Ellie's foster mother and asked to see the social worker in charge of their case. Lynette hurried to the lobby.

"I'll handle this," Lynette said to the receptionist.

Lynette ushered Mrs. Moore into the office, closed the door, and took a seat behind her desk.

"I heard you say you're Cassie and Ellie's foster mother, so I assume you're Penny Moore." Lynette acted as if she had never seen Penny before, but she felt in awe to be in her presence. Penny was even more beautiful than the pictures in the society pages, but there were dark shadows and worry lines under her makeup.

"Are you the one who met with my husband on the day he made arrangements to get Cassie and Ellie?"

"I am," was Lynette's only reply.

"I know something is not legitimate with the girls." Penny shook her head, refusing to sit down when Lynette motioned to the chair in front of the desk. "My husband is a very powerful man and knows how to make things happen. I've come across information that leads me to believe he knew Cassie and Ellie before they came to live with us. Did he?"

"I'm afraid I don't know what you're talking about, Mrs. Moore," Lynette told her, trying to act casual.

"You know very well what I'm talking about," Penny said in a hushed but firm voice. "Is my husband their father?"

Lynette was genuinely aghast at Mrs. Moore's question. From the way Moore spoke of the children, she never imagined they could be his. He seemed to have only contempt for them and for the fact they were in his care. It was something Lynette always pondered—why take them in when they so obviously disgusted him? Though she supposed a love child was rarely convenient, especially for a man like Moore.

Penny was waiting for an answer. She stood with her arms folded and her eyes unwavering.

"Mrs. Moore, if you suspect your husband of infidelity, then maybe you need to have this discussion with him, at home."

"I will ask you one more time. Did my husband know Cassie and Ellie before they came to live with us?"

"I never saw your husband before he came into my office the day he asked me to pull your file and see if there were any foster children available. I never saw Cassie and Ellie before receiving the information they were in need of a foster home. I asked your husband if he would be interested. I don't know how he could've known the children before then." Lynette had rehearsed her spiel so many times she almost believed it herself. She did her best to stick to the truth.

"I don't know anything about the possibility of Mr. Moore being their father."

"Did you know they're missing?" Penny looked at the nameplate on the desk. "Ms. White? Has my husband or any of the men who work for him been in here?"

"No, he has not, and I don't know anything about the men who work for him. What do you mean by missing? Did they run away? Have you gone to the police? Are they issuing an Amber Alert?" Lynette remained calm, thinking back to Jim's visit the day before.

"No, but I intend to."

Not one to be bullied by rich socialites, Lynette held her ground. "If Cassie and Ellie are missing, you need to fill out a report, and I need to call the police. Is that what we need to be doing here, Mrs. *Moore*?" Lynette stared coldly at Penny as she asked the question.

"No," Penny said after a moment's thought. "Cassie and Ellie are fine."

"So, they're not missing?"

"Of course not," Penny snapped. "I just wanted to find out what you knew about my husband. I should be getting home now." Penny turned to go.

"Mrs. Moore." Lynette stood. Penny turned her head to look back at her. "Be careful."

Penny's confident expression faltered for a split second before she pulled back her shoulders. "Thank you, Mrs. White," she said before leaving the room. "I would advise you to do the same."

Lynette sat back down. She hadn't missed the look of fear on Mrs. Moore's face when she mentioned calling the police or the knowing look when Lynette warned her to be careful. Did Mrs. Moore not want the police called, or had her husband forbidden it?

Lynette hoped those little girls were all right. She took a deep breath and picked up the phone to call Jim. Maybe it wasn't such a good idea to keep Moore's secrets any longer, and she could trust Jim. Couldn't she?

She hesitated before letting out a long, shaky breath and placing the phone back in its cradle.

***

Penny's heart thumped erratically as she drove home constantly checking the rearview mirror. Once home, she breathed a sigh of relief that Alex's car was not in the driveway. She raced inside, nearly knocking over Teresa in her haste.

"Es everything okay?"

"Sí, Teresa. Everything is fine. I have a headache and wish to be left alone."

She fled to her room before Teresa could ask any more questions.

Penny swallowed two Xanax tablets and crawled under the covers.

***

Before

After several dates, Penny invited Alex to a home-cooked dinner at her place. It was snowing, and snow always brought out her domestic side. She looked forward to impressing Alex with her cooking skills. She wasn't sure where this thing with Alex would lead, but she was willing to find out, especially if she ended up getting up what she wanted.

Penny set out the ingredients on the granite countertop for one of her favorite starters, Maryland Crab Soup. Once the soup was simmering and dinner was in the oven, she surveyed her surroundings, trying to decide where they should dine. The dining room was easily the nicest room in the house with its one-of-a-kind crystal chandelier and Louis XIV furniture that Penny bought in an antique shop in St. Michaels on Maryland's Eastern Shore. She and Joe loved to entertain, and the dining room was their showplace. But tonight, Penny thought the large chairs and table for ten seemed too impersonal for dinner with Alex.

Her kitchen was cozy and warm, both figuratively and literally, with a round oak table in the middle between custom made cabinets at one end and at the other, a large stone two-sided fireplace that looked into the living room. It was the perfect place to sit with close family and friends and enjoy a home-cooked meal. Tonight, however, was not about family and friends. It was about getting what she wanted from Alex. Penny continued to ponder the perfect setting.

Deciding on cozy but intimate, she carried a tablecloth into the great room and spread it over the antique seaman's trunk she used for a coffee table. She turned on the fireplace and reached to the mantle to take down pewter candlesticks. She set them on the trunk.

Penny turned on the stereo hidden inside the armoire that served as an entertainment center and selected one of Joe's light jazz CDs. As she surveyed the scene, the doorbell rang. She checked her reflection in the hall mirror on her way to the foyer.

When she opened the door, Alex handed Penny a bottle of expensive Chablis and an enormous bouquet of lilies.

"For you," he said as he reached for her other hand and bent to kiss it.

"My favorites. Thank you. Please, come in, Alex." She felt giddy as she led him into the living room.

"Why don't you open the wine and pour us each a glass while I get our starters," Penny instructed, showing him the mini-bar in the corner of the room.

She could see he was impressed by her home. The interior showed off her knack for decorating and confirmed she had money.

Penny put the tray of food on the trunk and sat on a cushion, then studied Alex as he lit the candles, trying not to compare him to her Joe. In looks, there was no comparison. Where Joe was movie star handsome, Alex's attractiveness was in his charm and presence. He was probably nearing 60, almost twenty years her senior, and had developed that middle age paunch of older men. His hair was gray and thinning, although he tried to hide that fact, which made Penny smile. She liked the man despite herself and thought she might enjoy this evening more than she planned.

"For you," Alex said, handing her a glass and sitting on the other cushion. "Forgive my awkwardness. I don't often eat on the floor."

"Oh, but it's so much more fun." Penny smiled and sipped her wine. She enjoyed the taste of the wine as it flowed over her tongue and down her throat. And she enjoyed watching Alex. "Oh, this is very good. I'm not much of a drinker, but I do enjoy a glass of fine wine with dinner." She smiled sensually and knew Alex was affected by her in more ways than one. It made her feel powerful, and she enjoyed watching the play of emotions on his face.

Alex continued filling the wine glasses as they ate the soup, then the main course, and talked in front of the fire. Penny wasn't sure if Alex was using the wine to suppress his urges or entice hers.

"I don't think I've ever had Chicken Marsala as good as this." Alex complimented Penny as he chose and opened a bottle from Penny's own selection. He complimented her repeatedly that evening, and Penny let the alcohol go to her head. She was soon giggling at everything Alex said, brushing his arm with her hand as they leaned back against the leather sofa. It was unlike her to lose control, but she dismissed the voice in the back of her head telling her to take it easy on the wine.

When Alex told her goodnight, he bent and kissed her, stirring feelings she had long since let die. Before tonight, Penny thought his affection for her was one-sided, but she decided she was quite fond of Alex Moore.

CHAPTER TWELVE

After

Jim left Susan's house and headed toward the station. He had more questions now than when he arrived. He called Agent Morelli as he drove.

"Can you get me a warrant? I don't want to get one locally."

"What's it for?"

Jim told him the whole story about Cassie and Ellie. He told his FBI handler he hoped to find out more from the Social Services file.

"Do you think this has something to do with our investigation?"

"I'm not sure," Jim answered honestly. "But if my instincts are correct, these girls may help us find another way in. They may be the key to getting inside Moore's estate."

"I can have it for you later this afternoon. Will that work?"

"Sounds good, Tony. Thanks."

Jim hated to wait even a few hours, but his hands were tied. He hoped they could afford the wait.

By mid-afternoon, Lynette needed some fresh air. She'd been in the office all day, and she was a nervous wreck. Many questions plagued her. Was Jim going to return with a warrant? Would Mrs. Moore be back? And when would Mr. Moore decide to make an appearance? She didn't want to be there to find out.

"I'm leaving early," she told the receptionist as she walked out the door.

Lynette knew just what to do to take her mind off what was going on. She drove toward the mall and cranked up the radio. Classic rock from the 80s poured through the speakers. *There's nothing like Bon Jovi to take your mind off your worries*, she thought with a smile.

As Lynette left the town limits and headed toward the shopping center, a black Mercury Capri with rental plates kept pace with her a couple cars back. When she put on her signal and pulled into the parking garage, the Capri followed her in. Lynette swayed to the tune of Billy Joel's *Uptown Girl*. She had no idea the driver of the Capri watched her every move.

Turning off the car, Lynette grabbed her purse and opened the door just as the man in the Capri stepped out of the car.

"Lynette White, fancy seeing you here," he said with a smile, and Lynette stiffened at the sound of the familiar voice.

"I didn't recognize you. It's been a long time. What are you doing here?" She closed the car door, her keys dangling in her hand. A sudden chill ran across the back of her neck, and she regretted getting out of the car.

"It has been." He walked closer, his hands casually stuffed in his pants pockets. "You still look as beautiful as always," he said with a sly grin.

She recalled how he'd made her uncomfortable back when they briefly dated. There was something about him she could never quite name. She was glad when he stopped calling.

"Can I help you with something?"

"Lynette, I don't really have time for small talk."

Lynette braced herself, noting the change in his demeanor.

"I need some information about two of your foster children. I believe they go by the names Cassie and Ellie."

Lynette paled.

"This is kind of a strange place for a meeting, don't you think?" She swallowed and swept her gaze around the garage, hoping to see someone else nearby. "I didn't know you knew Cassie and Ellie. What is your connection to them?"

"I've known them for years," he said, ignoring her question. "Let's just say I have strong feelings for them."

Lynette didn't like the look in his eyes or the way he was inching closer to her with every word.

"Look, I need to go. I'm meeting some girlfriends, and they'll be worried if I'm late."

He was on her at once, pressing her against the car, his knees gripping her legs, his hands darting out from his pockets to her waist and throat. He was wearing gloves, and the realization sent her into a panic. She tried to breathe, but his grip around her throat tightened.

"Don't lie to me, Lynette," he said as he pressed against her, wedging her between his body and her Honda. "Tell me where they are."

"I honestly don't know," she gasped, terrified by the hatred she saw in his expression. She couldn't scream with his hand cutting off her air. She choked out, "You can ask the police. I told them the same thing."

"I won't be asking the police, Lynette." His other hand reached under her bouse, and she felt something cold and sharp against her side. "If you know what's good for you, you'll tell me where they are."

The cold feeling turned warm. She felt it spreading down her side.

"What are you doing?" she gasped.

"Who has them, Lynette?" he demanded. "Tell me now or I go deeper."

Instinctively, she tried to scream, but she couldn't find her breath.

"Please," she whispered, almost inaudibly. "You must believe me. I honestly don't know where they are."

She felt the blade enter more deeply into her side.

"Last chance, my sweet. Where are Cassie and Ellie?"

"I don't know," she gasped as the knife made its final thrust into her flesh.

She struggled to breathe and felt the blood pouring down her side as she had one last realization. She suddenly knew who the father was, and those girls were in grave danger.

"I always liked you. Too bad it had to be this way, but I don't want anybody else questioning you about those brats." He twisted the knife and tore it through her middle before pulling it out.

"Jim," she sputtered, blood filling her mouth. "I'm sorry, Jim." Her body went limp.

Jim was at home, working on his laptop, when his cell phone rang. As he listened, his throat went dry, and the fingers of his free hand froze over the keyboard.

"Yes, Sir." He jumped from his seat and grabbed his jacket. "How long ago did it happen?" Jim's superior gave him the gruesome details.

"Any ID? Security video?"

"No ID and no video, as far as we know" the chief growled. "The responding officers are waiting for you to give orders. Coroner's in route."

"Okay, on my way," Jim breathed as he ended the call. "I'll be there in ten."

He shoved the phone into his jeans pocket and grabbed his wallet from the desk as he raced out of the room. He hoped this new case didn't halt his investigation of Moore.

"Hold on, hold on," Susan said to the singing phone as she finished doctoring the store-bought marinara sauce. She put a lid on the pan and checked the clock. It was just about five.

"Hello," she said, peeking into the living room to check on Cassie and Ellie.

"Be ready to move immediately if I say so." Jim's tone was hushed but hurried.

"What is that supposed to mean? Move where?"

"I don't know yet," he barked. "Just start thinking of a safe place to go. And not your mother's or any friends' houses."

"That doesn't leave me a lot of options, Jim. What's going on? You're scaring me." Susan leaned on the counter, holding one hand to her forehead, which did nothing to stop the blood throbbing in her temple.

"I'm sorry, Susan. I don't mean to scare you." He sighed. "I just want you to be prepared so you're safe. And rest assured I'm going to do my best to keep you safe. Just do as I say and keep your cell nearby and turned on. Don't use your house phone. If I call and tell you to leave, then leave. Go somewhere people won't think to look for you, but get word to me somehow to let me know where you are. Don't use your cell in that case. In fact, take the battery out if you can."

"You've got to be kidding," she said in disbelief. "Where am I supposed to go, and how am I supposed to leave word for you? I've got a business to run, a house being renovated, and two children to think of. What is going on?"

Susan didn't realize she had raised her voice until Ellie came in and grabbed her hand. Susan saw the questions and fear in Ellie's little face. She squeezed her hand and forced a smile to assure the child everything was going to be fine.

"I'm not saying you're going to have to go anywhere. Just be prepared. Things are heating up. I have to go." With that, Jim was gone, and Susan was left wondering what to do next.

Suddenly Mannie was in the kitchen. "Susan," he said, "whatever you need, wherever you need to go, I'm here to help."

Susan, grateful for Mannie's friendship, sank down into the chair, pulling Ellie onto her lap. With Mannie's hand on her shoulder, Susan took a deep breath and tried to formulate a plan. The first thing she needed to do was assure Ellie everything was okay.

"Let's go see what Cassie's doing, okay?" Susan smiled at Ellie. The little girl nodded, and they went into the next room.

Once Ellie was settled and she and Cassie were playing in front of the television, Susan led Mannie back to the kitchen and told him everything.

"Please forgive me for not telling you the truth. I wasn't sure whether it was safe to tell anyone else, for your sake as much as theirs." She motioned to the girls. She went to the cabinets and reached for a glass, then poured Mannie a Coke and filled her glass with water. "I didn't believe Jim thought there was any real danger, but apparently he does now." She sat back down at the table.

Mannie listened quietly, nodding his head and sipping his soda as she talked.

"There are just so many questions left unanswered. I don't know what to believe, or think, or feel." She sighed and closed her eyes, resting her head on her hand.

"Susan, come stay with us. We will help."

"Mannie, I know you and Gina would help. Gracias. But I'm not going anywhere yet. You, on the other hand, have been here all day. You should be gone by now. Please go home to Gina and the children."

Mannie looked at her for a moment before nodding.

"Susan, I think…"

"Mannie, I'm fine, and I'll tell you if I need help. I promise."

Susan finally persuaded Mannie to go home though he wanted to stay on her couch. She assured him Gina needed him more than she did, and Jim would be there soon.

Cassie and Ellie sat at the table, playing Candy Land, as Susan finished preparing dinner. Six o'clock came and went, but they hadn't heard back from Jim. Susan had managed to eat a little spaghetti with the girls before putting them to bed. She watched the evening news in awe as the reporter told of the mysterious death of Lynette White, a social worker in Lakespring. Susan blinked back tears as she watched the story unfold.

When she heard the knock on the door, Susan ran and flung it open. She saw Jim and instinctively fell into his arms, trying her best to stay strong but allowing him to hold her together.

"Let's get inside," Jim said, closing the door behind him. Susan took a deep breath and led him to the kitchen. She made a cup of tea, handed Jim a soda, and sat at the table. Jim sat across from her.

After a few minutes of silence, Susan spoke. "What is going on?" She shook her head in wonder. "What happened to Lynette?"

Jim reached across the table and grasped her hands in his. He groaned. "Murdered. In the mall parking lot near her house. I can't believe it. I've known Lynette for a long time. I blame myself for what happened to her." He opened his eyes and looked at Susan. "I won't let anything happen to you; I promise."

Susan held his gaze and asked, "Her death, was it because of..."

"I don't know, but I can't help but think it might be," he conceded. He sat back and let go of her hand to rake his curly hair. "Nobody saw anything. There's no security video. According to her co-workers, Lynette left work early, unusual for her, and didn't tell anyone where she was going. Nobody knows why she was at the mall. A woman went to put her baby in his car seat and saw Lynette's body lying between their cars. Her screams alerted other shoppers and the security guard. Lynette was already dead."

"The reporter said she'd been stabbed."

"Yeah. If that's what you want to call it. The knife was twisted so far inside of her, he pulled out part of her... Well, it was bad." He took a drink before continuing. "I ID'd her on the scene. Her purse and keys were missing. We've got a team at her house and office. We did find a pair of bloody gloves and a knife in a nearby trashcan."

"Really? The killer had to know you'd find them."

Jim shrugged. "I guess he didn't care. He knew there was no other evidence, and there were no prints on the knife. Better to ditch them than to get caught with them. And maybe he's so brazen, he doesn't think he can be caught. Who knows what he was thinking?"

"It's 2013. What about DNA on the gloves? Surely, you have the technology."

"Sure, but it's not a quick process. It can take six months or more for results to come back."

Susan frowned. "That long? You're kidding me."

Jim shrugged. "The average turnaround time in Maryland is 110 days, but that depends upon how many cases there are. I've seen it take twice that long."

"Wow. But what does this have to do with Cassie and Ellie? Couldn't it be a coincidence? Maybe she was just in the wrong place at the wrong time."

Jim shook his head. "I don't believe in coincidence. I questioned her yesterday, and today she's randomly murdered after leaving work in a hurry? That can't be a coincidence. And there's more. The administrative assistant at Social Services said a woman wearing sunglasses and a long cape visited Lynette's office shortly after ten this morning. The woman claimed she was Cassie and Ellie's foster mother, but the admin told me she couldn't recall ever hearing of any children named Cassie and Ellie. Lynette intercepted the woman and took her into her office and closed the door. The woman left about fifteen minutes later. Lynette left shortly after that. When the other employees heard the news, they shut down the place and went home. By the time I got a hold of the admin to let me into the office, somebody else had beaten me there."

"Lynette's keys," Susan said.

He nodded, finished his drink, and continued. "Probably. At first everything seemed fine. The doors were locked, and the lights were off. Lynette's office was locked, as were most of the filing cabinets."

Jim looked at Susan and reached for her hand.

"But her computer was gone. Not the whole thing, just the CPU."

The implication of his words sunk in as Susan watched Jim's face. She laid her free hand over his.

"Would the girls' whereabouts be on there?" Susan looked around.

"I don't know. We don't know what background info was on the computer, if anything at all. There was no paper file on the girls. Whoever killed her either took it, or it never existed." He shook his head, and a scowl crossed his features. "I left my card with Lynette, more like threw it at her. She didn't have it on her, and it wasn't in her office, so I have to go on the assumption that her killer took it. I don't know if she wrote down anything about my visit, so whoever did this may not know why I was there, but he, or she, most likely has my card. Unfortunately, we have no way of knowing what other information he may have gotten out of Lynette."

"You cared for her, didn't you?"

"Is it that obvious?"

"It's the way you say her name, *Lynette*, not like someone you dated casually."

"It was more than casual, but not quite serious. At least, not on my end. She wasn't..." He looked away, shook his head. "We broke up on good terms." His free hand brushed through his hair again as he paused and took a deep breath. He held it and exhaled. "I think she may have been working for Moore."

"Then you may be in danger." Susan squeezed his hand with hers.

"I'm a cop, Susan. I'm always in danger. Nothing you've done could've changed that."

"But I've added to it. I've put you in danger by asking you to investigate this."

Jim let go of Susan's hands and moved around the table to sit next to her. He took her chin between his fingers and looked her in the eye. "And where would you be now if you hadn't come to me? At least I can try to keep you safe."

A familiar twinge in her gut pulled at her.

"Now," Jim said, "I need something very important in order to continue protecting you."

"Okay, what is it?" Susan said with resolve, strengthened by his touch and closeness.

"Dinner," Jim said seriously. "I need dinner. I'm starving."

On the other side of town, Alex answered the phone. The girls hadn't been found. Before hanging up, he was told to turn on the evening news. Alex switched on the television in his study and watched the breaking story.

He went into the kitchen where he found Penny watching the news as dinner burned in the oven behind her. She had a drink in her hand. The police at the scene declined to comment on the murder.

"Did you have a nice talk with the social worker this morning?" Alex said to his wife.

Penny felt the shock. "How did you...?"

"I know everything you do. Don't you know that by now? You can't go anywhere or do anything without me knowing or finding out." He pointed to the TV. "Are you happy? She didn't have to die, Penny. All you had to do was keep quiet and let me handle this. But no, you had to go to Social Services and let them know the girls were missing. That made someone very angry. Way to go, Penny. I hope you feel good about yourself."

Alex left the room in disgust as Penny put her head on the table and wept.

Penny locked the door to her room that night. She knew nothing could keep Alex out if he wanted to come in, but it made her feel better to turn the lock.

She walked to the mirror and stared at her reflection. She had aged over the past week, more than ever before in her life, but that wasn't what bothered her. What made her squirm was the lack of recognition of the woman gazing back at her.

The beauty pageant queen, with all her confidence and poise, was gone. Staring back at Penny was a defeated woman, someone with no spine, no confidence, and no hope for her future. Slowly, over the past five years, Alex had beaten it out of her, verbally, emotionally, and physically.

⚬

Before

The morning after their dinner, long-stemmed, red roses arrived at Penny's door. She blushed like a schoolgirl when she read the card, her thoughts still a bit fuzzy, but her body sending her signals she couldn't deny. She liked Alex. The thought astounded her. Penny found herself drawn to the man.

Despite any lingering doubts, Alex became the perfect suitor. He didn't overpower her but gradually gained her trust. He asked her to join him at several fundraising events until their names became linked in the social columns.

A year and a half after Joe's death, Alex and Penny attended a fundraiser together, and on the way home, Alex surprised Penny with a question.

"Penny," he said, his hand on her knee in the back of the limo. "I'm going away on business this weekend. I'd like you to come to Atlantis with me."

She was up half the night, trying to decide what to do. Maybe going to the Caribbean with Alex would be the thing she needed to get him to open up. It had been well over a year since she first called him, and while she was enjoying his attention and their many dates, she was growing impatient.

Did he really see a future with her? Or was all this just a ploy to get her into his bed? She couldn't bring herself to ask him that question, but she knew she could use her womanly charms to make him level with her. She may be naïve when it came to Alex's world, but she knew how to get a man to talk.

CHAPTER THIRTEEN

After

Alex paced his home office, his blood boiling, and not from the bourbon in his hand. This was all Denny's fault.

Denny Simpson was the son of a prominent congressman and grew up in the political arena. It was always assumed he would follow in his father's footsteps although he took a more local route than national. Simpson began at the grass roots level, working on campaigns, becoming a member of the Central Committee, County Council, and finally Mayor.

Alex had been part of his political dynasty from the beginning, and he enjoyed the power, the money, and the women. He was the best man when Denny married June in a lavish outdoor wedding on the shore of the Chesapeake Bay. June Simpson adored her husband and did anything he asked, which was something Alex could never fathom. She was too good for Denny. She was totally in love and had eyes only for him. Denny's eyes, however, never stopped wandering.

Alex had gotten him out of numerous romantic entanglements over the years, and he always felt bad for poor, unsuspecting June. Alex, at least, had always been loyal to whichever woman he was married to.

Denny loved his wife, but he loved the thrill of an affair even more. Every liaison was fleeting. Often, they were married women. Over the years, Alex cleaned up many bad situations for his friend. He even got mixed up in a police brawl years ago when Denny got involved with a policeman's wife. The cop threatened Simpson, but Alex stepped in to make sure the cop realized with whom he was dealing.

The cop had a good reputation but kept looking for ways to embarrass the mayor and pry into their business ventures. Eventually the cop became so obsessed with Simpson's downfall, he lost his hold on everything else and was forced to resign as chief of police by the Town Council. Alex later heard that the cop came to terms with his wrecked life and career by drinking his troubles away.

⚬

Jim quickly finished the reheated, delectable Italian meal. Susan was a great cook, which surprised Jim for some reason.

"Where'd you learn to cook?" He was unable to hide his amazement.

"What's that supposed to mean?" Susan asked with narrowed eyes.

"It means this is really good. I didn't know you could make anything other than chocolate chip cookies."

"There's a lot you don't know about me, Jim," Susan said casually as she stood up and took his dishes.

"I know you make a darned good marinara sauce," Jim said, wiping his face as he stood to help her clean up.

The sound of giggling flowed down from the top of the steps.

"Girls?" Susan called up as she made her way from the kitchen. "What are you doing up?"

"We heard Jim laughing and decided to see what you were doing."

He insisted they call him Jim. He thought, if they felt more comfortable with him, more like friends, maybe they would trust him.

"Well, if it isn't my favorite little girls. Come on down, and tell me goodnight. It's getting late."

Both girls ran down the stairs, and Jim crouched at the bottom of the steps. They leaped into his outstretched arms. Jim reached down to tickle Ellie. Her laugh deepened. He wondered if Ellie's more frequent laughs and giggles were signs she might speak soon.

"Okay, girls, Jim has to go soon, and you need to get back to bed."

"Can you come back tomorrow?" Cassie asked.

"I hope so," Jim answered honestly.

"Jim, look at my new nightgown. Do you like it?"

"Very nice, Cassie," Jim answered. "Did you brush your teeth?"

"Ages ago," Cassie said. "And we're still not tired" She looked up at Susan.

"Okay, five more minutes while we finish the dishes."

"Yay!" Cassie cheered as they went to the kitchen.

"Don't you girls think Miss Susan is a great cook," Jim asked, taking the parmesan cheese from the table. The girls nodded.

"My mom's a pretty good cook, you know," Susan said, returning to Jim's earlier remark. "I learned from her."

He put away the cheese while Susan talked and wiped down the table.

"Mom taught me a lot when we were on our vacations. We usually stayed at places with kitchens, so we didn't have to spend a lot of money eating out."

"I hated it when you went on vacation," he said, placing his glass in the dishwasher. "I used to count the days until you'd get back."

"No, you didn't," Susan said with a click of her tongue. "You probably counted the days until I left. I followed you everywhere."

"That's not how I remember it," Jim said, taking a rinsed plate from her hand and brushing her fingers with his. They both stopped and looked at each other. Jim's heart skipped a beat.

She's so beautiful, standing there with the glow of twilight coming through the window. What have I done without her all these years?

Susan and Jim continued to smile at each other as Cassie and Ellie twirled around the kitchen, their nightgowns billowing around them. Despite the gruesome event of the day, the evening felt almost magical to Jim.

Later, as Jim drove home, he thought about Susan. She was right. There was so much he didn't know about her anymore. What was her favorite movie? What did she like to do in her spare time?

His cell phone put an end to his thoughts as he recognized the number of Ron's Bar. His long day was about to get longer. He answered the call then headed toward the oldest bar in town.

It was also the only bar in town. There was the sports pub that opened in a strip mall on the other side of town, and one of the fancier restaurants had a bar at its center, but Ron's Bar was a real bar—what would be called a honky-tonk in a southern state—with dim lighting, beer on tap, country music on the juke box, and Ron, a bartender with a heart.

The bar struggled for a short time after many Maryland counties banned smoking, but Ron's was still able to turn a profit. Most of Ron's patrons were retired, old men who quit smoking years ago. They came for a drink, a frozen burger tossed on the blackened grill, and fries cooked in oil as old as Jim—the only food Ron served—and the reassurance he would make sure they got home safely.

When Jim arrived, his father was clearly agitated, more so than Jim had ever seen him.

"He's been agitated all evening," Ron said.

"Is he making any sense this time?"

"Not really. Just more of the usual. I wish I knew what he meant."

Jim gave a nod. "I hear you. Thanks, Ron."

Jim helped his father out to the car. His dad looked up at him and said the same thing he'd been saying for years. "I wish I could've done more. I tried, you know. I tried to stop him."

"I know Dad. I know." Jim never knew to what his father was referring, but there was no use asking him. By morning, he would be back to his normal stoic self, the tough, retired cop who never let anyone, including his own son, into his private thoughts. It was only at night, after a couple hours at Ron's, that Mike Russell let his defenses down. Unfortunately, he never elaborated on his regrets.

Cassie and Ellie lay in their beds, both awake, staring at the ceiling.

"Something bad happened today, Ellie," Cassie told her sister. "I think it might have been because of us." She turned on her side and faced Ellie. "I don't know what to do."

Ellie didn't know either. Cassie always had all the answers. She blinked back the tears that were threatening to spill from her eyes and tried to swallow the lump in her throat. She liked it here. It reminded her of home, their real home. She remembered so little about her mother, but she knew their mother loved them very much. She felt Miss Susan's love, too.

The little girl rolled away from her sister's gaze and faced the open window where the curtains blew in the breeze.

"Ellie, I know you don't want to hear this, but you have to listen," Cassie demanded. "If anything else happens, we're leaving. Do you understand? We can't let him hurt Miss Susan. Ellie, do you understand?" Cassie's voice was firm.

Ellie gave no signs of understanding or even hearing Cassie. After a minute, Cassie turned the other way and stared at the wall.

The moonglow cast on the room should have made Ellie less afraid, but instead, it gave her an eerie feeling, as if it were shining a spotlight on their whereabouts. Despite her age, Ellie wasn't naïve. She'd seen a lot in her short five years. She knew her sister was right. She knew there were bad men after them, and she just wanted them to go away and leave her and Cassie alone.

<hr>

After Mannie and Gina put their children to bed, Mannie closed the door and turned to his wife. He sat on the edge of the bed and pulled her to him.

"You've been so serious tonight, my love. What is wrong? Did something happen at Susan's?" Gina sat next to him and took his hand.

"Does your cousin still work for those rich folks on the other side of town?"

Gina looked confused. "Yes. Why do you ask?"

"I've always thought there was something strange about the arrangement—her coming here so quickly and unexpectedly, not wanting you to know where she lives, and how she's allowed so little contact with you. I'm surer than ever something is very bad in that house."

<hr>

The man sat at the desk in his hotel room and smiled. He marveled at his own genius at times. He had a hunch everyone would clear out of the Social Services building when they heard the news about Lynette, and his hunch had been right. He'd timed it perfectly so he could be in and out before the cops arrived to search it.

Of course, getting in wasn't a problem. He had a key. Always organized, Lynette had placed small stickers on each of her keys—SS, OFC, FC, DK, and HM. It didn't even take his high IQ to figure out her system—Social Services, Office, Filing Cabinet, Desk, and Home.

He had located the security system keypad on the wall and disengaged the alarm, a piece of cake for him. Lynette's nameplate was on her office door, and he used the OFC key to get inside.

The search only took a few minutes. He hadn't needed to worry about unlocking the filing cabinets. Just as he suspected, the file was in the desk drawer, which he conveniently opened with the DK key. He assumed Lynette would have it nearby. He doubted she ever kept it in the filing cabinet to begin with. She wouldn't take a chance on one of her co-workers coming across forged documents. He planned on making the contents of the file public in due time, but not before taking care of some other, unfinished business.

He had taken the CPU with him and made sure to lock everything up and turn off the lights as he left. Walking right through the front door, he tipped the baseball cap with a fake logo to a passerby and walked around the block to his car. Once he was out of sight of the building, he pulled into a parking lot and ripped the magnetic strips off the car that displayed the logo of a fictitious company.

Techies to Go

Make your blue screen our problem!

He waited until dinner to get back to work. He watched the news, gloating when the police chief admitted the motive for the killing was "unknown at this time."

After finishing off an expensive bottle of Argentinian Malbec, he was ready to hack into the computer for the rest of the information he needed.

Lynette's password was the name of her street. Anyone who knew her could figure that out, or anyone with her driver's license in his hand. He almost chuckled to himself as he thought about it.

A quick look at her files confirmed his assumption. Penny Moore was listed as a foster parent, but her record was labeled 'No Longer Available' without any mention of the children currently in her care. According to the computer, Penny hadn't fostered any children. As far as Social Services was concerned, Cassie and Ellie didn't exist. Soon, they wouldn't exist at all.

CHAPTER FOURTEEN

After

The next day, the parking garage was still roped off with yellow tape. Lynette's body was at the morgue, but her car had not been picked up. The forensics team was long gone, but the police officer assigned to guard the scene was alert when Jim arrived. He wanted to take another look around, though he knew the chances of finding anything were slim. Still, Jim felt he owed it to Lynette to look again.

Other than the clean knife and probably useless gloves, the only clue they had was a partial bloody footprint. The killer hadn't even tried to hide his steps back to his car. Jim knew there was little chance they could trace the prints to anyone. Still, they had taken the appropriate pictures, calculated the size of the shoe, and were working on determining the brand. That was where it would end, though. Miraculous crime links only happened on television, especially with the same gym shoes being available at every department and discount store in the nation.

This guy was smart, but he didn't really have to be. There were no security cameras, and without a witness or any hard evidence, it wasn't likely Jim, the FBI, or anyone else would be able to identify Lynette's murderer. Jim knew it, and he was sure the killer knew it, too.

* * *

Lynette's killer was back in his office, working diligently. He'd hidden the file until after he finished phase two of his plan. Phase one had been implemented weeks ago when he began attempting to contact anyone the brats had met since moving to Lakespring. He'd even sent a letter to the wife of Moore's young protégé, Eddie Reynolds, telling her Eddie was involved with another woman. Part of him regretted using Eddie that way. But the traitor refused to cooperate and needed to be eliminated.

The next step was to find the brats, but he might not have as much time as he hoped. Lynette may have talked to the police about them after all, judging by the card he found tucked into the file.

He held the business card in his hand and read it again—Detective Jim Russell, Lakespring Police Department.

Jim—the same name Lynette whispered with her last breath. Were they acquaintances, friends, lovers, or was he there on business? Was the card a coincidence? If he was there on business, did she call him, or did he go to her?

He'd have to see what the cop knew and determine whether to get rid of him, too. Not yet though. He couldn't risk it so soon. He needed to be seen in his office and to look like he was working as usual.

Phase two would begin soon. It would take a couple days to make the right contact, but once he put the feelers out, he would find the right person.

He hoped he could find the kids on his own and avoid hiring someone. It would cost him a heavy sum if he had to put a hit on the cop, and he didn't want to go that route for him either. Hits on kids and cops weren't taken quickly, even by the most entrepreneurial assassins. If he had to, he'd hired someone to do the kids first. If he could get rid of them, that would be enough. That had been the goal all along once he learned about them—to eliminate Cassie and Ellie.

<hr>

It took a couple days to find the time, because of the ongoing murder investigation, but Jim managed to make a visit to The Bentley School. He was shocked, but grateful, that Moore hadn't reported them missing yet. It confirmed Jim's suspicions that the girls knew something Moore didn't want known to the world.

Jim asked for a private meeting with the headmistress, who must not have been happy to have a police officer show up at the school. He was put in his place right away by being told to wait in the hall until she was able to see him.

While he waited, Jim took in the artwork along the walls. These kids were learning specifically about the Maryland state dinosaur, *Astrodon johnstoni.*

Maryland has a state dinosaur? Jim shook his head in disbelief.

"Dr. Peterson will see you now," the secretary told him from the doorway of the main office. She led Jim back to the private office of the headmistress.

"What can I do for you, Officer?" Dr. Peterson peered at Jim over her glasses while folding her hands on the desk in front of her. She wasn't even going to give him enough time to make it worth removing her reading glasses.

"I'm working on a case that involves two of your students. I believe go as Cassie and Ellie Moore." He paused, waiting for a response, but she simply stared at him. He continued, "Cassie and Ellie are now in protective custody. I cannot disclose where, why, or with whom."

"Detective Russell, I am aware that the Moore children have missed school, but I have not been notified by their foster parents nor any other agency saying they are in police custody. Do you have something with you now proving that to be a fact?" Her tone was businesslike, not friendly but not antagonistic either.

"You're being notified now." Jim kept his own tone even as he produced a paper from his pocket he obtained from Agent Morelli. It said very little about the situation, and Dr. Peterson eyed him suspiciously.

"This says the children are no longer with Mr. and Mrs. Moore. I'm sure you don't have them in a holding cell somewhere." Her smile was forced. "Where are they now?"

"I'm sorry, ma'am. I can't tell you that. As I said, this is part of an ongoing investigation."

"I see. Is there something you want from me or the school, Detective Russell, or is this just a friendly visit to inform me of the situation?"

"Actually, Dr. Peterson," Jim said, taking what he hoped was a more agreeable track." I'm hoping to get whatever work the girls have missed over the past couple weeks and would like to continue to pick up their work while they're in custody." Getting information out of tis woman without a warrant was going to be difficult, but this might ingratiate Jim with her.

The headmistress thought this over. She removed her glasses and closed her eyes, pinching the bridge of her nose. "I think that can be arranged, Detective, but you will go through me and no one else. You will not have the freedom to walk around the school and will not have contact with any teachers or staff at this institution." She looked at Jim, her expression serious but compassionate. "Are Cassie and Ellie all right?"

"Yes, they're fine. They're safe and well. We're taking good care of them."

Dr. Peterson nodded, seemingly satisfied with his answer.

"We do ask that you not contact Mr. or Mrs. Moore, and speak to no one about this situation or about the girls in general."

"Am I to assume I should not answer any questions from Mr. and Mrs. Moore should they contact me?"

"That's correct, ma'am. The Moores do not know the whereabouts of Cassie and Ellie and are not to be told of any contact you have with the police."

"Are the Moores being investigated for something?"

"I'm sorry. I'm unable to divulge that information."

"I understand. You may return tomorrow for the class and homework information. You will be given access to their Edmodo accounts so you may see what their assignments are. They may turn in their work through the online portal." Dr. Peterson put her glasses back on and stood, motioning to the door. "Thank you for coming."

Jim assumed their meeting was over. He was glad Susan had the girls and not him. He had no idea what language the headmistress was speaking.

Mannie walked into the kitchen while Susan was making herself a cup of tea. Cassie and Ellie were still in bed, but Susan had been up for hours trying to figure out how to rearrange her travel schedule.

"Susan, we need to talk."

Susan met his gaze. She could hear José using a drill in the sunroom.

"What do we need to talk about? Is everything all right with the room?"

"Sì, it's about the girls."

The mug in Susan's hand stopped halfway to her mouth. "The girls?"

"Sì, Gina's cousin es Teresa. Señora Moore is her boss." Mannie looked at Susan and waited for her reaction.

"Mrs. Moore is her employer?" Susan repeated slowly. Mannie nodded.

"Mannie, does Teresa know Cassie and Ellie are here?"

"No, Susan. I will not tell anyone. Neither will my nephew."

"Does Teresa know what happened? Why the girls ran away?" Susan sat her mug on the counter, her eyes going to the window, suddenly worried Alex Moore could show up any minute.

"I do not know. We don't hear from Teresa much. Es a very strange situation."

She fingered her mug and watched the steam slowly rise from the tea. She pondered whether to involve Mannie any more than he already was.

"Mannie?" She hesitated but pressed forward. "Could you see if Teresa knows anything that might help us figure out why the girls left? Do you think she could find out anything for us?"

Mannie shook his head. "If I can talk to her, but es very hard. Teresa es scared of Señor Moore, and our contact with her is limited. Something is not right there or with her coming to America..." Mannie stopped there, and Susan knew he had his suspicions about the legality of Teresa's immigration.

"It's okay, Mannie. Thanks for telling me."

Mannie looked at Susan for a moment then went back to work.

He knows something but isn't sure how to tell me or what it means. I'll have to think of a way to find Teresa myself.

⚜

Penny stood on her balcony overlooking the empty back yard and took a heavy gulp of red wine. The swings blew in the breeze. She pictured the girls running around the yard, zipping down the sliding board, and swimming in the pool. They loved the pool, an exact replica of one of the pools at the Atlantis Resort where Alex had proposed. What a fool she'd been. Her marriage had cost her so much. The price was her confidence, her mind, her soul, and maybe her life.

Before

When Penny stepped onto the resort's patio in the Bahamas, she acted giddy with excitement.

"Oh, it's so beautiful here."

The patio led to an infinity pool with cobalt blue water flowing into the Caribbean Sea. Palm trees danced in the breeze as the sun glistened on the water, the white sand beaches and Easter green golf courses were at their beck and call.

As Alex led her through the maze from the grand foyer, with its elaborate Murano glass décor and high-priced designer boutiques, Penny soaked in her surroundings. He didn't take her immediately to their room. She knew he was trying to intoxicate her with all he could offer her, and she was ready to play her part.

She let him show her how to put a twenty-dollar bill into the slot on the machine, as if she'd never seen one before. Three plums lined up in the machine's windows. Bells chimed, and Penny screeched as she realized she had won $100. Alex hit the cash out button and held up the slip of paper showing her winnings.

"Beginner's luck." Alex laughed. "I knew bringing you here was a good idea."

Alex motioned for drinks and handed her one. She was thirsty and drank it right away without thinking about what was in it. Alex handed her another.

After they played a few more rounds, they walked along the outside of the building and strolled through the private swimming area. When Penny was finished with her third drink, Alex suggested they go to their suite and change for a romantic dinner.

In the famed Café Martinique, they feasted on escargot, Caribbean lobster, Crème Brulé, and even more alcohol. They finished the evening with a moonlight stroll on the soft sand, their toes caressed by the warm waves gently washing onto the shore. They held more drinks between their fingers, and Penny appreciated Alex's strong, steadying hand on her back as they made their way to their suite.

The next morning, Penny awoke with a long-stemmed rose on her pillow and attached to it, a small black velvet box. Her head was pounding, and her thoughts were jumbled.

The room seemed to be in motion, but she knew she wasn't in her room, the room where she had changed clothes the previous night. Somehow, she ended up in bed in the other room, Alex's room. But how?

She had on a nightgown she'd never seen before and knew Alex must have undressed her and put this on her. How many drinks had she downed? How had she let herself lose control? It had been a long time since she and Joe drank all night in lavish settings, but she thought she'd be able to handle her alcohol.

Her head throbbed, and the aroma coming from the breakfast tray made her feel nauseous. Her legs were weak as she slowly stood from bed, leaving the velvet box on the pillow. She reached for a nearby chair and attempted to cross the swaying floorboards, but she didn't feel steady enough to go far. It felt as though they were at sea. She slid to the floor and looked around for Alex. Not seeing him, she pulled herself up and stumbled to the bathroom. She barely recognized the woman in the mirror.

Her head suddenly felt as if it would explode, and she sat on the commode to ease the queasy feeling in her stomach.

She tried to remember what happened after their walk on the beach. She saw the empty bottle on the floor.

She was already quite drunk by the time they arrived on the beach. She had a fuzzy memory of Alex kissing her on the lips, the neck, then down...

The familiar longing she had stifled for so long after losing Joe had taken control of her, and she had given in to the sensations her body so eagerly craved. Even now, thinking about how Alex had touched her, she couldn't believe the things they'd done, the things she'd done.

She cried as she wondered what kind of person she had become.

She caught her reflection in the floor to ceiling mirror. She looked like a woman who had enjoyed a night of passion: tussled hair, full red lips, her cleavage spilling out over the top of her nightgown. Even in her youth, she had never given in to any of her suitors. She and Joe had waited until their wedding night to become intimate.

She supposed she'd allowed this to happen by agreeing to go away with Alex. She should have known he wouldn't allow her to resist his advances, and she wouldn't have been able to resist them if she had wanted to. She thought she could play this game, but she was wrong.

Penny downed a glass of water and the ibuprofen Alex had knowingly left for her on the bathroom counter. She walked back to the bed, opened the box, and slipped the ring on her finger.

CHAPTER FIFTEEN

After

Two days passed without incident, but Ellie still hadn't spoken. Cassie refused to elaborate on why.

"Cassie, you do understand there's a reason why Ellie won't speak." Susan talked in a hushed tone while she and Cassie made sugar cookies. She peeked into the living room where Ellie was doing a puzzle with Patrick and Ida.

"I think so," Cassie said. "I mean, I know it's because she's scared, but I'm sure she'll get better. Won't she?" Cassie bit the side of her lip and lifted her gaze to Susan.

"She may not unless she gets help, Cassie. She needs to see a doctor."

"Why? I told you, she's not sick," Cassie insisted.

Susan held a ball of dough in her hand and looked at Cassie. "It may be more than that, Cassie. She might have something wrong in her brain that is causing her not to talk."

"Don't say that! Don't say she has something wrong. She's not stupid!" Cassie threw a piece of dough on the counter.

"Cassie, calm down. I'm not saying that." Susan took a deep breath and tried to figure out what to say. Taking Cassie gently by the shoulders, she locked their gaze. "Look, Cassie, I'm not good at this. I don't know how to explain things so you understand."

"How are the cookies coming?" Ida asked, walking into the kitchen and peeking into the oven.

"Okay," Cassie sulked.

"I bet Ellie likes cookies. Does she have a favorite kind?" Ida picked up a cookie cutter and cut out a bear-shaped piece of dough.

Cassie shrugged. "I don't know. I never asked her. I think it's Oreos," she said quietly.

"Do you know what she wants to be when she grows up?" Ida placed the cookie on the tray without looking at Cassie.

Again, Cassie shrugged.

"Do you know what her favorite book is? Do you know when she doesn't feel well? When she's hurt?"

Cassie shook her head and slowly looked up at Ida. "Miss Susan says she has something wrong in her brain. Do you think she does?"

Ida looked at Susan, who shrugged in defeat.

"No, honey, not something wrong. I think her brain is trying to protect her. It won't let her talk because it's afraid she'll say something that could get her hurt or remind her about what happened. If you won't tell us what happened, will you at least let us try to help Ellie talk again?"

Cassie was quiet for a while before nodding her head.

"I'll call someone tomorrow," Ida told Susan. "My former school psychologist retired a few years ago but is still in the area. I'll see what I can do."

"Thank you." Susan let out the breath she was holding and hugged her mother.

Jim was becoming a regular guest at dinner. The first night, they played Candy Land. The next evening, Jim showed up with a DVD for them to watch together. Jim wanted the girls to feel safe, and he looked for ways to make their lives seem normal. Each night, after Cassie and Ellie went to bed, Jim and Susan compared notes.

Jim already felt comfortable with this new routine, but he was wary that something bad could happen at any minute and was always alert and on guard. He worried Susan and the girls no longer saw the danger in the situation.

When the night's movie ended, Jim and Susan tucked the girls into bed and settled next to each other on the couch. Susan's eyes were heavy, and Jim knew he should go, but he couldn't make himself leave. He continued talking, soft and low, when Susan laid her head on the back of the couch and her eyes slowly closed. He watched her, resisting the urge to caress her cheek.

Suddenly, Susan jolted and sat up, blinking her eyes. She smoothed her hair as her face turned pink.

"It's late," she said, unable to look at him. "You should've woken me."

"You were only out for a few seconds, and you looked so peaceful," Jim whispered, reaching over and stroking her hair. "I didn't want to disturb you."

And I didn't want to leave you and go home alone.

Susan tilted her head up to look into Jim's eyes. "I, I guess you should be going." She rubbed her arms. Jim looked down and saw goosebumps crawling across her flesh.

"Are you cold?" He pulled her into his arms and grabbed the blanket from the back of the couch.

Susan yawned and settled against him as Jim tucked the blanket around her. Their friendship came back so easily, as if they'd never been apart, and Jim couldn't help but wonder if 'friendship' was all she felt.

Just then, they heard screaming from upstairs. Susan jolted again, and Jim was sure his look of horror matched hers, before jumping from the couch. They ran up to the bedroom where Cassie and Ellie were both sitting on Ellie's bed. Cassie held her and tried to soothe her fears.

"She had a nightmare," Cassie told Susan and Jim.

"Oh, Ellie." Susan sat on the bed and wrapped her arms around both girls. "It's okay now, Sweetie. Everything is going to be okay."

Ellie gave a little nod as she tried to gulp down her sobs.

"Can I do anything?" Jim felt helpless.

"I don't think so," Susan said.

Cassie wore a creased brow and tight lips. She looked as worried as he felt. He pulled her from the bed and onto his lap, putting his arms around her.

Ellie's crying grew quiet, and her shoulders stopped shaking.

"Better now?"

Ellie nodded at Susan.

After a few more minutes, Ellie snuggled back under the covers and yawned. She closed her eyes, and rolled over, her breathing becoming a steady rhythm. The room was quiet. Jim tucked Cassie back into bed but continued to watch her until she fell asleep.

"Do you think she's coming around?" Jim asked Susan as they went back downstairs.

"I hope so," she told him. "Though, it's not the first nightmare she's had since she's been here. I can't help but believe it's about whatever happened to them."

"I hope not." He ran his hand through his hair and wondered what Moore had done to those children.

Alex sat at his desk, unmindful of the late hour, a glass of bourbon in his hand. He had exhausted all leads and had no idea where the girls were. His hired man had not found them either, and Penny was beginning to act peculiar. Alex suspected she'd been snooping in his office, going through his files, learning more about where the children had come from and why. He'd always been particular about his desk, and though the drawers were all locked, Penny was resourceful enough to find a way in. He knew his wife, and she had a knack for not leaving well enough alone.

Now he had to worry about what she knew as well as what those brats knew. At least there'd been no news reports about two lost or missing children. And with Lynette out of the picture, nobody would ever find out where the girls had come from.

I should've taken care of her long ago before she could be connected to their disappearance.

Alex stared off into space as he pondered how they could have vanished into thin air and whether Lynette had known where they were hiding.

Too bad it had to be this way, he thought, shaking his head. She was a real looker. But in the end, her death made his life easier. She would never be able to come forward about the girls' invented past.

He threw back the rest of the bourbon, and the expensive libation slid down his throat. As if he didn't have enough problems already, Simpson was on the verge of a nervous breakdown, and Eddie Reynolds' wife reported him missing. What more could go wrong?

He had to find a way to stop those kids from talking. He was sure they'd seen or heard something, and no doubt they wouldn't keep their mouths shut for long.

⸺ ⬦ ⸺

"I talked to the psychologist," Ida told Susan on the phone the next morning.

Susan walked out of the upstairs bathroom, where the girls were brushing their teeth, and lowered her voice. "Will she see Ellie? Does she have any ideas?"

"I didn't tell her everything, of course. She thinks Ellie is my great niece by adoption and may have been abused by her foster parents in another state. She can see her on Friday if that works for you."

"I guess so. I've got to go to Denver soon." Susan was trying to figure out how she was going to keep her business afloat while the girls were in her care. She walked into her office, opened her calendar program, and looked at the appointments on the screen. "Yes, Friday should be okay. I have an appointment tomorrow in Baltimore, and I think I can put Denver off for another week. They're anxious to get their network set up, but they're not on a strict timeline."

"Just let me know how I can help, Susan. You know your father and I are here if you need us."

"Thanks, Mom. I know you are. I've also been thinking of calling Daisy and asking for her help. Jim knows and trusts her, so I think he'd be okay with that. I hate to put everything on you."

"That's a good idea. Playing with her girls might do Cassie and Ellie some good. The three of you began playing together when you were their age."

Only Daisy and I stayed friends, and Jim drifted away.

Susan shook away the thought and decided to call Daisy that night. She would mention it to Jim when he called. She felt guilty about avoiding her best friend and not returning her calls all week.

They said goodbye, and Susan turned back to the computer to plan her workday with two little girls under foot.

"Have you heard anything, Alex?" Penny asked over breakfast. She held her tongue after the death of the social worker, but her mind was working out a plan.

"Not yet, Penny. I told you I'm working on it."

"I'm worried about them, dear. Where could they be? They're just little girls."

"For heaven's sake, Penny. I'm sick of your whining and acting helpless. Go find something to occupy yourself, and let me take care of finding Cassie and Ellie."

I'll find something to occupy myself. As soon as you leave for work, I'll be occupied with the files in your office.

She sipped her cappuccino and concealed her smirk with the newspaper.

"Do we need a warrant for that?" Jim was on the phone with Morelli for their daily briefing.

"Patriot Act, Jim." Morelli confirmed what Jim was thinking. "We can make it work for us. Do you think Lank can handle his part?"

"Like most of the young guys around here, he was born with a mouse in his hand. He won't have a problem. Now explain to me again how this works?"

"The Carnivore is a pretty sophisticated piece of software that will intercept all his emails, web searches, and shared documents. We'll be able to see any and all of Moore's network communications."

"Even if they're encrypted." Jim repeated what he'd been told to make sure he comprehended everything.

"That's correct," Morelli told him. "If he's doing or saying anything related to our investigation, via email, online storage, or shared folders, we'll know about it."

"And all Lank has to do is use this gadget from his car in front of Moore's house," Jim verified.

"Correct again. Anything else?"

"No, that's it. I'll have Lank meet your guy at two o'clock to get set up."

"He'll be there," Morelli said before hanging up the phone.

Jim never thought he would be this grateful to two little girls. Cassie and Ellie running away had been the perfect opportunity to set in motion the electronic surveillance Jim had wanted and needed all along. And they'd given him an in with Susan as well. Jim's work and social life had both benefitted from the girls' misfortune.

I'll make it up to them somehow. That's a promise.

"Goodnight, Jim." Cassie hugged him and gave him a kiss on the cheek.

"Goodnight, Cassie." He smiled, enjoying playing the daddy role. "Thanks for reading to me tonight. You did a super job."

Cassie beamed at the compliment. Ellie was sound asleep in her bed.

Susan turned off the light, and Jim followed her downstairs, anxious to tap her techie brain.

"So, it's called a sniffer?" Jim was amazed by Susan's knowledge of the software Morelli was providing and was eager to learn more.

"Yeah, that's the street name for that type of software. The FBI has been using them for years, or so it's believed, but they're commonplace these days with all the spy shops opening everywhere. That's why it's so important to have passwords on everything, including home networks. Most people still don't." She paused at the kitchen counter and reached for glasses. "Drink?"

"Yeah, I'll have a soda. No glass."

"How can you drink so much caffeine and sleep at night?" She reached for a teacup for her herbal tea.

"I don't have time for much sleep," Jim shrugged as he took a can from the fridge. "So, what else do you know about these sniffers?"

"At one time, they were only used by governments and then by hackers. Now anyone can buy one along with spy cams, bugs, and any other devices that steal our privacy. Of course, nobody cares about privacy anymore with the advent of social media and the government snooping on everyone." She took her tea and moved toward the living room.

"I never thought I'd need so much computer and technical knowledge to be a detective."

Jim waited for Susan to settle on the couch and sat next to her.

"You always did want to be a police officer, didn't you?" Susan asked, stretching her legs out onto the coffee table and propping a pillow under them. "Most kids change their minds a dozen times, but you never wavered." She turned to Jim.

"After all those years of watching my dad and granddad do it, I guess I always knew I would, too. I wanted to branch out a bit. I studied a lot of criminal psychology, profiling, forensics, that sort of stuff. I never stopped wanting to be a cop, but I knew I could be more. There's not much more offered in our little department, but I've had my share of interesting investigations as a detective."

"Like what? Not much happens in Lakespring. At least, not until recently."

"That's not true." Jim feigned being insulted. "Just last year, I had to use my investigative prowess to find out who was stealing flowers from Daisy's greenhouse."

"Well, thank Heaven you were there!" Susan laughed. "I remember that. It was a teenager down the street, attempting to woo the girl he hoped to take to the prom. He had to do community service, delivering flowers for Daisy. When his hours were done, she hired him!"

"A reformed man. Gotta like that." Jim took a deep breath as his thoughts turned serious. "I wish things were always that easy and quiet. The sniper case back in '04 was really trying."

"I didn't know you were involved in that," Susan's voice conveyed surprise and admiration. "I was away at college. Scary time back here."

"The Metro Sniper was the first big case I ever worked on, fresh from the Academy. It was exciting for a rookie, but I'll admit, all that national attention and the suspense it created was a little scary. Nobody knew where they would turn up next. Every department worked closely with the FBI during those few weeks. It was a good training ground for me."

"And the FBI didn't whisk you away from here?" Susan teased.

"No, I was a little too green back then," Jim said with some honesty. Jim's affiliation with the FBI hadn't come about for several years after that, and they still hadn't 'whisked him away' as she put it. "You know, I like what I'm doing. I feel like I'm picking up where my dad left off."

"How's he doing, now that he's retired?"

Jim was certain Susan knew about his struggle to keep his father sober. Things like that were hard to keep quiet in a small town.

"Not well. Even though he's not on the job, the guys let him come and go as he pleases, out of respect. He hasn't been to the office in a while, stays out of Baltimore altogether these days. Unfortunately, he spends most of his time down the street at Ron's, looking down his nose into a bottle." Jim shrugged.

"I'm sorry. Was it the stress of the job?"

"No. It was losing my mother." He sneered, feeling the familiar irritation creep up his spine.

"Really?" Susan said with surprise. "I don't remember him having a drinking problem when we were kids. In fact, I always thought he spent way too much time at the department while you took care of yourself. If he had a problem then, he sure hid it well."

Jim thought for a moment. "Now that you say it, I guess he didn't drink as much back then. He's been like this for so long, I never stopped to think about when it started. From the way he always talked about my mother, I just assumed it was because of her."

"I remember the day your mom left. She put you on the bus that morning and was gone when you got home. You thought it was your fault for a long time. It always made me so sad."

"I know better now. She was never cut out to be a cop's wife. She moved here from the city, thinking country life and marriage to a cop was what she wanted." Jim choked out a mirthful laugh. "Dad says it was because she got pleasure from watching her daddy blow his top that his money might someday go to a do-nothing cop. After six years of trying to persuade my dad to make more of his life, she gave up. I was only five when she went crawling back to her daddy, asking for forgiveness and money for an annulment. I don't even know if she ever told her parents or anyone else I exist. I've never heard from her or from them to this very day." Jim chugged down the rest of his drink.

"I'm so sorry, Jim." Susan reached over and laid her hand on his arm. "I remember how much it hurt you. I would've done anything to take that hurt away."

After all those years hanging out together, this was the first time Jim had ever talked about his mother, and it felt good.

"Don't be sorry. As I said, she wasn't cut out for life with a cop. Not everyone is." He looked to Susan for a reaction.

Susan squeezed his arm. "I'm sure that was her loss."

Jim smiled at Susan. She always knew just what to say to make him feel better, and she'd given him an idea.

As he sat in Susan's driveway, Jim couldn't stop thinking about their conversation. She was right about what a good cop his dad was. Jim checked the clock. If his dad wasn't at Ron's, he might still be up. He put the car in reverse and headed to the house down the street.

"You're investigating who?" his father demanded when they were both seated in the kitchen that hadn't changed since Jim was a child.

"Alex Moore, the Baltimore mayor's chief of staff." Jim subconsciously traced the fake marble pattern on the green 1970-something table that had been around since his dad was a kid.

"Alex Moore?" Mike seemed surprised and confused.

"Yes, Dad, Alex Moore. I thought you were sober."

"I am sober," he said hotly. "I'm always sober."

Jim rolled his eyes. "Anyway, like I said, I was hoping to get your opinion on my case."

"The Alex Moore case?"

"Yes, the Alex Moore case. Come on, Dad. Can I talk to you about the case or not?" Jim stood up and paced around the room.

"Yeah, yeah, what's up?" His voice quavered, but his eyes were clear and bright.

"Do you remember Susan O'Neil?" Jim sat back down on the peeling vinyl chair that matched the table.

"Susan? Of course, I do. I never could understand whatever happened between the two of you. She's not involved with Moore, is she?" Alarm was written all over Mike's face.

"No, not directly. She found these two little girls hiding behind her house. It turns out they're the foster children of Alex and Penny Moore. They ran away after witnessing something, but I don't know what. I wish I did. Anyway, they saw or heard or know something that made them run, and they're scared to death to go back." Jim's hand went to his hair. He prayed that sharing this news with his dad was a good idea. He was beginning to have his doubts. "I've been looking into Moore, Simpson, and their company, trying to see if I can come up with anything, but they've covered their tracks well. That's where you come in."

"Me?" His father asked in surprise.

"Dad, you're the best cop I know. I'm against a brick wall and need to know I'm heading in the right direction." Jim saw the color rise in his dad's face and knew his father more than appreciated the compliment.

"I'll do whatever I can to help, Son."

Jim told his dad everything he knew about Moore and Simpson. He told him he was certain the disappearance of Eddie Reynolds had something to do with Cassie and Ellie. He just didn't know how to prove it.

"Have you talked to Reynolds' family?"

"I've tried. His wife has completely disappeared. I thought maybe she'd gone to her parents' place in Virginia, but they won't answer my questions. I'm planning on contacting his parents as soon as I have a chance. Between intercepting and analyzing Moore's computer communications, watching over Susan and the girls, investigating Harbor Supply, and solving Lynette's murder, I haven't had time." Jim's hand went back to his hair, and he sighed in frustration. "I need help."

"Son, that should've been a top priority, tracking down the wife. Water under the bridge, though. Tell me what to do."

"Let's start with what we've got, then we'll figure out what you should do. What do you know about Moore?"

His father backed up Jim's belief that whatever Moore was up to, Simpson was involved as well. He gave Jim the name of a friend at the PNC bank in Lakespring who might be willing to confirm Jim's findings of Moore's financial situation.

Jim was amazed his father knew so much about Moore and Simpson, and he suspected there was much more than his father was letting on to.

"Now, first things first, son. You need to start looking into Reynolds' disappearance as soon as possible."

⸺⬥⸺

After Chief Mike Russell's wife left, he felt he had nothing going for him but his son and his job. A career police officer, Mike was as honest a cop as one could come by, and that was saying a lot for Baltimore City. He did everything by the book and made it clear he would not tolerate any officer in his department who didn't do the same. He had no patience for mistakes or cover-ups, and all his men knew he would prosecute, to the fullest extent of the law, any officer who dared be so brazen as to break the law. He didn't have to worry; no officers were as loyal to their superior as his men were to him.

It was no secret, within the department, why the chief's wife left. She'd been involved in a torrid affair with a local businessman, Denny Simpson, and poor Mike had caught them red-handed.

Not long after that, Mike got a tip that Simpson and his buddy, Alex, were visiting a local bar. Mike stopped by to remind Simpson he was not welcome in Lakespring. Moore had gotten pretty roughed up, trying to keep Mike off Simpson, but Simpson left unscathed.

Ron, a friend of Mike's from high school, told Mike about his conversation with the pair and about their inquiries into whether that bar, or any others in town, might be interested in hiring some cheap help for the cleaning crew. It was all the information Mike needed to start his own private investigation. And from that day on, Mike watched Ron's back, and Ron watched his.

Before

While on a routine patrol through the city, a rookie cop recognized the chief's wife walking into a cheap motel. A few minutes later, a man he couldn't identify knocked on the door and entered the room. Uneasy about what he'd seen, the cop kept it to himself until guilt got the better of him.

Once the chief heard the officer's story, he took up surveillance outside the motel a few days a week. It didn't take long before the day came when Mike spotted his wife entering the motel. Soon after, a man joined her. The smile on his wife's face, and the way she pulled the man into the room, told Mike all he needed to know.

He waited an hour before he pulled his car into a space in front of the door and sat on the hood, cigarette in hand, like he had all the time in the world.

When Simpson walked out, with a smirk on his face, it was more than Mike could stand. His calm melted like ice dropped into boiling water, and he lunged from the car and grabbed Simpson, beating him until his wife's pleading brought him to his senses.

"You'll regret this day for the rest of your life," Mike told Simpson.

"I wouldn't bet on that," Simpson said, his hand catching the blood that dripped from his nose. His mouth turned into a bloody grin. "I think I will remember it as one of my best."

If the same young cop hadn't been driving by and recognized the chief, Mike would've killed the Baltimore City councilman right then and there.

When Denny and the officer were gone, Mike turned to his wife. "Go home and pack your things," he hissed.

She started to protest, but he turned his back on her. "I said go, now." She didn't even ask about her son.

Mike knew what he had to do. He would file for divorce and seek an annulment. And he would convince his son that his mother chose to walk out of their lives.

By the time Jim returned from school that day, his father was waiting at the bus stop, and Jim never saw his mother again. As Chief Mike Russell held his sobbing son, he made a vow that he would take down Denny Simpson, if it was the last thing he ever did.

CHAPTER SIXTEEN

After

Clint Jacobs was a ruthless hit man with no soul. Find and kill two children? Not a problem. If anyone else was involved, including the police, take care of them too.

He was to hit the girls first. He had extensive background information and descriptions. He wasn't told why they ran away or why they needed to be eliminated. He couldn't have cared less.

Whoever his employer was, he was loaded. Clint knew better than to anger or disappoint someone with that much money. Money meant power, and he didn't want to be on the wrong side of a powerful man. The sooner this job was over, the better.

Clint left for Maryland on a sunny, Sunday afternoon. Later that day, Clint read over the notes on his assigned hit as he sat outside the private school the girls attended. He was trying to get a feel for their lives and where they might be. He was as puzzled as his employer.

They couldn't hide for this long without help. Where on earth could they have gone?

They supposedly didn't know anyone except for the foster parents, but the kids were nowhere to be found.

On Monday, Clint tried hanging around the schoolyard at drop-off and again at dismissal to see if somebody was bringing the girls to school and picking them up, but he never saw them either time. He was getting a lot of looks from the over-protective moms going to pick up their privileged kids. He didn't fit in, it seemed, at this high-class school with its fancy iron gate and three turf-lined athletic fields.

What kind of elementary school paid for turf?

Just when he was beginning to think he was wasting his time at the school, there was an interesting development. A man went into the school who Clint recognized. When he emerged a few minutes later, Clint held up the picture on his phone. He was sure the cop was Jim Russell, his next possible hit. Seeing as how Jim was unmarried and had no kids, his leaving with schoolbooks raised Clint's suspicions. This tied him to both the dead social worker and the kids' school.

Jim Russell was one of many names and faces his employer had sent him. They were people the girls may have met since being with Moore or people with some connection to the disappearance. Jim's visit to the social worker just before her death made him a liability.

Some of the other names he had were dead ends—Teresa the maid, too dumb and too scared of Moore, in his opinion, to be hiding them; various teachers from school, too busy with their own lives to deal with two more brats; Moore's business associates, also too scared of Moore to get involved.

One person interested him above all—Susan O'Neil, single, thirtyish, owned her own company. She'd run a computer camp the older girl took the previous summer.

She was a possibility—young, smart, and with the means to hide and protect two children who didn't want to be found. And if his research was correct, a friend of Jim Russell. That, combined with the information the older kid had a knack for technology, put her at the top of Clint's list.

Clint pulled his car out of its spot and followed the unmarked police car, hoping it would lead him straight to the girls.

⸻ ◆ ⸻

Jim's father was right. It was high time he pursued the disappearance of Eddie Reynolds, assistant to Alex Moore. He'd been itching to sink his teeth into that case for days, and now that his dad was going to help with some of his research, Jim made a point to get to work. After a brief visit to the school to pick up schoolwork and thank the principal for keeping things quiet, he headed to his office.

Jim's superior within the department was waiting for more information on Lynette's murder. The manager at the mall was calling him daily as was the DA and the town's mayor. There didn't seem to be any concrete evidence shedding light on who murdered Lynette or why. Jim had a strong suspicion Lynette's murder and Reynolds' disappearance were related, but Moore was the only connection, and he couldn't find a link between Reynolds and the girls. He asked his boss for some leeway in the investigation. Luckily, his superior didn't question his methods or ask for many details. Jim didn't want Alex's name brought into the investigation just yet.

Eddie Reynolds was reported missing by his parents within the same time frame Cassie and Ellie found their way to Susan's. Nothing new had come through any of the police wires about his disappearance. Though Jim checked the John Doe alerts every day, looking for any bodies found matching his description, nothing surfaced. His wife couldn't be reached for comment, according to the police report, and she wasn't returning Jim's calls. He hoped she wasn't another victim in the case.

Jim found Kayla Kelly Reynolds on Facebook, but her profile was private. Eddie didn't have an account. Nor was there anything on Twitter or LnkedIn. The kid truly was a shadow in today's open world.

The police report didn't tell Jim anything he didn't already know. According to the report, Eddie worked at Harbor Supply. He started as an intern for Simpson, when he was a councilman, before working for the mayor's office and then becoming supervisor of the human resources department for Harbor Supply. Jim knew that's when Reynolds became an informant.

According to Moore, Eddie was having marital problems and had been acting irrationally lately. The case was still open but cold, classified as a disappearance due to domestic problems—a case of a husband trying to escape a bad marriage. Jim was certain that was not the whole story. Of course, the report said nothing about Reynolds being an informant for the FBI.

The report listed Eddie's parents as Mr. and Mrs. Gerald Reynolds of Phoenix, Arizona. Their address and phone number were on the report. Jim checked his watch. It wasn't too early to call. In fact, the day was getting away from him.

"Hello," answered an older-sounding man.

"Mr. Reynolds, Mr. Gerald Reynolds?"

"Yes, who is this?"

"This is Detective Jim Russell of the Lakespring Police Department, near Baltimore City."

"You've found him, haven't you? My son is dead." The man wasn't asking, and his voice didn't falter. He was already resigned to the fact that his son was gone.

"No, Sir, I haven't found him. I wish I could tell you I had. But that's why I'm calling. I'd like to ask you some questions."

Mr. Reynolds let out a great sigh of relief—maybe not so resigned after all. "Yes, yes, I'll answer anything. Who did you say you were with?"

"The Lakespring Police Department, sir, outside of Baltimore. I'm working on a case involving two missing children, and I think your son's disappearance may be connected."

"No!" the man shouted, his voice at a fever pitch. "Heaven, help me. EJ and Todd, are they okay?"

Jim was momentarily confused until he recalled the intel that Eddie had two sons.

"Sir, your grandsons are fine, as far as I know. These missing children may have witnessed or overheard something your son was involved in. Or your son may have witnessed something that involved the children. They disappeared around the same time, and they share a connection that leads us to believe one disappearance may have to do with the other."

"Stop talking in riddles, man. Do you think my son did something to these children or that they're together?" The man's anger was evident.

"No, Sir, neither," Jim said quickly. "We have reason to believe the children and Eddie may have come across each other through a mutual connection. I'd like to know about Eddie's background and his connection to Alexander Moore."

"Moore, huh?" he said in a huff. "That SOB. Eddie always looked up to him, wanted to be just like him. I never liked the man and never understood what Eddie saw in him."

"How did Eddie and Moore meet?"

"Through the mayor's son. I don't remember the kid's name. He and Eddie helped with the mayor's campaign, and Eddie got in good with Moore. I think the mayor was named Sampson, or something like that. The son was a jerk, but Eddie thought he was the coolest kid at Yale. I don't know why we ever let him go to that school. Eddie was bright, is bright, I mean." He paused, his voice cracking. Jim waited for him to compose himself.

"Eddie and the mayor's kid got into all kinds of trouble together in school. Whatever that kid suggested, Eddie was right there with him. By some miracle, and probably the kid's money, they graduated.

"I thought they'd go their separate ways, and that would be the end of it, but no such luck. They stayed in touch, and after the campaign, the son helped Eddie land an internship with the mayor when the man was on the Baltimore city council. Eddie was always fascinated with politics, and he was in heaven working there. His degree was in business even though he loved politics. He thought that gave him more options..." Mr. Reynolds paused, and Jim wondered where his thoughts went.

"Did your son continue to work for Simpson through college?"

"Yeah, in the summer, and then he went to work for Moore after he got his MBA. He didn't stay friends with the son. They had some kind of falling out. For some reason, after a while, the son didn't like Eddie working for his dad even though he'd helped my boy get the job. Eddie never really told us why or what happened. The son left the area and never went back as far as I know."

"As far as you know, were things going well at work for Eddie? And at home?"

"From what we could tell, things were fine. Eddie and Kayla have two boys, great kids. The family comes out every summer for two weeks. Kayla went to Yale, too, and majored in business, but she got pregnant right away after they got married and stayed home. Ironically, they met through the Sampson kid. Eddie went to a party with him one weekend, and that's where he met Kayla. She's a real nice girl, and we've always loved her. The separation came as a real shock."

"Separation?" Jim asked.

"Yeah, Kayla called us the day before Eddie disappeared. She'd decided to leave him and was filing for a legal separation. Said the boys could still come out this summer if we wanted 'em to. Of course, we want them to." Mr. Reynolds sniffed and took a breath. "They were deeply in love, Kayla and Eddie. You could tell every time you saw them together. He worshiped her, and she thought he walked on water. Like I said, a real shock."

"Did Kayla say why she was leaving him?"

"Nope, just that she had her reasons. We still can't understand why, and we haven't heard from her since. She's okay, though, because the boys still call every couple of days. In fact, they called last night."

"Do you know where they are?"

The line was silent for several moments before Reynolds answered. "Chincoteague Island. Had a hard time learning to pronounce that one. It's where Kayla grew up."

Jim noted the information then asked, "Why did you report Eddie missing, Mr. Reynolds?"

"After Kayla called, we tried calling Eddie to see what happened. We called him at home, at the office, and on that phone he carries in his pocket. His mother emailed him at least twenty times, but he never answered. That's just not like Eddie. He would never purposely let his mother worry like this."

"What did the Baltimore City Police tell you about Eddie's disappearance?"

"Nothing. They never called us back. Do you think you can find our son, Detective... I'm sorry, I didn't catch your name."

"Russell, but please call me Jim. I don't know if I can find him, but I'm going to try. And whatever I find out, you can bet I'll call you back and let you know."

Jim hung up the phone and wondered why the wife was never questioned. She would've been his first suspect. Why would the Baltimore Police let her disappear and not try to track her down?

The answer dawned on him.

Someone in the department, or higher up, didn't want Eddie to be found.

Before

Eddie Reynolds was a good kid and a good man. He loved his wife and their two boys. He was loyal to a fault and never wanted to do anything to hurt or upset those he cared about. He was an honest man and assumed everyone else was honest, too.

On a 'boys' weekend out' in Pennsylvania a few years back, he saw something that made him question everything he thought he knew. When he went back to Alex with what he'd witnessed, Alex told him not to tell a soul, and he started sending Eddie monthly checks to keep him quiet. Eddie never cashed them. They went against all his beliefs.

He quietly started looking for employment with other businesses in Annapolis, D.C., and even Virginia, near his wife's family, but Alex found out and threatened to blacklist him. Eddie was miserable being under Alex's thumb, but he had a family to support. He just hoped he never had to tell his best friend what he saw.

As it turned out, he didn't have to. The mayor's son told him one night, before moving away, that he already knew what Eddie had witnessed. It was the last time they ever spoke.

CHAPTER SEVENTEEN

After

Susan waited for Mannie and her parents to all arrive at the house before leaving for the city to attend her meeting. She worried about leaving the girls, but her parents assured her they would be fine, and Mannie was there, which eased Susan's anxiety.

Over dinner that evening, Cassie gushed about their visit to Daisy's house. "Their rooms were so pretty. Rose's room is decorated with roses, of course." She giggled as she described every detail. "And everything in Camilla's room was covered with white flowers. It was so cool!"

Daisy Bloom's family owned the local florist. Her mother was named Iris, and Daisy's sister was Lily. They were like a family in a Hallmark movie.

Susan laughed and told the girls about Daisy's childhood room, decorated in daisies. She turned to Jim, but her smile fell as her stomach twisted into a knot. She'd known Jim her entire life, and she knew those lines in his brow and tightness of his jaw meant he was angry.

"And Miss Daisy said we can come over any time, and we can help her in her greenhouse whenever we want." Cassie chattered throughout the meal.

Jim's tension was palpable as they cleared the dishes. When they went to take the girls to upstairs, Jim grabbed her arm.

"I'll say a quick goodnight, but then I have to head back to work." His jaw clenched, his eyes as hard as steel. "But we need to talk about what happened today."

"What's wrong? I suggested to Mom we should get the girls together with Daisy's girls. I thought you'd be okay with that."

Jim shook his head, and his Adam's apple bobbed. He spoke through clenched teeth, "Well, I'm not. This isn't a game, Susan. They're not here on vacation."

Susan swallowed. Just then, her phone rang from where she left it on the kitchen counter.

"Go on," Susan said. "Let me make sure it's not Mom. You're making me worry."

"Good," Jim said as he turned and walked up the steps.

Susan stood, open-mouthed, until she remembered the phone and headed back to the kitchen. She hesitated before taking the call but answered anyway, hoping tucking in the girls would calm Jim down.

"Hey, Susan. I hope it's not a bad time," Seth said. This time she recognized his number and voice.

"Seth, not at all. It's nice to hear from you." She'd nearly forgotten about his late-night call the previous week and his desire to get together when he came to town.

She asked how Ed was doing and if the server was working well. They chatted for several minutes about the network and compared the weather in Seattle and Lakespring, before he told her he did have some questions he'd like to talk to her about if she had time to see him. They made dinner plans for the following night and said goodbye.

Susan frowned. Ed's network was a pretty simple one. Someone like Seth shouldn't have any trouble figuring it out. Perhaps he had some ideas about how to boost its capabilities and didn't want to say anything over the phone. He might not want to insult her by having her think he was questioning her knowledge.

Oh, well, I'll find out soon enough.

When she went upstairs, Jim had both girls in bed, sound asleep.

"They're out already?"

"You were on the phone for a long time," Jim said, avoiding her gaze. His manner was stiff and distant as he went out into the hallway. "Important call?"

"Just a work colleague," Susan said vaguely, sensing a shift from his earlier irritation to full out anger.

"A work colleague, huh? At this hour?"

"Sometimes that happens." Susan was irritated by his tone and implication. The hall felt small and cramped with Jim's ire hanging between them. "Do you have a problem with that?"

"No, no, not at all." Jim raised his hands in protest. "You can talk to anyone you want, any time you want. It's none of my business. Just don't expect me to be happy about being a babysitter. I'm exhausted, and I've got a case that's not getting solved because of the time I spend here. Maybe I'll see you tomorrow and maybe not. I do have to work, you know, and your parents didn't make my job any easier today. They were supposed to stay here with your friend, Mannie. Who knows how many people they put in danger." With that, Jim brushed past Susan and went down the stairs. The house shook when he slammed the door.

"What on earth?" Susan wondered out loud, astonished by his behavior. This was about more than her parents taking the girls from the house. She shook her head and went to kiss them goodnight.

"He likes you," a sleepy Cassie said from bed.

Susan jumped, caught her breath, and went to Cassie's bedside. "You scared me! I didn't know you were awake, Sweetie. What did you say?"

"Jim likes you, Miss Susan. Can't you tell? He didn't like you talking to another man on the phone."

"That's ridiculous. He's just tired." She hoped Cassie hadn't heard everything Jim said in the hall. The girls loved and looked up to him, and they certainly didn't think of him as a babysitter.

"He might be tired," Cassie said, "but he sure asked a lot of questions about who Seth is and if you talk to him a lot. I told him I'd never heard of him." She yawned, turned over, and closed her eyes.

He did, did he? If that's true, why didn't he just ask me? Why not tell me how he feels?

She sighed and shook her head.

Because that's what he did before. He let me think we had a chance, then he disappeared from my life for over ten years. Why should I be surprised?

⸻ ◆ ⸻

While Jim was at Susan's house, someone else was at Jim's. He took a calculated risk coming back to town, but it was necessary. Besides, if anyone suspected him of Lynette's murder, he'd know by now. Not that he was worried. Before last week, he hadn't been back in years, and nobody knew he and Lynette briefly dated. They'd kept their relationship casual and private, and they were practically kids back then.

The detective's driveway was lined with tall, old trees. Once a car started down the drive, it would be impossible to identify it. The intruder smiled at the irony.

Cops always warn people about dangers like this, but they're so paranoid about their private lives, they don't take their own advice.

The sky was cloudy, and there was no moonlight to alert anyone to his presence once inside the columns of trees. He used his know-how to operate the automatic garage door and hid his car right inside Jim's own garage, just in case. He was brazen and bold and everything his arrogant father had raised him to be, including a killer.

His penlight led him through the kitchen. Empty Coca Cola cans lined the counter. A crayon drawing of a man and woman with two little girls was taped to the refrigerator. One of the girls had what appeared to be curly blonde hair; the other had straight brown hair. Interesting. His body tingled with excitement.

Are these the girls? Who is the woman?

He followed his light into the living room. A small bookcase sat in the corner. Books on the criminal mind were mixed with psychological thrillers. A picture of a little boy and an older man sat on top the television. They each held fishing poles and wore matching hats.

He entered a door to the left where he found a desk littered with papers and files. The bookcase held dozens of books on criminal psychology, unsolved crimes, and famous serial killers.

No wonder the guy is single. He has a one-track mind.

Against the far wall were three filing cabinets. Each one was clearly labeled:

Moore and Simpson - business ventures

Moore - personal and financial

D. Simpson - personal, financial, and political.

The drawers were half empty, but Russell must've high hopes of filling them. Why people kept paper records was a mystery to him, but paper or computer—it didn't matter. Either was easily accessible.

He began rifling through the existing files, throwing them on the floor when he was done. No need to be as careful as he had been in Lynette's office. He wanted Detective Russell to know he was on to him. It made the chase that much more exciting.

He went over reports about Harbor Supply and Distribution, Simpson's political campaigns, campaign finance reports, and personal financial records. As interesting as this was, there was nothing there he didn't already know. What he needed to know was if the detective knew about the girls.

He went to the desk and rifled through the papers. There, he found what he was looking for—notes about Cassie and Ellie. Bingo. Jim Russell did know about them. He combed through the papers for information, but he stopped short when he came across a name—Susan O'Neil. Was she...? Were they...?

Suddenly his elation at confirming Jim knew the whereabouts of the girls turned to anger.

"They've been this close all along," he said out loud, his anger turning to pure rage.

He swept his arm across the desk, sending papers across the room and the phone to the floor. He eyed the telephone lying on the carpet, the dial tone filling the silence in the room.

He placed the phone back on the desk and started pushing buttons. Names and numbers scrolled across the small display area. Then he stopped on the one he wanted. Susan O'Neil was listed. He scrolled through all twenty-five numbers in the phone's memory. She called more than once in the last couple days. This was not a coincidence. She had to have them.

He pulled his iPhone from his pocket and tapped the Maps app. He already had her address and should've gone there to begin with. He could go right now and end this thing, but he inhaled deeply and tamped down his rage. He needed to calm down, think things out. He took another breath as he stared down at the phone in his hand, and a plan began to form.

"They've been through everything, Tony." Jim talked to Agent Morelli over his cell phone. "Every doggone file in my house. My house, for heaven's sake!" He kicked the door to the office, causing it to bang against the wall and bounce back toward him.

"Do you want me to send someone now or in the morning?"

Jim wondered what to do. "I guess it can wait until morning. Whoever did this is gone. Do you know how he got in? Through my own garage! It was wide open when I got home. I know I closed it."

"Jim, I can send someone right now if you want."

"No, thanks. I've got a bag in my car, so I'll go ahead and start dusting and collecting whatever I can find. No need to bother one of your guys tonight."

"It's your call. Normally I'd send someone right over, but I know you can do the prelim stuff. What about bugs?"

"I'll do a cursory check." Jim kicked himself again for having dinner with Susan and then spending hours at the department. If only he'd been home when the guy showed up, but he didn't have access to all the department's online stuff here.

"I'll let you know..." His words drifted off as he caught sight of the phone. Why was that the only thing not on the floor.

What the...?

"Tony, I have to go," Jim said quickly, remembering the phone had a built-in caller ID.

"Is everything alright?"

"I don't think so. I've got to check on something."

"I'll have someone there at—" Jim hung up while Morelli was in mid-sentence.

Careful not to touch the unit, Jim bent down to get a look at the information it displayed, and it was just as he feared.

O'Neil, Susan 410-555-7846

Jim cursed as he hit the speed dial on his cell phone. He ran into the small backyard in case there were bugs in the house.

"Lank, here."

"Are you watching? Are they okay?"

"Yeah. Everything's fine. Susan turned the lights off about an hour ago. All the security lights are off. Nothing has triggered them. I haven't taken my eyes off the house for a second."

Jim breathed a sigh of relief. "Okay, Lank. Keep watching. He may be on to them."

Lank sat up straighter. "Moore?"

"Yeah. Somebody broke into my house. They've been through all my files on Moore and Simpson. They may know Susan's involved. Just don't let them out of your sight, and call me if you see anything. I mean anything." He hung up and ran to his car to grab his forensics kit.

Every instinct told him to go to Susan's, but he trusted Lank, and he wanted to do the search himself. Though the FBI would be there in the morning, this was his home, and he'd be darned if he was going to feel like he had to have his guard up in his own house.

⋯⋯◆⋯⋯

Three hours later, after numerous breaks to call Lank, Jim had dusted every surface in the house. Nothing but one set of prints, probably his own. Whoever broke in wore gloves.

Just like the person who killed Lynette.

Jim dropped into his chair and closed his eyes, running his hands through his hair.

He yelled a stream of curses and slammed his fists down on his desk as the rain beat on the roof above him.

How could I have been so stupid? I knew that darned thing kept track of every number until it was full. Why didn't I clear it after every call?

He resisted the urge to go to the department and check his office. There were too many people there for someone to gain access to it. Unless it was an inside job... But then, why come to his house? They could easily access his online files from anywhere in the department.

Jim's mind raced with possibilities, all of them fuzzy. He needed to get some sleep. He dragged himself up the stairs and collapsed on the bed.

CHAPTER EIGHTEEN

After

At seven the next morning, Jim's groggy brain registered a noise, startling him from a deep sleep. He grabbed his gun and leapt from the bed.

When the doorbell rang for the second time, Jim slipped the gun into the waistband of his shorts, pulled on a shirt, and chastised himself for being so jumpy. He padded barefoot down the hall to the door.

"Detective Russell?" A young man in a business suit stood on the front step, an umbrella over his head, and handed his badge to Jim. "Brian Ross, sir."

The man reached out his hand, and Jim shook it as he handed back the badge and gestured for the man to come inside. He stuck his head out into the rain and scanned the yard before closing the door.

"Early, aren't you?" Jim could barely open his eyes in the morning sunlight.

"Yes, sir. I was told this was a top priority."

Jim led him through the house.

"The office is down the hall. All the other rooms seem okay."

Agent Ross put his briefcase on the desk. When Ross opened the case, Jim saw several technical gadgets. Ross took out what looked like a walkie-talkie and turned it on. He said to Jim, "I need you to turn off any device that is wireless or Bluetooth enabled."

"You don't have to worry about any other devices on my end," Jim told him as he turned off his phone. "My computer isn't wireless, and I don't own anything else."

"Are you sure?" Ross asked incredulously. "You don't have a wireless network set up, no iPad or other tablet, no Bluetooth headset?"

"You're kidding, right?" Jim could tell by the look on the tech's face that he wasn't kidding.

Ross rolled his eyes in disbelief and began to tune in his equipment. The walkie-talkie-looking device started to beep when he held it out in front of him and walked around the room. The beeping on the device became more constant until it was a steady high-pitched tone.

Jim watched as the agent stopped in front of the picture of Jim and his father above the desk. It was the same as the one in his office at the department and had been taken the day Jim was promoted to detective. His father beamed with pride. The tech started to take the picture down from the wall.

"Be careful with that," Jim cautioned. "It means a lot to me and cost an arm and a leg to have blown up and framed."

"I may need to take it apart, but I won't break it," Ross assured Jim.

Jim watched as he turned the picture over and carefully examined the frame. A small slit had been made in the brown paper covering the back of the picture. Ross carefully lengthened the slit and peeled up the paper. Between the picture and the brown paper was a small device about the size of a dime. He used tweezers to extract the device. He never said a word as he dropped the device into a plastic bag and sealed it. He labeled the bag, opened a metal box, and dropped the bag inside of it. He went back to using his contraption and headed toward Jim's desk phone.

"How does that work?" Jim motioned to the device.

"This," Ross said, pointing to the box on the desk, "hones in on radio waves produced by a bug and sends a tone letting me know when it locates one. It's no more complicated than what you saw."

As he spoke, he began to take apart Jim's phone. Within a few minutes, he had removed the smallest listening device Jim had ever seen. "You shouldn't have any more problems in here," he told Jim. "At least, not until they get back in and install more."

"I figured there was one in there, but it's a lot smaller than what I looked for. I didn't even see it. I wish I knew how long it's been there."

"No way to know," Ross said, taking out a piece of equipment that looked like a pocket camera. He turned it on and swept it around the room. Nothing seemed to happen.

"Mind if I ask what that is?"

"It's a laser video detector. It doesn't appear there are any hidden cameras in here."

"I looked last night, but then again, I looked for bugs, too."

"Surveillance tools are getting harder to detect without the right equipment. I'll go ahead and check the rest of the house."

"Be my guest. If you don't mind, I'm going to brush my teeth, splash some water on my face."

"Show me the way first. I'll start in the bathroom and work my way out."

Ross followed Jim through the bedroom to the bath, where Jim waited until the agent removed another device from behind the dresser. He gave Jim the all-clear to do what he needed to do in the bathroom. After setting his gun on the counter and freshening up as best he could in a hurry, Jim found Ross in the kitchen-living room area.

"One in the kitchen phone but nowhere else out here. No cameras." Ross told him.

Jim just nodded. What was there to say? His home had been broken into, his privacy violated, and Susan's number noted. Jim realized it was after eight and felt a sense of panic.

I've got to check on Susan.

He ushered the agent to the door, thanked him, and went back to the kitchen. He picked up the phone, stared at it for a moment and hung it back on the wall. He went to his office and retrieved his cell. He dialed Lank's number on his way back to the kitchen, filled a mug with water, and shoved it into the microwave. No time for real coffee this morning. He reached for the jar of instant coffee as Lank sleepily answered the phone.

"Did you get any sleep?" Jim hoped it was more than he'd gotten himself.

"Not much. I left at sun-up when her handyman got there. I'm glad he's an early riser. I couldn't have lasted much longer," Lank said through a yawn.

"Are you awake enough to work?" Jim stifled a yawn himself. "I need you to follow Susan today."

"Yeah, I'm good. Just need some strong coffee."

"Good." Jim carried his poor excuse for coffee back to his bathroom. He needed a shower. "She has a meeting with one of her clients in the city again today. She'll be dropping the kids off at her mother's and going downtown to the Chase Manhattan building. You are absolutely not to let her out of your sight, especially in the city. Got that?"

"Yes sir." Lank paused for a moment and took a deep breath before continuing. "Boss, does she know what's going on yet? I mean everything?"

Jim was quiet for a minute. Lank was the only person to whom Jim had confided his position with the FBI. He told him everything on the night they sat outside Susan's house. After Lynette's murder, Jim was glad he'd decided to let Lank in on the investigation. He needed someone he trusted to be his backup and look after Susan and the girls. Or to contact Morelli if anything happened to him.

"Not everything," Jim told him. "She knows about Moore's connection to the girls, but I haven't told her I've been investigating him, or about my affiliation with the FBI, or that you were the one following her that day."

"Boss, I know it's none of my business, but—"

"You're right, it's not." Jim cut Lank off and turned on the shower.

"But boss, I see the way you look at her, and I know you've got feelings for her. Don't you think she's going to be upset when she finds out you haven't leveled with her? Not to mention, she's in even more danger than she knows, and she deserves to be told."

Jim put the phone down and took off his shirt. When he picked up the phone, Lank was still talking. "Jim, are you there?"

"I'll tell her when I need to, Lank," Jim said curtly. "I'm still trying to figure the implications of what her parents did yesterday. For now, just get out of bed, and don't lose her this time."

He disconnected the call and put it on the counter. He took off his shorts before reaching for the phone again.

"One more thing, Lank."

"Yes, sir."

"It's not safe to call my home phone and maybe not the office either. I'll explain later, but don't let on to anyone what you're doing for me. If anyone asks, you're following leads on Lynette's murder."

"Got it, Boss. Is that all?"

"I'm getting a new cell phone, and I want you and Susan to get new ones, too. But not yet. Get to her and wait for word from me. I don't want her left unguarded for another second. Try not to call me on this line unless you have to."

"Got it."

"Good." Jim turned off the phone and stepped into the shower.

He knew it was wrong not to tell Susan the truth, and he knew the time was coming when he'd have to come clean. About everything.

⚬

As soon as Penny felt Alex had been gone long enough, she sent Teresa to the market. She felt bad sending her out in the rain, but Penny had to take every chance she could to get into Alex's office.

The wood paneling, mahogany desk and bookshelves, and leather furniture made the room seem eerily dark as she slipped inside. The office was completely different from when it was her former husband's. Joe never locked anything, and his furniture was cozy and inviting. Alex sold all of it as soon as they returned from their honeymoon without even consulting her.

With little sunlight coming in through the windows, there was hardly a difference when Penny closed the heavy drapes to hide her movements from the outside world. When the office had been Joe's, there were no blinds or heavy curtains. How he loved the sunlight coming in to brighten the room. Even on days like today, he enjoyed watching the rainfall and the ever-shifting clouds.

Penny turned on the small desk lamp and felt under the center drawer. Alex wasn't very clever. It had taken her no time at all to discover his filing cabinet key taped to the drawer's underside. She unlocked the desk and began removing files.

Penny copied as many documents as she could in fifteen minutes. It was all the time she allowed herself in the office each day. She attempted to copy as many things as possible that linked Alex and Denny to whatever might be of interest to the authorities. She was running out of space in her safe deposit box, and she sensed she was running out of time.

Lynette's killer was up and dressed shortly before eight. He went through his plan.

He needed to catch Susan off guard. He needed this to be over. Soon, people would start questioning why he was away so much. He could lose his job, not that he cared about the job itself, but he'd been forced to work ever since... He scowled and pushed away his anger.

Placing the gun under the seat gave him a thrill no woman ever had. He started the car.

Two women down, and three more to go.

He felt smug. He was getting good at this. Nobody connected him to the first woman he'd killed nearly two years before. He only wished the girls had been with her.

———◦———

Jim's doorbell rang for the second time that morning. He was surprised to find Tony Morelli on his doorstep. He welcomed the man into his house and asked if he was there because of the bugs Ross found.

"No, Jim. I'm here for another reason."

Jim eyed Morelli with curiosity. Morelli was not one to beat around the bush and had never shown up at Jim's house.

Without a word or explanation, Morelli reached into his coat pocket. As usual, he wore a dark suit and white shirt. He handed Jim a leather case. Jim took the case tentatively, not sure he wanted the responsibility he presumed it held.

"It's been decided you should have this in case you need to delve further into anything you've found."

Jim opened the case and stared at the gold shield inside. The letters *FBI* protruded from the shield as though his doubts made them more prominent. He raised his eyes to Morelli's.

"I'm not sure what to say."

Morelli frowned. "Is there a problem?"

"No, not exactly." Jim ruffled his hair with his empty hand. "It's just that, I always imagined, if I ever got one of these, there would be a bit more pomp and circumstance, so to speak. I've never studied at Quantico, haven't filled out an application, and am not sure I'm even worthy of the honor of carrying this."

Morelli smiled. "That attitude, Jim, is precisely why you're the perfect man to hold that badge and handle this case. Just to clarify, you're not an agent. Your badge is different from mine. My hope is that you'll apply for a position at Quantico when this is over. That's the only way in for an agent. For now, you're considered an Intelligence Officer. We'll talk about the future later."

Jim wasn't sure how to respond. He was filled with emotion, though he was uncertain as to what the primary emotion was. He wished there was someone with whom he could share this. His first thought was, Susan, but perhaps his dad...

"Thank you," Jim managed to say.

"You're welcome. It's temporary, you understand?"

Somehow, that made Jim feel better. "I do, and I will do my best to fulfill my duties with honor."

"I'm sure you will." With that, Morelli bid his farewell.

Jim stood in the open doorway as Tony pulled away. The open case felt heavy in his hand. He never knew how much he wanted this until that moment. Perhaps, when this case was wrapped up, he might give some thought to that application Morelli mentioned.

Susan had Cassie and Ellie packed and ready to go. They were taking their coloring things, schoolwork, and Candy Land to play with Grandpa Patrick. They were on the way out the door when the phone rang.

"Don't talk," said Jim. "Just listen. There's a pay phone on the corner of Laurel and Jefferson where the gas station is. Do you know where I mean?"

Susan thought for a moment. There was no Laurel Street in Lakespring. Come to think of it, there was no Jefferson Street either. "No." She hesitated. "I'm not sure where you mean."

"Think, Susan. It's where Laurel and Jefferson meet. We used to go there as kids."

Susan thought harder, trying to identify landmarks around town and places where she and Jim used to hang out. "Oh! I do know where that corner is. Do you want me to call you from there?" She gripped the phone harder, knowing something was wrong.

"No, I'll call you there in ten minutes. Hurry. You'll be escorted by Officer Lankton. You'll know the car."

Jim hung up, and Susan told the girls to run to the garage and get in the car. Jim didn't have to tell her something had happened. She'd been waiting for this call since the day Lynette was murdered.

"We don't have our jackets on yet." Cassie protested as she watched Dora the Explorer on TV.

"Put them on in the car. We need to go *now*."

Cassie turned to Susan and nodded, her eyes wide with understanding. She switched off the TV, grabbed Ellie's hand, and ran toward the door.

Susan knew she had scared the girls. She was having a hard time hiding her own fear. She took one last look around the kitchen before heading into the garage and wondered when they would be able to return.

———◆———

Lynette's killer pulled to a stop across from the house, trying to gauge whether anyone was home. The house was dark. With no sun and the pouring rain, there should be lights on.

Where could they be?

He hoped he hadn't made a mistake leaving the detective's place a wreck. He should've gone in, gotten what he needed, and left. He checked his phone for messages but had no notifications. That was good. For now, everything was still in place. He would be back tonight, and then it would all be over.

CHAPTER NINETEEN

After

Susan willed herself to stay calm as she drove through town, the windshield wipers swishing to the rhythm of her beating heart. She paid keen attention to everything and everyone around her, unwilling to be caught off guard. She watched owners and managers opening the bakery, the pharmacy, and the video rental store that was going out of business. She was reminded of how hard the little town struggled to maintain its rural atmosphere as she drove past the two-hundred-year-old buildings, some camouflaged by the massive growth of vines. The town had gone through several rebirths since Susan's youth. So many businesses changed hands over the years. Every so often, the shops changed to reflect the current fad.

Susan turned the corner where once stood a soda fountain where she and Jim spent their allowance on root beer floats and homemade ice cream. It was a specialty coffee shop now. Next to it was, at one time, the Quilting Bee where she had gone with her Girl Scout troop to learn about sewing. It was now a chain craft store with very few fabrics left and a multitude of scrapbooking supplies.

Susan stopped at the light on the corner of Washington and Carroll Streets, one of only three lights in the town. Jim's cousin owned the jewelry store on the corner. Susan could see Daisy's car already parked outside her shop across the street.

She checked her rearview mirror when the light changed. There was a car following her, but she didn't recognize it like Jim said she would. She was almost to her destination but wasn't sure whether to go there. The car had been back there for some time, and she didn't want to take any chances. She turned into a convenience store and parked right in front of the door. The car kept going, and Susan breathed a sigh of relief.

"Why are we here?" Cassie looked around.

"I think I forgot my phone," Susan lied, picking up her purse. "No, here it is. Never mind. I just need to stop at a restaurant ahead and do something for Jim."

"Is he meeting us at Grandma Ida's?"

"I don't think so, Sweetie." Susan answered as she backed out of the space. It was then that she saw the familiar blue sedan at the other end of the lot.

Susan drove another block to the town's vintage movie theater where she and Jim spent half their childhood. It used to show all the latest releases, but the megaplex at the mall just outside of town had taken its place many years ago. The newly renovated theater housed the local actors' troupe and showed old Tinsel Town classics. It was running Laurel and Hardy movies every night this month.

Beside the theater was the oldest inn and restaurant in town, Thomas's Inn and Tavern, said to have been frequented by Jefferson himself. Susan recalled that the Revolutionary era building had a pay phone in its lobby. The restaurant to the right of the lobby could be seen through the windows from the parking lot. She noticed the waitresses, dressed in 18th century clothing, already setting up for lunch.

"Stay here," she told the girls. "I need to run into the inn for a few minutes, but you'll be safe." A car pulled in beside her, and Susan knew it was the same blue sedan that had followed her a week earlier. She recognized it the previous morning after Jim assigned someone to watch her house at night. She intended to give Jim a piece of her mind about not telling her it was his guy who had followed her the other day, but Jim's hasty exit after her call with Seth hadn't allowed her to say anything.

"The man in the car next to us works for Jim. He's one of the officers who has been watching the house at night. If anyone tries to get in the car, he will stop them."

"Does he have a gun?" Cassie's eyes were wide with fear.

"Well, he is a police officer, so I would assume so. Don't worry. Police officers are trained not to use their guns unless someone tries to hurt them first." She motioned to the man that she was going in and leaving the girls. He got out and waited for her to unlock the doors before getting in on the passenger side.

"Hey, Ms. O'Neil. I'm officer Lankton." He reached for her hand.

"Nice to meet you. I'll be right back. Jim should be calling that pay phone any minute."

Susan jumped out of the car and quickly opened her umbrella. She ran to the building, splashing through puddles, and walked inside as the phone started to ring.

"Hello," she answered, surveying the lobby and trying to remain calm and observant.

"Good job, Susan. I knew you'd figure it out."

"What's going on, Jim?"

"My home was ransacked last night."

Susan gasped. "Jim, are you okay?"

"I'm fine. It happened either when I was at your house or at the department. But Susan, every file was gone through. We did a sweep this morning, and the phone and office were bugged. I don't want you calling the house or the department anymore, especially from your house or your mother's."

He continued. "I don't want you using your landline or cell at all except for business. Stop by Walmart sometime today and pick up two of those pay-by-the-minute phones. One's just a backup. Lank, Officer Lankton, is getting one, too. He'll make sure you have the number. Once you have the phone, give the new number to your parents and to him. Text me. Nobody else. Understand?"

"Yes, I understand," she said quietly into the phone. She turned to check on Cassie and Ellie. She closed her eyes and leaned onto the wall for support. "Do they know about me? That I have the girls? Are my parents going to be safe after I leave them?"

"I don't know how much they know. I'm positive they saw your number on my caller ID, but Lank won't leave you for a second. You'll be safe, I promise."

"But my parents... the girls..."

"I'll send someone over there. They'll be okay."

"Jim, about last night..." Susan began.

"Not now, Susan. We'll talk later. Now, write down this number, and give it to your parents."

She did as told.

"Okay, listen. Lank is going to be close by all day. If you need him for anything, just give him a sign, and he'll be there in an instant. He knows everything that's going on, and I trust him with my life. Now I'm trusting him with yours. Go about your business as usual today so you don't raise any suspicions. I'll be in touch. And call me if you need me."

"Wait Jim, I need to tell you some—" He was gone before she could finish.

⚬

Lank followed Susan as she drove past his old high school. He was on the football team and had big dreams, but they ended in a fiery flash one fateful night. The field was empty now, but in a couple months, a group of boys with big dreams would gather in the hot summer sun to give it their all.

Lank turned back in time to see Susan make a turn onto a residential street. The sun was trying to peek through the clouds as she slowed down in front of a modern colonial with blue shutters. Lank parked across the street and watched the garage door open. Susan pulled in, and the doors began to shut again, but not before Lank saw the older man standing in the garage waiting for Susan. Lank smiled at Coach O'Neil and for just a minute, he lost his focus as he remembered how much he admired that man.

⚬

"Señora Moore, Cassie and Ellie have been gone for over a week." Teresa smoothed the fresh sheets she'd put on the king-sized bed. "I know they not go to friend's house. They run away, sí?"

Penny didn't know what to say to her anymore. Teresa had made it clear she didn't believe the girls were visiting friends, and Penny would never be able to convince her now that they'd been gone for so long.

"Si, Teresa." Penny sighed. "They have run away. Alex is trying to find them."

"You call the police?"

"Not exactly." Penny hesitated. "You know Alex has connections with Baltimore City. He's using his contacts there instead of the local police."

"I do not understand." Teresa stopped making the bed and looked at Penny. "You love them, no? Why you not call the police? You not want them found, or Señor not want them found? He a bad man, Señora."

"Teresa, he truly is trying to find them. You've got to believe me."

Teresa snorted and looked at her with disapproval. She picked up a pillowcase and furiously forced in a pillow.

"I not argue with you. I think he no want them found. I not understand why you let him stay this long."

Penny was speechless.

The longer Teresa worked for her, the more she made her thoughts and opinions known. She never said a word around Alex even though he was the one who hired her through his company. Penny was learning more about that every day, and she hated knowing what Teresa had been put through and was probably still being put through every night when she returned to whatever abomination she called home.

———— ◆ ————

Susan hugged her parents and scooted the girls into the living room before telling Ida and Patrick about her conversation with Jim. Ida slid onto a kitchen chair and covered her face with her hands.

"Did we do this? Is it because of yesterday?"

Susan shook her head. She'd had little time to think about that, but she didn't believe her parents had given anything away.

"I don't think so. If he knew you had them, and they're what he wants, he would've taken them. No offense, Dad" she said, giving him a pointed look. "He could probably overpower you."

"I knew this was going to happen. I knew you were in danger. We never should have involved Daisy and her family." She tried to stifle her crying.

Susan bent down and put her arms around her mother. "Mom, I'm fine. I'm going to be fine. Jim will take care of us."

"And where is he now?" Ida raised her voice. "Where is he at night when you and the girls are alone? He wasn't home when this person broke into his house."

"He has police officers watching the house all night, Mom. You know that."

"But it's not the same. I know he'll protect you with his life. He needs to be the one there making sure nothing happens. I don't even care if he stays the night!" Ida was becoming hysterical. "I only care that you're safe. It's a good thing that we..." Ida stopped herself and looked up at Patrick.

"It's a good thing you *what*, Mother?"

When Ida didn't answer, Susan moved her gaze to her father. "Dad, is there something you want to tell me?"

"No, Susan. Your mother is just upset. She's been saying multiple Rosaries a day, praying for your safety. She didn't want you to know how worried she is."

She shifted her gaze shifted back and forth between her parents. Her mother was hiding something, but she didn't have time to dwell on it.

"All right," she finally said. "I need to go. I'll have to break every speed limit between here and Baltimore to get to my meeting on time. It's a good thing I have a police escort."

"Don't you dare speed in the rain," Her mother called after her.

Lank followed closely behind Susan as she sped into Baltimore City. It was a wonder neither of them got pulled over or ended up in the ditch. That would be just what they needed. Jim would have his badge for sure.

Getting pulled over was just one of the many fleeting thoughts going through his head as he watched Susan's car and thought about the task that lay ahead of him.

Lank was following Susan O'Neil, and he'd be darned if he let anyone hurt her. He'd had a crush on Susan in ninth grade when he first met her on the football field. She was home on college break, helping her dad put lime on the yard lines, and he thought she was the most beautiful girl he'd ever seen.

This case was important for his career, but it was important to him for other reasons. He'd been waiting a long time to find a way to thank Patrick O'Neil for all the long hours spent helping Lank walk again, run again, and feel like a person again after he'd broken his back. This was his chance to finally do something for the man who meant more to him than anyone in the world, the man who was like a father to him. And no matter what, Abe Lankton was not going to let his old coach down.

—◦—

Susan drove through the rain, with Lank close behind, past crumbling brownstones and condemned storefronts until they reached the bustling downtown. The sidewalks were a sea of umbrellas as men and women rushed to their offices. Most newer buildings had underground parking, but space was limited.

Charm City, as it was called, had little charm on rainy days. The Inner Harbor was vacant of sightseers, and nobody was around to feed the only creatures walking on the brick docks who didn't mind the rain. The ducks were watching the few passersby hoping for a morsel of food.

Susan made sure Lank was still behind her as she turned onto a street lined with skyscrapers and multi-level shopping centers.

When they reached the Chase Manhattan Building, they both pulled into the garage. Susan gave her name and the name of her client to the security guard.

She motioned to Lank behind her and said, "He's my assistant. Can he park here, too?"

"I don't know if we have any extra spaces today, ma'am, with the rain, you know. Let me check." Susan watched the guard go into the little glass office and check a clipboard on the wall. He returned to her car nodding his head.

"Go to the next level down. There should be spots open there." He motioned which way to go and waved Lank on to follow her.

They both parked, and Lank jumped out of the car and hurried over to her.

"Where are you going to be while I'm in my meeting?" Susan tried to remain casual as she spoke, in case someone was watching.

"With you. I was told not to let you out of my sight."

"But I have business to take care of," Susan said with exasperation. "I thought you'd be hanging out in the lobby or something. What are you supposed to do, sit in the back of the room and ask to see the ID of everyone who comes in?"

"If that's what's necessary. Look, Miss O'Neil, I'm sorry to do this to you." Lank felt a bit sheepish around her. "I know this is awkward, but I really do need to stay with you."

"No, I'm sorry. I'm on edge, and I'm worried about Cassie and Ellie and my parents. I'm not sure I'm even fully prepared for this meeting, and..." She glanced at her watch. "On top of that, I'm late."

They got into the elevator where they decided Lank would pose as Susan's new employee, coming along to learn the ropes.

CHAPTER TWENTY

After

Jim spent the day at home, going through his files after a quick outing to get his phone. The badge felt heavy in his pocket.

He tried to determine if any files were missing and exactly what information the intruder had gotten. After some time, he called his dad.

After years of spending half the night at Ron's bar, Mike Russell finally seemed to be spending less time in the bottle. His conversation with Jim lit a spark Jim hadn't seen in years.

Mike arrived less than fifteen minutes after he and Jim ended their call.

"What's all this?" The filing cabinets were open, and papers were strewn everywhere. "There's more than just a week's worth of work here." He eyed Jim suspiciously.

"Dad, I think you'd better sit down."

Mike looked for a place to sit and ended up pulling in a chair from the kitchen.

"I haven't been up front with you about the Moore case. I'm a lot more involved than I've led you to believe." Jim paused.

"It looks that way." Mike surveyed the mess in front of him.

Jim tried to think of the best way to tell his dad about his covert life. He stood from his chair, pulled out the leather case Morelli had given him earlier that day, and handed his father his badge. Mike looked stunned.

"When did this happen? Why didn't you tell me?"

"I couldn't. I was told not to tell anyone. And I'm not an agent, just a temporary intelligence officer." Jim told his dad about the day Agent Morelli showed up at his office and about the work Jim was doing.

"Tony Morelli," Mike mused. "I haven't seen him in years."

"How do you know him? He never mentioned meeting you."

"We went to the Academy together."

"The Police Academy?"

Mike shook his head.

"You went to *the* Academy? As in the FBI Academy? I didn't know that. Why didn't you ever tell me? Why didn't you work for the FBI?"

"I dropped out." Mike shrugged. "I met your mother, and you came along." His father blushed, and Jim understood the implication. "After we got married, your mother didn't want me to be away. She asked me to come home, so I left."

Jim was stunned. He had no idea his father had gone to the Academy, even for a short time. He assumed his dad always wanted to be a small town cop, and he couldn't imagine his father doing anything just because his mother asked him to.

"Back to you, son. Want to fill me in on the past year? You obviously know more about the case than you've let on. Have you contacted Reynolds' parents?"

"Yes, and it was an interesting conversation. Seems Reynolds was friends with Simpson's son." Jim told his father what he knew. When he finished, Jim sighed and pulled his fingers through his hair.

"There's more," his dad said. It was a statement and not a question.

"What do you mean? I told you everything I know."

"I don't think so, Jim. I know you. There's something bothering you."

"It's Susan," Jim said with a shake of his head. "She doesn't know what's going on, with the FBI that is. I know I need to tell her. I just don't know how. She'll think I'm just using her to get to Moore."

"Are you?"

"Of course not!" Jim frowned at this father. "I'm trying to protect her, and Cassie and Ellie."

"I think there's more to it than that. For days now, I've heard you talk about Susan, these little girls, your concern for them. Your feelings run a lot deeper than a cop just protecting his charges." Mike looked at his son. "Are you in love with her?"

Jim stared at his father. Was he? He got up went to the window. It was still raining, but the sun was trying to break through the clouds. Everything outside looked fresh and clean. Jim thought about Susan and the new chance they'd been given.

He did have deep feelings for her. Now that Susan was back in his life, he knew he wanted her to remain in it forever. He wanted hers to be the first face he saw every morning, and the last one he saw each night. He wanted to spend the days thinking about her and the nights making love to her.

"Ahem." His father cleared his throat, reminding Jim he was still there.

"Yeah, I love her," Jim said, turning around. "I always have." He laughed and shook his head. "I even love those girls."

"Then you have to tell her, Jim. About your case and your feelings. Trust me. There's nothing more important in a relationship than honesty and communication. Once trust is gone, it's hard to ever get back."

Something in his dad's voice made Jim wonder if his dad had more experience in this area than Jim knew.

"Tonight," Jim said. "I'll tell her tonight."

⚬

It was after five when Susan and the girls returned home. Susan was afraid Jim might not want her to go back, but while she was gone and Mannie was working, Jim had a police tech sweep the house. Luckily it was clean. Mannie, at Patrick's request, had added a security light by the front entrance, and deadbolts now adorned the doors. The back gate had a new padlock.

She dug her new phone out of her purse and laid it on the counter. She thought of Jim as the phone rang.

"Hello," she said tentatively.

"You're home," he said. Not a question. "How was your day?"

Digging through the pantry she found a box of macaroni and cheese and some rice. She walked into the living room and held them both up. Ellie pointed to the mac and cheese. Susan rarely had food in the house on a normal basis. She'd had time earlier to pick up a few things, but there wasn't a much to offer her guests.

"Good. The meeting went well. I like the local ones. I really hate flying. I'd like to expand my business to a team of techs based around the country, so I don't have to do so much traveling." The words were out before she realized she was thinking them. Had the girls done that to her, made her think of being home more and traveling less?

"Makes sense to me. Is your business at the point where you can afford that?"

"I think so, to a small extent anyway. In fact, I think I know someone who'd be a great hire out west."

"Then talk to that person. See if you can make it happen."

"Maybe I will." She smiled as she reached into the refrigerator. *Maybe tonight.* "Which reminds me—"

"Hey, Susan, I've got to go. Dad's here, and he's motioning to me about something. We're almost done cleaning up my office."

"Will you make it over for dinner tonight?" Susan hoped the answer was yes.

"Absolutely. I'll be there around six. I've got something to talk to you about."

"That doesn't sound good." Susan opened a bottle of steak sauce and poured some over a tray of steaks she'd just seasoned. It was too early to put them in the broiler, so she left them on the counter.

"No, nothing bad, just some things I want to clue you in on. I'll tell you when I get there."

"Sounds good. I'll see you then."

"See you then."

"Darn." Susan looked down at the phone in her hand.

"What's wrong?" Cassie asked, and Susan jumped. That girl was practically a panther.

"I didn't have a chance to tell Jim my friend is coming over for dinner."

"The guy from the phone?" Cassie asked, her tone dubious.

"Yeah, him," Susan said with a sigh, catching Cassie's eye roll as the little girl turned away.

———— ◆◇◆ ————

It had been an interesting night. After leaving town to take care of another client, Clint returned to town in time to see someone turn down Detective Russell's driveway. Someone who was not the detective. He'd stayed for an hour or so before leaving. Russell arrived at home a few hours later.

Early this morning two guys showed up—one right after the first one left. After, Russell hurried to Walmart but was in and out of the store in minutes. He spent the rest of his day at home. Clint was able to identify his only other visitor as Russell's father.

When it didn't appear Russell was going anywhere by mid-afternoon, Clint made a quick dash to the convenience store around the corner. He hurried back and returned to his surveillance of the driveway, having no idea Jim was already gone.

———— ◆◇◆ ————

Lank was parked in front of Susan's house, waiting for Jim to get there. At one time, he thought he was going to be the next superstar of the NFL, but that wasn't possible after he broke his back. If it hadn't been for Coach O'Neil and all his help and encouragement, Lank probably wouldn't have joined the police force. And he almost didn't. The department was worried about his injury and what could happen if he had a spasm, or worse, while on the job.

But Jim saw potential in him from the start. He convinced the department to let him take Lank on as his protégé. He trained him and even let him in on his biggest secret—that he was working with the FBI. And now Jim had Lank protecting the woman Lank was sure Jim was in love with. On top of that, she was Patrick O'Neil's daughter. Maybe his mother was right all those times she told him his injury happened for a reason, that he had a purpose in life. He didn't believe it back then, but now it all made sense.

A sudden movement outside snapped Lank out of his thoughts. He sat up and peered out the window. He thought he saw something, or someone, lurking in the bushes outside Susan's house. Before Lank had a chance to get out of the car, he saw another figure running out of nowhere. The figure ran into Susan's yard and leaped into the bushes tackling the man who was peering into Susan's window. Lank jumped out of the car and yelled, "Stop, police!"

The two men continued rolling on the ground, wrestling with each other, ignoring Lank. They both stopped when he pulled his gun.

"Stop! Police!"

Lank recognized one of the men. He was a large man with dark hair and light brown skin and an all-access pass to Susan's house. What was the handyman's assistant doing at the house this time of night? And who was this other guy? He wore expensive clothes and was getting the worst of the beating.

"Don't move, and don't try anything stupid," Lank told them. "Just put your hands up where I can see them, stand up, and get against the wall."

Susan came running out of the house and yelled, "Officer Lankton, what are you doing?"

"Just go back into the house Miss O'Neil. Call Jim on his cell and tell him I've apprehended two men." Lank always wanted to say that. He had to stop himself from smiling. This was the best night of his life

"Lank, neither of these men is trying to hurt us. Let them go."

"What do you mean let them go? I saw them. That one was trying to spy on you through the window, and that one came running up and tackled him." Lank stopped and thought for a second. "Why did you tackle him?"

"That's what I'd like to know," said Susan. "Why on earth are you sneaking around here at night, José? And why, Seth, were you spying on me?"

"You know him?" Lank asked in disbelief.

Both men looked like deer caught in headlights. They looked at Susan and then away. Lank lowered his gun and told everyone to go inside as Jim pulled into the driveway.

"So, you invited this man here without asking me if I thought it was okay?" Jim gaped at Susan, his tone and expression showing his disbelief mingled with anger.

"Well, this is my house." Her voice rose with indignation. She'd tried to tell Jim about Seth earlier, but he cut her off. It was his own fault. "I didn't know I wasn't allowed to entertain company."

"You were planning on 'entertaining' him?" Jim roared. "What is that supposed to mean?"

"It doesn't mean anything! He's a colleague!" Susan shouted back.

"A colleague? A colleague who comes to your house?" Jim lowered his voice, but the animosity remained. His face was inches from hers.

"Guys, hello, over here," Lank interrupted. "We were trying to get to the bottom of all of this, remember?"

"I am getting to the bottom of this." Jim's eyes were locked on Susan's. "I'm getting to the bottom of why a woman, under police protection, invites some guy she hardly knows into her home without telling the police. I've got men watching this house twenty-four-seven, and you think nothing of leaving me out of the loop about strange men coming over?"

"You're under police protection?" Seth choked. "For what?"

"It's complicated," she said to Seth before turning back to Jim. "And you're being totally honest with me?"

"Here we go," Lank chimed in.

Jim turned to him "You stay out of this." Then to Susan, he asked, "What's that supposed to mean?"

"I tell you I was being followed, and you act like you know nothing. Furthermore, you scold me for not telling you sooner, and it was *him* the entire time!" She motioned to Lank who looked away from her angry stare. "So much for honesty!"

"That's different!" Jim retorted. "I was trying to *protect* you."

"By lying to me?"

"By not letting on to you about how much danger you're actually in!"

"And how much danger is that?" Seth asked, his voice quivering.

Jim and Susan ignored him. They never took their eyes off each other. The room seemed to empty of everyone but them. Jim's eyes conveyed... what? Anger? Fear?

For several moments everything was quiet. It was Cassie who broke the silence.

"Miss Susan, are we ever going to eat dinner? Me and Ellie are starving."

Susan noticed at the girls for the first time since she told them to hide at the sound of the commotion outside. She wasn't sure how long they'd been standing there or what they heard or understood.

"Ellie and I," she said. "And of course, we're going to eat, Sweetie, but I think we're going to need to set more places at the table."

⸙

The meal was tense. Jim refused to look at Susan. He knew he was being foolish and juvenile, but he was so angry with her. And so darn in love with her at the same time. When he pulled up and saw Lank holding his gun on the two men, Jim nearly had a heart attack. His first thought was that something had happened to Susan.

Jim kept an eye on Seth throughout the meal. Seth tried to hide his annoyance but didn't do a very good job. It was obvious he was interested in Susan, colleague or not. Lank and José were the only ones who enjoyed their food and greedily continued to reach for more. That only added to Jim's irritation.

José explained that his Uncle Mannie was paying him extra to hang around and keep an eye on Susan. Susan thanked him but told him he could go back home after dinner and let Mannie know that it wasn't necessary. Jim sneered at Lank for not noticing the kid sooner.

Susan didn't say anything more about being followed, but she continued to scowl at Jim, which just made him angrier. He wasn't the wrong one here.

After Seth and José left, he offered to help put the girls to bed.

"Are you sure? I know how busy you are." Her words dripped with scorn, and Jim bit his tongue.

"I'm sure." He clenched his teeth as he brushed past her but smiled sincerely at the girls when they took his hands and led him up the stairs. Jim knew Susan followed but didn't look back in her direction.

As he watched her tuck the girls into bed, all his anger faded away. The domesticity of the scene warmed his heart. All he wanted was to take Susan in his arms and let her know why he'd been so angry earlier—angry she had behaved so recklessly, angry Seth was in the picture, and angry she didn't even seem to notice how much he cared for her.

"I'll wait downstairs," he said quietly as she kissed them goodnight.

When Susan leaned down to give Cassie a kiss, the little girl grabbed her hand. "Don't be mad at Jim. He's just trying to protect us."

"I know he is, Cassie," Susan said. "Now go to sleep."

"He loves you, Miss Susan. He's worried about you."

"I don't know about that, but I know he loves you, and so do I." Susan kissed Cassie on the cheek and gave her a hug.

"I love you, too, Miss Susan," Cassie whispered, closing her eyes.

Susan smiled and shook her head. She never knew what to think about the things that came out of that girl's mouth. If only all Cassie's words were true.

Susan remembered how strong her feelings were for Jim when they were growing up and how much she loved having him around now. He made her feel complete when she hadn't even known something was missing. She found herself watching the clock in the evenings, waiting for it to be dinnertime, listening for his car in the driveway. If only the words of a child could make something be true.

Susan turned off the light and headed downstairs. She noticed Lank on his phone in the sunroom. Jim was waiting in the kitchen. He put the last of the dishes into the dishwasher and turned toward Susan.

"Susan, look—"

"Jim, it's okay. It's been a long day. I'm sorry for yelling at you and for being angry. I know you were doing what you thought was best."

"I'm sorry, too." He paused. "About Seth…is there anything going on between you two?"

"Would it matter if there was?" Susan asked quietly, averting her eyes from his.

Jim took his time answering, and Susan felt her heart fill and then deflate at his words.

"Yes, Susan, it matters because I need to know if he might show up again sometime, so Lank doesn't have to hold him at gunpoint." She lifted her gaze, expecting to see that twinkle in his eyes, his mouth twitching at the corner, but all she saw was the uptick in his jaw and frost in his eyes. He reached over and picked up his keys from the table.

"He just might," Susan said, feeling hurt. If Cassie was right, why couldn't Jim just say so? "I did make a life for myself between ninth grade and last week, you know."

Jim gave a curt nod, and she saw his jaw tense again. "Noted. I'd better get going. I have a lot to do tomorrow." Jim walked to the door but turned back to her "Shoot. I forgot to ask when you're supposed to go to Denver."

"Not until a week from Friday. I moved the meeting so I wouldn't have to leave Cassie and Ellie. I thought maybe by next week…" She shrugged, not wanting to think about them being gone. "Why do you ask?"

"I'd like you to go earlier, tomorrow if possible."

"Tomorrow?" Her head snapped up so she could meet his eyes. "You want me to leave?"

"Just for a day or two. Until things cool down here. Mannie can keep an eye on the house during the day, and

Lank can stay here at night and get some sleep. I can do some more digging, and you'll be safer away from here."

"Okay," she said slowly. She checked the clock. It was six in Denver. Could she reach anyone tonight? "I'll let them know I've had an opening and can be there tomorrow. I'll have to book a flight and see if Mom and Dad can watch the girls."

"No," Jim said. "Take them with you. I'd rather all three of you get out of town for a couple days. And don't tell anyone where you're going. Did Lank give you the ID cards I had made?"

"Yes, and I can't believe the names you gave them." Susan smiled.

"What little girl wouldn't want to be named after a cartoon princess? Isn't it every girl's dream to be a princess?"

Only if it leads to Prince Charming, Susan thought.

"Will I talk to you while we're gone?" She busied herself with a piece of lint on her shirt, trying to hide the eagerness in her voice and the tears in her eyes.

"I'll try to check in," Jim said as he opened the door. "Just let me know what your flight plans are." With that, he was gone.

A stunned Susan stood in the doorway and watched Jim drive away. Didn't he say he had something to tell her tonight, something important? Maybe that was it. He wanted them out of town, maybe out of his life.

That's what it felt like—like he had walked out of her life all over again. Susan couldn't tell what his thoughts and feelings were. He was jealous of Seth. That much she knew. But why? Because he cared for her or because of his male ego? Her heart ached as much as it had on that day almost twenty years ago.

Putting thoughts of Jim out of her mind for the time being, she sent a short text to Seth, apologizing about the evening. She offered to talk to him over the phone about whatever questions he had.

Susan opened her computer to check flight possibilities. Hopefully their new ID cards wouldn't raise any red flags with airline security. She needed to figure out what to do with them while she had her meeting, but at least they would be safe if they were out of town.

Nothing bad can happen to them if Moore can't find them, right?

Susan called her client as soon as she confirmed there were flights available and asked if tomorrow would work. The client was thrilled, arrangements were made, and Susan scheduled their flight for early the next morning. They would have an evening in Denver before her meeting the following day.

I ought to bill the police department for the fees I had to pay to pay for these tickets at such short notice.

She shook her head. The money was worth it to be away from Jim for a few days. Maybe they'd be lucky, and he'd solve the case by the time they got back.

⸺❖⸺

Jim headed home, hurt, angry, and confused. The flowers were on the seat where he left them when he jumped out of the car earlier. How could he have been so stupid? He had no idea she was seeing someone, and he almost let his feelings compromise the case.

He hit his hand on the steering wheel. He knew there was something going on with the late-night calls from

Seth. Why hadn't she told him the truth? Why toy with him? Did she think it was funny? Was it to get back at him for kissing her all those years ago and then pretending she didn't exist?

At least he wouldn't have to face her for a few days, and she'd be safe. Getting her out of town would be the best thing for them both.

———◦———

He was furious with himself for not getting the job done, but how could he? His attempts to get rid of the brats and Susan had been thwarted twice in one day. Where had all those people come from?

Now he had to try again tomorrow. This time, he'd be there even earlier. He'd get them before they had a chance to leave the house again, and then he'd get out of this town and back to work.

For moment, he wondered if he'd made a mistake coming back here. Were the cops onto him? Were they checking him out? How close were they to figuring out the truth? He shook his head.

No, they're all too stupid for that. I'm the smart one. I'm the one with all the brains and know-how. I'm the one running the show now.

CHAPTER TWENTY-ONE

After

"We're going on a little vacation," Susan told Cassie and Ellie when she woke them up.

"We are?" Cassie asked. "Where are we going? To the beach, to Disney World?" She scurried out from under the covers and sat on the edge of the bed.

"Cassie!" Susan laughed. "It's not beach weather, and no we aren't going to Disney World. We're going to the mountains, to Denver, Colorado."

"Denver, Colorado?" Cassie repeated, her voice filled with excitement. "I know where that is on the map! That's almost on the other side of the country! Are we going to drive all the way there?"

"No," Susan replied as she dug into their closet. She pulled out a suitcase she stored there. "We're going to fly there, this morning."

Cassie and Ellie jumped up and started dancing around the room. Susan watched and laughed. She could hardly believe they were the same little girls she found just over a week ago. So much had happened since then, and they'd undergone a dramatic transformation. They didn't look like companions of Little Orphan Annie anymore. They seemed like happy, normal, little girls.

———⚬———

He watched the young police officer pull away from the curb and head down the street. The Mexican was there, much earlier than usual, but he was alone.

He may be big and strong, but I'd bet my life he's no match for me in the brains department. This shouldn't be too hard.

He formed his plan carefully. There were many houses on the street, and he was certain most of them housed working adults who would be leaving for their jobs soon. He'd waited most of the night; what were a couple more hours? Soon the brats would be gone, and whatever secrets they'd told Susan, she would take to her grave.

An evil smile crept across his face as his anticipation grew.

This will be even better than killing their mother. I couldn't witness her death, and the thrill of the kill with Lynette was short-lived in that public place. But this time, I will enjoy every minute of it. Maybe I'll kill them first while Susan watches, then I'll watch her die a slow, painful death.

He was practically giddy with excitement as he hid in the shrubs bordering Susan's yard. He watched as the Mexican, as he liked to call him, looked around as if he knew he was being watched.

He wished he'd been able to install bugs and video equipment in the house. The ones in the cop's house were no longer working, so he assumed they'd been discovered. This little town's police force must have better resources than he thought.

He'd been reckless. He was too cocky, too sure he could pull this off in just a day. Things were taking too long, and he feared Russell might begin putting the pieces together. But none of that mattered this morning. He would silence Susan and the brats, take care of one last loose end, and disappear forever.

He took the latex gloves out of his pocket and put them on. He could feel, in his blood, the timing was right. The man was hard at work in the back yard, alone this time, measuring sheetrock. He wouldn't have time for a final prayer.

He slid the gun out from inside the shirt identifying him as a cable repairman and attached the silencer. He aimed the gun at the back of the man's head and placed his finger on the trigger.

"Mannie," Susan called from the house. "Could you back your van up to the garage, please? I have some things I'd like you to take to the Salvation Army for me."

His hands froze. Maybe he'd be able to take them all down in the house after all.

He watched as the man went around the house and backed his truck into the driveway and up to the garage door.

•◦•

On the other side of town, Penny, in dark glasses and hair as black as ebony, walked into the First Maryland Bank in Lakespring and signed in to access a safe deposit box under her former name, Adams. She took out what she needed and left the rest behind. When she was finished, she asked to see the manager of the bank.

When the manager, Mr. Graves, left his office to greet the woman, he blinked, his mouth agape, clearly realizing *Ms. Adams* wore a disguise. He looked around before hastily ushering her into his office.

"I'd like to give permission for someone else to access my safe deposit box," she said quickly.

"Is the person here with you, Ms." He cleared his throat. "Adams?"

"No, he's not. Is that a problem?"

"Well, it's very unusual to allow safe deposit access to someone who hasn't signed the permission form in front of witnesses."

"I understand that, but this is a special circumstance." She spoke in hushed tones even though they were behind a closed door. "Mr. Graves, I am willing to sign a certified document allowing Detective Jim Russell, or any person working on his behalf, access to the box. *However,* the person must be able to prove he is, in fact, Detective Russell or someone working with him." According to the Internet, Russell was the detective in charge of Lynette White's murder. Penny assumed he'd make the connection between her husband and the social worker just as she had.

"This is highly irregular, Ms. Adams. I'm sure you'll understand if we take some time here to properly document everything."

"I most certainly understand and will do whatever is necessary to have my wishes carried out. One other thing, Mr. Graves..."

"Yes?"

"I also want a certified document forbidding the opening of the box by Alexander Moore, Dennis Simpson, or any member of the Baltimore City government or Baltimore City Police Department." Mr. Graves eyed her suspiciously, and for the first time, she wondered if he was in Alex's pocket, too. "And I want Detective Russell notified immediately of the box in the event of my death."

The bank manager's eyes widened, and he hesitated.

"Mr. Graves, is there some reason you would refuse to comply with my wishes? A loyal customer of this bank for over twenty years? A reason you would be against following my instructions to block the contents of *my* box from Alex Moore or Mayor Simpson?"

Again, he cleared his throat, and his voice took on an air of umbrage. "Certainly, not, *Ms. Adams.*"

"Very well. Let's get this paperwork done, shall we?"

When Penny got back into her car, she removed her black wig revealing her auburn hair. She needed to find out if there was a train that stopped near the Outer Banks and how to purchase a ticket for it.

Penny assumed, based on all the movies she'd watched, she could just show up at the station and purchase a ticket with cash if necessary. She'd never been on a train, and she thought it was the last way Alex would expect her to travel. With all the sleuthing she'd been doing, she felt a little like Agatha Christie preparing to journey on the Orient Express.

Penny was grateful she never told Alex about the house she inherited from her long-deceased father. It was still in her biological father's name, a name she only vaguely remembered, having been adopted by her stepfather at a young age. In a bag beside her was another gift from her father—all the cash she would ever need.

Before

Their marriage went smoothly for the first couple years. Penny stayed busy, helping with numerous big-name events. She knew she was a terrific hostess and meticulous with details. Alex could turn over to her all the particulars of an event, and it would run smoothly without any mishap. Penny had always loved the limelight and found she enjoyed socializing with Alex's friends, though some she preferred more than others.

Her desire to have children remained, but Alex assured her there was time. After all, she was barely into her forties. They had plenty of time to look into fostering, or even adoption. He told her he wanted to spend his days and evenings with her, and his romancing won her over every time. Taken with her new social status and the endless round of parties, she put her wishes for children on the back burner.

One evening, after playing bridge, just a week before the mayoral election, Penny arrived home early and was surprised to see several cars parked in the driveway. She recognized them as belonging to the mayor and his security detail. She soundlessly entered the home and heard the mayor speaking. The room went quiet when Alex spotted her and held up a hand to Denny.

Alex pushed himself from the table and grabbed her arm. He dragged her to their room and pushed her onto the bed. When Penny asked what was going on, Alex hit her for the first time.

"Don't push me, Penny." Alex slammed the door as he left.

Penny tried the door, but it was locked. She waited for hours to be able to confront Alex, but she eventually fell asleep. The next morning, her husband was gone when she woke. That evening, he arrived with red roses and a bottle of one of Penny's favorite wines.

He told Penny her desire to have children was going to be fulfilled. He'd been working on it for quite a while and had just found out they'd been approved. They would have two children by the end of the week.

Penny had mixed thoughts about the children. What kind of home was she bringing them into?

Her mother always told her a woman could never be too careful and should always have a bank account her husband didn't know about. Penny had never been so happy to have heeded her mother's advice.

With the wellbeing of the children in mind, she visited her bank and withdrew a large sum of cash. She placed the money and several copies of documents into a safety deposit box she once shared with Joe—insurance policies, as she liked to think of them.

Penny continued to add her little 'policies' to the box over the next two years, both money and documents. She knew there would come a day when she would need it.

CHAPTER TWENTY-TWO

After

Jim hated himself for making Susan leave, especially since he didn't have the chance to tell her any of the things he wanted to. On the other hand, maybe it was for the best. She hadn't given Jim any sign she might have feelings for him, nor she did deny anything was going on with Seth. So that was that. Their relationship was nothing more than two old friends helping each other out. She didn't see it as anything else, so why should he?

Jim plunged into his research. Every day he got a little closer to finding out what Moore was up to. He was getting better at doing his own online research, thanks to Susan, but he still relied on printed police reports more than the Internet. He picked up the phone and called the forensics department to see if they had any leads on the knife that killed Lynette. He had more important things to do than think about Susan. At least, that's what he told himself.

He crept closer to the house and heard them saying good-bye.

"I'll be back soon."

"Thanks, Mannie. See you later."

He watched as the van pulled down the driveway. When it was out of sight, he made his move. He went toward the back door and peered into the house. The TV was on in the living room, but he couldn't see anyone watching it from his angle.

The stupid man had left the door open, letting him sneak in without being heard. He followed the woman's laughter up the stairs to a closed door, his back to the wall, gun drawn. He didn't see or hear the brats, but he could hear Susan talking to someone. Her voice was muffled behind the closed door.

He swung the door open and raised the gun, ready to shoot.

"Call me later," a phantom voice said in the empty room.

He stood there, unable to move. What was going on? Susan wasn't there, but the computer was on, and her voice flowed from the speakers in a pre-recorded conversation.

"Goodbye, Mom."

Enraged, he shouted profanities and sent the laptop flying across the room.

He checked the other rooms, but they were empty. He barely touched the steps as he raced back to the living room where the TV was still blasting. The kitchen was neat and tidy. There were no signs of Susan or the girls.

It's a trap, he thought suddenly. *I have to get out of here.*

He ran back outside and through the hedge. He tucked the gun back into his jacket and headed around to the van. As he drove away, he thought about the laptop he'd left behind. Why hadn't he taken it? It probably held the answer to wherever they had gone.

He watched his mirrors the entire way out of town and hoped, if he had been recorded, this Podunk town's police department had fun trying to identify him behind the mask he wore.

"Thank you, Mannie, for indulging me and my wild imagination." Susan sat in the passenger seat of his van, her heart racing. "I know it was a silly thing to do, but I didn't want to take any chances after last night. Maybe Jim was right that I've been too reckless."

"No problem. I'm happy to help. Everything okay back there?" He could see Cassie and Ellie in the rearview mirror.

"Si, Mannie," Cassie answered. "We're buckled in and ready to go. That was fun!"

Mannie had carried them out in boxes Susan had stored in the attic. They thought it was a game and held their breath to see if they could stay in the box without giggling. Their suitcases and Ellie's car seat were also in boxes which Susan carried out and put in the van.

"Do you think anyone was watching, or am I just paranoid?"

"You can't be too careful, Susan."

"You be careful while we're gone, Mannie."

"Es fine, Susan. I will be fine."

"I hope so, I really hope so."

Susan, Cassie, and Ellie arrived in Denver, exhausted by the haste to leave and the day of travel. Susan never realized how hard it was traveling with two children. Flying cross country by herself had always been a piece of cake.

They took a cab straight to the hotel, and thankfully their room was ready. Susan sent a text telling Jim they'd arrived safely, but a single letter *k* was the only reply. They ate an early dinner at a restaurant within walking distance of the hotel before going to a Target in the same shopping center. Donning new bathing suits, they spent the evening in the pool until they were all too tired to stay up any longer.

In the middle of the night, Susan awoke to the sound of crying. Fearing another nightmare, she jumped out of bed and went to Ellie's side.

How I wish Jim were here.

Ellie was sound asleep and crying, but she wasn't screaming like previous nights. Susan didn't know what to do. Wasn't there a rule about not waking someone who was dreaming? Or was that sleepwalking? She reached down to touch Ellie's hair, but her hand stopped in mid-air when she heard a small voice amidst the cries.

"Please, don't find us. Please, please." Ellie said it repeatedly. Susan didn't know to whom she was talking or if it was a dream or a memory. What she did know was that Ellie could talk, and something deep down inside was keeping her silent.

Susan picked up her phone and texted Jim, telling him what she discovered. She asked if he had anything new and watched the phone for a few minutes, hoping she would get a message back, but it was barely morning on the East Coast, and there was no reply.

Ida was at the grocery store when the doorbell rang that morning. Patrick peeked out the window and was stunned to see his former football player standing on the porch in his police uniform. Abe dropped by now and then but not usually out of the blue, and never in uniform. Patrick's initial surprise at seeing Abe was replaced by fear.

"Susan, the girls, what's happened?"

"They're okay, Coach," Abe said quickly. "I'm sorry to alarm you. I just wanted to talk to you."

Patrick took a deep breath and put his hand to his chest. "Son, you came close to giving me a heart attack."

"I'm sorry, Coach. I didn't think about that, about you seeing me here in uniform with everything that's going on. I'm really sorry."

"It's okay, Abe." Patrick put his hand on Lank's shoulder. "It's good to see you. Come on in." They went inside, and Patrick led him to the kitchen. "Would you like something to drink?"

"Do you have any soda?"

"We've got ginger ale."

"That works. Thanks."

Patrick handed the can to Abe, motioning for him to sit down. Abe took a sip and noticed childlike drawings on the fridge and wondered if they were done by Cassie and Ellie.

"So, what brings you here today?" Patrick asked as he poured himself a cup of coffee and took a seat.

"It's about Susan, Sir, but nothing bad." The young man took a sip of his drink.

"Susan? You said nothing happened to her." Patrick held his cup midway between the table and his mouth.

"No, Coach, nothing's happened. I just wanted you to know I'm the officer who's been keeping an eye on Susan since she found the girls."

Patrick's eyes widened as Abe's words sunk in. "You're Lank, the 'rookie' Susan talks about?" He couldn't hide his astonishment.

"Yes, Sir. I just wanted you to know."

"Well, this is a surprise. I didn't know you were working that closely with Jim. Are you having any luck learning anything about the girls?"

"Not much. I'm pretty good with forensics, but I'm still learning the ropes as far as detective work. That's Jim's area, but he's brilliant and is teaching me a lot. I really wanted to work at the FBI or a high-tech crime lab, but they wouldn't take me. My back can still be a problem at times, if I sit too long or don't exercise." Abe, who Parick couldn't think of as Lank, shrugged. "I almost didn't get this job, but Jim convinced 'em to hire me and has kinda become my mentor. He said I was smart enough to be more than just a beat cop." Abe smiled sheepishly.

"I've known Jim his whole life," Patrick said. "He's a good man. I'm not surprised he saw the potential in you."

"I hope to prove him right. As I said, I've got a lot to learn about detective work." Abe drained his soda and placed the can on the coaster.

"It looks like you're doing all right to me. You've kept Susan safe, and Jim trusts you."

Abe smiled. Patrick acted nonchalant, but he was proud of the young man who sat across from him. The kid meant the world to him.

<hr>

Susan's meeting was successful, and the girls were angels under the watchful eye of the company's receptionist, a woman Susan had gotten to know and trust. The following day, Susan and the girls went sightseeing. Their first stop was the Colorado History Museum. They loved the exhibits about western frontier life, living in the mountains, and local Native Americans. Their favorite room was the History Express, where they could touch all the displays. They dressed up as Native Americans and mountaineers. They played games, made crafts, and pretended to mine for gold.

From there, they went to the Denver Museum of Miniatures, Dolls, and Toys. The girls were wide-eyed with amazement throughout the tour. Susan had as much fun as they did. The day was just what they needed.

Cassie and Ellie were enthralled by the Rocky Mountains surrounding the city. Never had they seen such vast mountains, and they couldn't believe they were still covered with so much snow.

"Our mountains weren't half as big as these," Cassie said over lunch.

"Your mountains?" Susan tried to sound casual though her heartbeat accelerated. "What do you mean, Cassie?"

"Um, well, I guess it's okay to tell you that." She shifted her eyes around the room. "We used to live in the mountains. Mama loved to ski, and she taught me when I was real little. She said we lived in the desert before then, and she never knew how much fun the mountains were. We didn't live there for long, though. We left after Mama...well, after she died." Cassie stared at her cheeseburger but didn't take a bite.

"Do you want to talk about it, Cassie?" Susan gently prodded.

Cassie pursed her lips and closed her eyes, and then she shook her head. "No, not yet. Is that okay?" She looked up at Susan, her eyes filled with sorrow. Susan smiled.

"Sure, Honey. It's okay." She reached across the table and grabbed Cassie's hand. Ellie put down her milkshake and slowly placed her hand on top of Susan's. Susan put her other hand on top of Ellie's, and they all giggled as they piled their hands on top of each other.

By the time they returned to the hotel, they were all exhausted. They ordered room service and a movie.

"I wish Jim was here," said Cassie during the movie. "He's fun to watch movies with. Why didn't he come, too?" She turned and looked at Susan.

"He had to work, Honey. He's very busy, remember?"

"Can he come next time?"

"We'll see." Susan was going to miss these girls when they were placed in a new home. "But you might have a new mommy and daddy and a new house to go to. This is just temporary, remember?"

Cassie looked down and frowned. "I remember. I just thought…"

Susan's phone rang, and Cassie scooped it from the table and answered before Susan had a chance.

"Hello?"

"Cassie?"

"Jim! It's Jim on the phone," she told Susan and Ellie. "I knew it was him calling! We miss you, Jim. Why didn't you come with us?"

"I really wish I was there, Sunshine. I'm busy trying to help you and Ellie, remember?"

"I know. I just miss you. And watching movies is no fun without you."

"Let me talk to Susan, okay, Sunshine?"

"Sure, Jim, hold on." She handed the phone to Susan.

"Hi," she said. "How's it going?"

"Great. I may be on to something. I got your texts, but I've been busy. I'm sorry." Susan heard a note of regret in Jim's voice, or maybe that was wishful thinking.

"That's okay, I understand."

"No, I mean, I'm sorry. I acted like a jerk the other night, again."

"No, Jim, we're both under a lot of pressure. It's okay."

"Has Ellie said anything, other than in her sleep?"

"No, nothing, but I think she's getting there. Maybe she will soon."

"I hope so."

There was a long pause in the conversation.

"I've been thinking." Jim finally broke the silence.

"Yes?" Susan's heart skipped a beat in anticipation.

"I'm hoping it won't be long before we break this case wide open. And that means you won't need my protection any longer, and you can go on with your life."

"Oh." Susan felt a painful tug in her chest.

"What I mean is…" Jim hesitated. "When this is over, I don't want you to go on with your life. I mean, I do want you to go on with your life, but I don't want you to do it without me."

Susan remained quiet. She closed her eyes and said a silent prayer. She waited for him to continue.

"What I'm trying to say is, I miss you, all of you. I never thought I could miss anyone so much. But now I know that I've missed you since high school when I let you believe I didn't have feelings for you." Jim took a deep breath, and Susan pictured him running his hand through his hair. "I've always had feelings for you, and I don't want to live without you again."

Susan smiled, and her heart did a somersault. "I miss you, too, Jim. I miss you a lot. And I don't want to go on without you either."

"That settles it then," Jim said with an obvious lift in his voice. "I'll see you tomorrow."

"But we'll be home really late."

"And I'll be waiting." She could hear the smile in his voice. "I'll see you tomorrow." And with that, he was gone.

Cassie looked up at Susan and beamed. "I told you so."

⋅⋅⋅◦⋅⋅⋅

Jim felt good when he disconnected the call. He hadn't exactly told Susan how he felt, but he hoped she knew. *I love you* isn't something you just blurt out on the phone, not if it's the real thing.

And this is the real thing. Life is good.

He'd also refrained from telling Susan about the letter that arrived at the station earlier that day. The letter listed several current and former hotel and restaurant owners in Baltimore, Lakespring, and the metropolitan area. The note advised Jim to question those listed about visits from Alex Moore over the past ten years.

Jim was taken aback by the contents of the letter, and a barrage of questions swarmed his brain. What was the sender's level of knowledge? Why not just come forward with the information rather than sending a cryptic note? Why not tell Jim in person? Why all the subterfuge? And how had he come upon all this information? Most importantly, what else had he been hiding?

The sender may not have signed his name, but Jim knew who it was. The handwriting, although obviously disguised, was more than familiar to Jim. It was very similar to his own.

Mike read over the pile of notes he abruptly stopped making sixteen years before.

After losing his wife and his dignity to Denny Simpson, Chief Mike Russell began investigating the councilman on his own. He knew about the human trafficking, but he didn't know how to tie Moore and Simpson to it. Witnesses could be bought off, or killed, and all Mike had as evidence was hearsay from a few friends, unwilling to talk on the record.

For years, Officer Russell thwarted every effort by Moore and Simpson to bring their business to Lakespring. In addition, he prevented them from infiltrating both the police department and the town council. Even after Simpson became Baltimore's mayor, Russell continued to amass information on the men that would lead to their downfall.

The day was finally near.

⋘⊶⊷⋙

Jim was working late, aware that Susan's plane wouldn't land for a while longer. When he finally packed up and grabbed his jacket, he heard the buffeting of rain on the roof as thunder crashed and shook the station. He hoped it would let up before Susan's plane neared the airport.

Her previous night's words played again in Jim's mind. It was hard to concentrate on anything other than her voice saying she missed him and didn't want to live without him. Jim stopped, a frown overtaking his face.

Susan and the girls were still in danger, and he still wasn't being honest with her. He may have told her he had feelings for her, but he still hadn't leveled with her about his initial involvement in the case.

How was he going to tell her about his secret life, the investigation, the information he was compiling and withholding from her? He should've told her already and was afraid she'd think he was using her, and wasn't he?

Let's face it. I am kind of using her just like I would've used anybody to get this close to the truth. But Susan isn't just anybody.

Every time he saw her, touched her hand, looked into her eyes, heard her voice, he knew she had never been just anybody to him and never would be. Now he needed to convince her of that before the truth came out.

A call came in from Lank, but Jim was re-reading the letter and let the call go to voicemail. He'd call Lank back in a minute. He had several guys out looking for Eddie's missing car and trying to track down his wife, Kayla. So far, they were striking out.

Jim walked out of his office and headed through the station. He noticed all the other officers watching the TV in the conference room and wondered what was going on.

"What's up?" he asked, poking his head into the room as his phone vibrated in his pocket.

"Big news," replied one of the officers, not taking his eyes off the screen. "A plane coming from Denver went down outside Baltimore, right in some farmer's field. Lots of casualties. Seems the pilot lost control during the landing."

All that registered with Jim were the words *plane*, *down*, and *Denver*. No, it couldn't be. He was too stunned to speak.

"Hey, Jim! Where're you going?" the officer yelled to Jim as he bolted out the door.

Once on the road, Jim managed to dial Lank's number. Lank answered his phone on the first ring.

"What the heck, Jim? Why aren't you answering? Susan's plane—"

"I just heard. What do you know?" He put the phone on speaker and accelerated the car.

"Not much. According to the news, things don't look good. The plane was ripped in half when it went down.

Most of the passengers are dead or believed to be dead. There's even talk of a possible tornado in the area."

Jim's throat went dry. It was all he could do to concentrate on the road amidst the pelting rain and jagged flashes of light in the coal black sky. The wind roared like a train racing through the night, and Jim's heart matched the cacophony of its chugga-chugga beat and churning wheels. Tornadoes were becoming less of a phenomenon in Maryland, and Jim tried not to think about the death and destruction they had brought to the state in the last several years.

"Jim? You there?" Lank asked, his voice hushed like a prayer.

Jim couldn't remember praying much over the course of his life, other than the Sundays he went to church with Susan and her family, but he found himself making every promise he could think of, begging God to let Susan be okay.

"I've gotta go," he said, flicking his gaze to his phone just long enough to find the *End* button.

He tuned the radio to a news station and jacked up the volume, praying he would hear something good.

CHAPTER TWENTY-THREE

After

What should have been an hour's drive to the town of Westminster felt like two, but Jim made it there in less than fifty minutes despite the weather. He didn't bother stopping to ask questions after jumping out of his car. He ran through the police line, holding up his badge and scanning the scene for Susan. He turned his gaze from the wreckage and swallowed his fears.

"Jim! Jim!"

He heard someone screaming his name and turned to see Cassie running toward him through the rain, her long, wet hair sticking to her face, eyes wild with fear. She had several cuts on her arms, legs, and cheeks and was covered with dirt. Ellie ran behind her, arms outstretched, her blonde curls soaked and drooping with rain.

Jim stooped and wrapped his arms around them both, looking past them for Susan as they crushed him with their shivering bodies.

"Where's—"

"We don't know." Cassie's voice was thick with emotion. Her tears mixed with rain, forming rivulets through the dirt and blood on her cheeks. "We're scared, Jim," she said through sobs. "We're so scared."

Jim held the girls to him, assuring them everything would be okay, praying it was the truth. They'd been through so much already, and now this. How could they ever manage a normal life after the events of the past few weeks? It was too much for any child to go through.

He released the girls and stood. He watched another stretcher descend from the plane.

"Stay here," he told them.

"No!" Cassie threw her arms around his waist. "Don't leave us!"

Jim met her eyes. "I'm not leaving you, Cassie. I promise. I need to find Susan."

"But..." Cassie started to protest.

"Cassie, Ellie needs you to be strong while I look for Susan. I know you can do this."

Cassie's frown and tear-filled eyes said otherwise. Jim scanned the emergency responders for a friendly face and spotted a uniformed officer, a woman, helping other passengers. He caught her eye and motioned her over.

"Can I help you, Sir?"

He showed her his badge. "I need to find their mother. They're all under police protection. Can you stay with them? Make sure they're okay and nobody gets near them?"

The officer bent down and smiled at Cassie and Ellie. "Sure, I can," she said in a gentle voice. She looked at Cassie. "Is that okay with you?"

Cassie gazed at the woman, then turned to look up to Jim. She slowly nodded, and Jim didn't hesitate before racing toward the plane.

He showed his badge and pushed his way inside, using the emergency ladder the rescue crew set up. The plane's stairs were gone. He stopped short as he boarded and saw the number of passengers, still in their seats, covered with yellow sheets. For a moment, he thought he might be sick. All the training in the world could not have prepared him for this. Only one thought kept him going. He had to find Susan, and he was determined to find her alive.

There was a sudden commotion in the back of the plane. Jim heard a woman scream.

"Ellie, Cassie! Where are you! Does anyone see my girls?" Medics were holding her down, urging her to be calm.

"Susan!" Jim yelled as he made his way down what was left of the aisle, past the medics and airline personnel who were trying to save whomever they could.

"Jim! The girls," she began.

"They're fine. They're just fine. They're outside waiting for you."

At that, Susan slumped into the seat and began to cry. Jim reached the seat in front of her and questioned the medics. "Is she okay?"

"She lost consciousness. Just woke up a few minutes ago and started screaming for her kids. Probably has a concussion. It's a miracle she's even alive. If she'd been just a couple rows farther up..." The medic stopped and shook his head. "Anyway, there's an ambulance waiting outside."

"Oh no, you don't." Susan protested. "I'm not going to the hospital. I have two children who need me."

Jim reached over the top of the seat and gently but firmly held her face in his hands and looked deeply into her eyes.

"Now you listen to me. What good are you to Cassie and Ellie if you pass out on them? Haven't they had enough tragedy in their lives? Do you want to be the source of more trauma for them? You will go to the hospital, and you will get checked out and do whatever they tell you to do. I'll take care of the girls. I'll get them cleaned up, and then we'll head to the hospital to check on you. When you're cleared, we'll all go home. Is that understood?"

A tear rolled down her cheek, and Susan gave a nod of understanding.

Jim leaned over the seat and kissed her gently on the lips before letting go of her face. He was too emotional to say anything else. Silently, he thanked God Susan was going to be okay.

Susan had never felt so happy to be in her own bed. The thought of spending the night at the hospital, away from Cassie and Ellie, was almost unbearable. Thank heaven for Jim, she thought. He had taken care of the girls, told them she was fine, and assured them they could see her as soon as the doctors said it was okay.

He told Susan that Agent Ross had swept her house while she was gone. No bugs were found. A state-of-the-art home security system was installed at Jim's expense. Susan protested that she could have done that herself, but Jim insisted it be done immediately. Surveillance cameras were strategically placed around the yard and porch. They'd also swept her parents' house and added security lights and cameras there, too. Nobody was getting close to any of them without Jim knowing about it.

The girls cuddled in bed with Susan, and Jim threw a sheet and blanket onto the overstuffed chair by the window. Despite Susan's insistence that a mild concussion was hardly a call for bedside attention, Jim was determined to stay the night, having promised the doctor—and himself—he wouldn't leave her.

Cassie and Ellie beamed as they watched the news. Seeing themselves on TV, even if it was just a quick shot of the passengers being lifted from the wreckage, made them forget everything else that happened.

Jim exchanged a worried look with Susan. That coverage would be all over the news and YouTube by morning. He hoped the small figures in the background wouldn't be recognized by anyone else.

⸻◆⸻

Jim woke Lank, who stretched as he peeled himself from Susan's couch. It was early, and the house was quiet. With instructions from Jim, Lank left and returned with a breakfast of freshly baked muffins, orange juice, and coffee.

While Lank made scrambled eggs, Jim filled him in on a call he'd made while Lank was out. He'd informed his boss, Chief Webb, that there'd been a break in Lynette's murder case, and he needed officers to help protect some witnesses who had information about the killer.

Jim then woke Cassie and Ellie and told them to get dressed and go downstairs so Susan could get some rest. She'd had a restless night, often letting out a soft moan, and Jim knew she was in more pain than she let on.

When she stirred around mid-morning, the girls served her breakfast in bed and excitedly told her that Lank was taking them to Grandma Ida's for the day. After fifteen minutes, Susan laid her hand on the side of her head, and Jim shooed the girls out. As they ran to get their shoes, Jim sat on the bed and reached for the pain medication on the nightstand. After he gave Susan her morning dose, he reached for her hand.

"I really thought I'd lost you last night. I've never been so scared in my life." Jim held her hand and gently caressed her cheek with his fingers. He carefully tucked a long strand of her dark hair behind her ear.

"I can't tell you what it meant to me that you were there," Susan said. "I don't think I could've handled it alone."

"Yes, you could've. You're the strongest woman I've ever known. I can't believe how lucky I am to have you."

Susan smiled, but her eyes grew heavy as the pain medication kicked in.

Jim kissed her lightly and stood to go. "I'll be back in a little while. I've got to get to the station. Another officer is downstairs and will stay here while Lank and the girls are at your mom's. You're all going to be watched twenty-four-seven now. I'm not taking chances with that news report."

Susan's head sleepily bobbed, and Jim watched her fall asleep, thoughts of the previous night tugging at his mind. It was all a blur—hearing the news, racing to the site, seeing the girls, finding Susan, watching her being lifted into the ambulance, talking to the doctor, bringing her home, then hearing her small gasps and mewing throughout the night. He closed his eyes. He did not want to leave her.

Jim adjusted the curtains to keep the light from stealing its way into the room. He remembered the white four-poster bed and dresser from her childhood room. That room was yellow, but this was a soft green. He recalled being there on her tenth birthday when she'd picked out the furniture.

She's spoiled, but you'd never know it. She has a heart of gold and a love of all things soft and simple.

He walked to the dresser and picked up the picture he'd noticed the night before. Her thirteenth birthday party. Susan sat at the kitchen table in front of a cake with glowing candles. Ida and Patrick beamed proudly from behind her chair. Susan's grandmother was to their left.

On one side of Susan was Daisy, her hair adorned with flowers. Their friend, Heather, who died in a car wreck when they were in college, was sitting next to Daisy. On Susan's other side, with his arm around her shoulders, blonde curls covering his eyes, was Jim. On his face was the look of pure happiness.

Jim replaced the picture, catching a glimpse of himself in the mirror. Gone was the thirteen-year-old kid who would screw it all up in another year. In his place was the man who vowed never to walk away from her again.

⚬

Hours later, Ida ignored the groans and turned off the television. "Let's get some yard work done and then have a picnic in the back yard to enjoy the fruits of our labors. The storms are over, and the day looks just glorious."

"A picnic?" Cassie and Patrick said at the same time.

Patrick frowned. "Outside?"

"Just in the back yard," Ida said as she handed them their jackets. "The fresh air will be good for them."

"Please, Grandpa Patrick, please?"

"Okay," he agreed reluctantly, shooting a dirty look at Ida. "But only if we can have some of those cookies you made the other day. Grandma Ida hid some in the freezer." He winked at Cassie.

"I was saving those," Ida protested.

"For today," said Cassie, winking back at Patrick.

"You win. But only if you get your shoes on while I pack the picnic basket."

Cassie and Ellie ran to retrieve their shoes from the foyer, and Patrick followed Ida into the kitchen. He pulled the picnic basket from the top shelf of the walk-in pantry. It was usually reserved for vacations and the 4th of July, but he knew Ida would want to use it for the girls.

"Where's Abe?"

"Someone called and said Jim wanted to meet him at the station."

Patrick shook his head. "Are you sure? I thought he wasn't supposed to leave the girls."

"Some kind of break in the case. That's why I suggested the picnic. I think this is almost over."

"If so, are you going to talk to Susan?" Patrick kept his voice low.

"Yes, when we take Cassie and Ellie back home tonight. I don't know what it would take for her to adopt them, but I think she should consider it once they're out of danger."

Patrick came up behind her and nuzzled her neck. "I hope it works out. Having them around makes me feel young again."

Ida laughed. "Go in with the girls and let me work, you dirty, old man."

"I can't help myself." He feigned being hurt. "Thinking about having grandchildren gets me excited."

"Go." She laughed and pushed him away, but she was excited, too, and hummed as she packed the basket.

<hr>

Jim was anxious to question the hotel and restaurant owners on the list in his pocket. He hoped the owners would be willing to come forward with whatever information they had, but something bothered him about the situation. Why had his father not investigated this himself all those years ago? What was his connection to Moore and Simpson? And why didn't he tell Jim in person instead of writing an anonymous note?

Jim tried calling his dad, but there was no answer. He wasn't at Ron's, and he wasn't at home. Where could he have gone? Jim racked his brain, trying to figure out what his father was up to. He was nearing the station and thinking about the possibilities when his cell phone rang.

<hr>

Before

Shortly after his mayoral rise, Simpson decided he'd had enough of Mike Russell. He sent a man to Russell's house with a message. The man entered the house while Russell was at work, and his sixteen-year-old son was at school.

The man was waiting at the kitchen table when Mike got home.

"Who the hell are you and what are you doing here?" Mike asked, reaching for his gun.

"I wouldn't do that if I were you. If anything happens to me, your son won't be returning from football practice today, or ever."

"What does that mean?" Mike was horrified. "What have you done to my son?"

"Nothing yet, but that can change in an instant. Right now, your son, James Steven, is at football practice. After that, he'll come home for dinner and do his homework until about nine o'clock, then he'll go to bed in the upstairs room facing the east side of the house." The man gestured toward the stairs.

"Tomorrow, he'll leave for school at exactly 7:35 and go to practice until five in the evening. His game will start at seven, then he and his friends, and probably some high school floozies, will go to that burger joint they all like to hang out at. He'll be home by his midnight curfew. He'll leave at seven tomorrow morning to go to work at Dan Miller's farm and be there until he gets off at three. Would you like me to go on?"

Mike sat in stunned silence. After some time, he shook his head. "I understand."

The man left the house, and Mike reached for a beer. Although he'd never been much of a drinker, it would be the first of many he would reach for over the next sixteen years. From that moment on, he stopped investigating Denny Simpson and Alex Moore.

CHAPTER TWENTY-FOUR

After

"Ida, stop what you're doing." Patrick hurried into the kitchen, taking the sandwich from her hands.

"What's going on?"

"Get the girls in the car. Don't open the garage door. Just get in and wait for me."

"Patrick?" Ida's face turned pale.

"Just go," he commanded. "Now."

Ida grabbed their jackets off the chair and hurried the girls toward the garage.

"Not this again," Cassie said. "Where are we going?"

"We'll explain in the car," Ida told her. "Patrick, what are you doing?"

"Shhh," He scribbled a note as Ida hurried the girls into the garage. He scanned the room for a second then opened the refrigerator door and put the note under the tub of butter.

Dear God, please let her find this, he prayed as he ran to the garage.

Just as Patrick shut the door, he heard the shattering of the sliding glass patio door.

When Clint entered the house, he heard the garage door being raised. He cursed to himself as he watched Ida and Patrick drive away with Cassie and Ellie in the back seat. He ran to his own car while pushing a button on his phone.

"They're gone. I'm going after them now. They won't get away this time."

When Clint entered the house, he heard the garage door being raised. He cursed to himself as he watched Ida and Patrick drive away with Cassie and Ellie in the back seat. He ran to his own car while pushing a button on his phone.

"Jim, I screwed up."

"What do you mean, you screwed up? Where are you?"

"On my way back to Coach O'Neil's. I got a call from someone at the station. Only it wasn't from the station. The guy said you and I were both being called in to meet with Chief Webb, but when I got there, you weren't there, and neither was he. He's on his way to Coach's house. The alarm company called the station."

Jim's heart missed a beat, and his breath caught in his throat. "I'm on my way." Jim shoved his phone in his pocket as he raced from his office.

"What do you mean, they're gone?" Susan cried when Mannie told her the news. He and the officer guarding her were standing in her bedroom, neither looking happy.

"We don't know, Susan." Mannie remained calm. "There was no sign of a fight, just a break-in."

"Someone broke in?" Susan said in alarm.

"Yes," the officer said. She knew his name, or had been told what it was, but her head was pounding, and she couldn't come up with it.

"The alarm company got a call, and a neighbor saw a man run out of the house and jump into a car down the street, but she has no idea what kind of car it was. The cameras caught him going in and out, but his face was covered. Your parents and the girls are gone. Their car was seen leaving the house the same time the alarm went off." He shook his head. "They didn't pack anything. Your mother's purse was still on the counter with her cell phone in it. Looks like they left in a hurry."

Susan's head was throbbing. She wanted to get up and go find them herself, but she felt dizzy when she tried to stand. Mannie jumped in to ease her back onto the bed.

"Don't get up, Susan. Jim is doing everything he can to find the girls. He and Lank brought in the police and they're going over everything in the house."

"The refrigerator," Susan suddenly said. She opened her eyes and sat up. "Call the house and tell them to look in the refrigerator. That's where Dad always left notes for me when I was in high school and got home after he left for practice. He knew I always headed straight to the fridge."

The officer called the house and relayed the message to Jim. He paused while Jim checked the refrigerator.

"It's written on the back of a grocery list and Jim doesn't understand it. You want to talk to him?"

"Of course, I do," Susan snapped at him. Catching herself, she blushed. "I'm sorry. I'm stressed, and my head is killing me. Yes, please, hand me the phone."

"No need to explain, ma'am."

Jim read Susan the note. *Gone fishing. Stay out of the water until I get back. I love you. Dad.*

Susan started to choke up. She knew how much her dad loved surf fishing. He would go to Assateague State Park and fish for hours, with others or by himself.

Susan never went near the water alone. Even though she was an adult when her parents bought the beach house, they always worried she'd be taken under by a wave if they weren't there to watch her. It had become a family joke.

"I know where they are, or where they're heading. They're on their way to the Eastern Shore. I'll explain when we're on the way." Susan didn't know whether to laugh or cry. "Come get me, Jim, please. I want to go with you. I need to go with you."

Jim reluctantly agreed, and Mannie helped Susan get out of bed. It was a struggle, but she managed to be dressed by the time Jim arrived.

⚬

Alex paced back and forth in front of his desk. Things were out of control. The girls should've been found two weeks ago. Now it was all over the news that two girls and an old couple had disappeared. It was just a matter of time before it was leaked that he was the foster father.

He watched as the newsreel continued.

"What are the police saying?" asked the news anchor.

"That's the funny thing, Alan. They're not saying much. According to neighbors, Ida and Patrick O'Neil were at home when a man threw a chair through the sliding glass door at the back of the house. When the police arrived on the scene, the couple were already gone, apparently having fled in their own vehicle." The on-scene reporter turned and pointed toward the house. "As you can see, the garage door is open."

The camera panned the scene. Yellow police tape was stretched in front of the door.

"One neighbor claims to have seen a man drop off two small children earlier, but she says the couple doesn't have grandchildren, just one grown daughter who has not been seen here today and hasn't been reached for comment."

"Are the children in the house now?" the anchor inquired.

"I can't confirm either way. We're told this is an ongoing investigation and that, at this time, the police have no comment."

"And no Amber Alert?"

"Not that I'm aware of, Alan."

"Thanks, Donna. We'll check back in our next hour."

Alex assumed the girls had to be Cassie and Ellie. Why else would the police be attempting to keep their whereabouts quiet? Either the cops knew where the girls were and that they were safe, or they hoped to find them before anyone else did. Either scenario was not good for Alex. He watched the rest of the report with great interest.

"Wow, an interesting situation," the anchor said. "We'll keep you all updated on this story and will run a story about Ida and Patrick O'Neil on the six o'clock news. Be sure to tune in to see what we find out about this couple and their mysterious disappearance—."

The anchor paused. "Hold on, folks. This just in. According to a source at the Carroll Hospital Center, Ida and Patrick O'Neil's daughter, Susan, was released in the early hours this morning after being one of the survivors of

United Flight 367 that crashed in Westminster last night. We don't know if the two events are related in any way. We'll bring you an update on that development as we get more information."

Alex cursed loudly. Now the press was involved. Alex knew those nosy reporters would keep digging until they came up with just what they wanted. Fortunately, most of the Baltimore-based reporters were on his payroll. He had to find a way to stop them from finding out who Cassie and Ellie were and hoped this story wouldn't be picked up nationally. Everything was, nowadays, thanks to the blasted Internet.

The phone on his desk rang, and Alex picked it up before it rang a second time.

"Alex, have you seen the news?"

"I can't talk to you now, Denny. You know what I'm dealing with."

"I know, Alex, and I've been thinking that maybe my office should release a statement to the press. Maybe get ahead of this, tell the truth, before it comes out."

"Are you crazy?" Alex yelled. "You let me handle this. You've screwed things up enough already. I'll fix this mess, as usual. Now stop talking about it. You know better than to say anything over the phone. It was your stupid phone call that started this whole thing two weeks ago." Alex hung up and tried to decide what to do next.

———◦◦◦———

Penny whispered into her cell phone from the upstairs bathroom.

"Yes, Sir. I may have information about the girls on the news. Yes, the ones who were with the older couple. No, Detective Russell cannot call me back. Just give him this message. Tell him to go to the First Maryland Bank on Washington Street. Ask to see safe deposit box 3074. He has full access to it."

Penny disconnected the call and turned off the phone. It was done. It was time to put her plan into action. She prayed the girls were safe.

The news report told her the time had come to get out of this town. It was an omen. Now she just had to find a way out of the house, fast.

Outer Banks, here I come. For good.

⸺⬦⸺

Jim called Lank and told him to get to the bank and cordon off the vault. He then called Agent Morelli's cell and left it on speaker as he drove out of town.

"Agent Morelli."

"Tony, I guess you've heard what's going on. I've got Susan, and she knows where they're heading. We're trying to catch up with them before Moore does."

"Are you sure Moore is the one after them?"

"No, I'm not sure of anything," Jim replied. "I just know whoever broke into my house was awfully interested in those files. They went through everything I had from the past two years. Our hunch that whatever happened with Cassie and Ellie has to do with his business dealings is looking more likely." He pounded the wheel with his fist, then tightened his grip in frustration. "If only I had kept electronic copies instead of those stupid paper files."

"He'd have gotten them anyway, Jim, one way or another. What do you need from me?"

Jim told Morelli about the deposit box. "I spoke to the bank manager and told him Officer Barnes, who I trust, would be hand-delivering a notarized affidavit giving you permission to open it. If whatever is in that box is related to Moore and Simpson, we might be able to blow this out of the water. It's imperative we get to that box before anyone else in the Lakespring Police Department does. I'd like to believe they don't have anyone on the take there, but I'm not willing to take any chances. We can trust Lank, your guy, Ross, and a couple guys from the department, but they don't know I'm working with the FBI, and for now, I want to keep it that way. Barnes was at the house with Susan and witnessed me notarizing the form, but all he knows is that this is related to Lynette's murder."

"Speaking of Ross, he wrote a report on the devices found in your house," Morelli told him. "They were pretty high-tech. More sophisticated than someone in your department or an amateur would've had access to. More like the ones we use here at the bureau. Not ours, of course. Moore might've hired a professional."

"So, there was nothing to give us a clue as to where they came from?"

"Nothing at all," Morelli answered.

Jim finished his call and closed his phone. He turned to Susan. The shock on her face felt like a kick in the gut to Jim.

"Susan, I can explain."

"Did I understand that correctly? Are you working with the FBI? How long have you been investigating Moore and Simpson? I know you lied to me about having me followed. Have you been lying to me about everything? What else have you been keeping from me *Agent Russell*?" The anger in her voice and in her eyes sent shock waves through Jim.

"First of all, I'm not an agent." He took a deep breath and continued driving as he told Susan everything. By the time they reached the Chesapeake Bay Bridge, the car was silent.

Jim kept his eyes on the road. He'd blown it with Susan again, and he couldn't blame anyone but himself. Lank warned him. His father warned him. There were plenty of nights, after Cassie and Ellie were in bed, when he could've leveled with her. Now, Susan refused to speak to him and wouldn't even look at him.

He didn't think he'd ever be able to convince her he was trying to protect her or that he felt a duty to the Agency not to reveal everything to her. He'd felt like he was between a rock and a hard place since the day she walked into his office and handed him the case. He was furious with himself for messing up the best thing that had ever happened to him.

———◆———

"You don't see him, do you?" Ida turned to the window as she had every thirty seconds for the past two hours.

"No, I think we lost him, but let's not chance a drive-through. He may spot us." Patrick slowed down and pulled off Route 50 onto a hidden access road.

Kay's Country Kitchen had been there for years. Locals and frequent visitors loved the old-fashioned fried chicken, crab cakes, and oyster fritters. Tourists usually drove right by, never knowing the great meal they were missing.

"Where are we?" asked Cassie as she stretched after a long nap.

"We're in a little town called Cambridge," Ida told her. "It's one of our favorite places to stop and eat. Anyone hungry?"

"Starving," groaned Cassie. "We never had our picnic."

"We had a change of plans," Ida told her. "For now, we'll get something quick. We don't want to be late." She knew Patrick was in just as much a hurry as she was. She hoped his idea of stopping here was a good one. If they were still being followed, they could very well be trapped.

⁂

After they ate, Cassie began wondering about their situation.

"If we're going on a trip, how come Miss Susan didn't pack us a suitcase?"

"Because she didn't feel up to it, Honey," Grandma Ida told her. "And besides, we told her we wanted to spoil you with all new clothes."

"Where are we going, and how will Miss Susan know where to find us?"

"Don't worry," Grandma Ida assured her. "Susan and Jim will join us as soon as Susan is feeling better."

"Jim's coming?" Cassie asked excitedly. "All right! Miss Susan said maybe he'd go on a trip with us someday."

"And she was right. I'm sure they'll both be joining us soon."

Grandpa Patrick looked at Grandma Ida with a raised brow.

"Well, you don't think he'll let her come alone, do you? I have a feeling, after all that's happened in the last twenty-four hours, he'll never let her out of his sight again." Ida sat with a smug smile on her lips.

"You and Abe," he said. "He thinks Jim's in love with her, too."

"I always knew Abe was a smart young man."

"He's definitely in love with her," Cassie agreed.

"Oh, really?" Grandpa Patrick said. "How do you know that?"

"Because," Grandma Ida said before Cassie had a chance to answer. "I can tell by the way he looks at her, the same way you've always looked at me. And I think we're both fools for not intervening years ago."

"I agree with Grandma Ida," said Cassie. "Even if I don't know what inter-veen-ing means." She smiled and turned toward the windows where flat fields raced by.

"Why do you think so?" Grandma Ida asked, turning around to look at Cassie.

"It's like you said. He looks at her a special way, not the way Mr. Moore looked at Miss Penny. He's always staring at Miss Susan when she's not looking and smiling at her when she does something silly. He always looks happy to be with her. And he doesn't have to be touching her all the time and kissing all over her. Yuck. I've seen him just reach over and hold her hand, and that's so romantic." Cassie sighed and smiled as she watched the world fly by.

"What do you think, Ellie?" Ida asked, turning around as much as she could to see behind her.

Ellie smiled a broad, beautiful smile. She nodded and then giggled. Cassie didn't hear her giggle often anymore, but it was a beautiful sound when she did.

— ◇ —

If only I had told her the truth. Now she won't even look at me.

What Jim was aching to do was reach over and hold Susan's hand, stroke her cheek, but Susan sat with her arms folded across her chest, her face turned toward the window. When Jim attempted to talk, she held her hand up for him to stop.

The sound of Jim's phone finally caused her to look his way.

Jim picked up his phone, placed it to his ear and answered, "Russell here."

"You won't believe this," said Morelli. "It's all here. Everything we need to know. We've got enough on Moore to put him away for a long time, and probably Simpson as well."

"Yes!" Jim exclaimed, punching the air with his fist. He quickly grabbed the wheel again as the car swerved a little to the left. "When we catch up with the O'Neils, we'll be able to head back home."

"Hold on, Russell," Morelli said. "I wouldn't do that if I were you. I'm not convinced Moore is the only one after the girls. Let me explain why..."

"Hold on, Tony. I want Susan to hear this, too." He handed the phone to Susan, and she tapped on the speaker button.

Jim couldn't believe what he was hearing. When they said goodbye, Susan closed the phone and slowly put it down.

"Oh, my gosh." Susan said.

Jim breathed the word, "Wow." He stared out the window in disbelief before finding his words.

"They were there. They're witnesses," Susan said.

"Those poor girls." Jim's heart broke for them. "No wonder Ellie won't talk."

"Oh, Jim. What are we going to do? What did Reynolds know about the girls? How do we know they'll be safe even if Moore goes to jail? Agent Morelli thinks someone else is involved, someone connected to them who knows who they really are." Susan bit her lip as though she might cry, and Jim reached for her hand. "We don't even know who they really are."

"It's going to be okay. I'll keep digging until we know the truth." He prayed he wasn't wrong.

Alex left the house and went for a drive. He had to think things over. He needed to tell Penny the truth about the girls. He worked so hard to make sure there were no loose ends, but who would've thought Eddie Reynolds would figure it out? If he was able to put the pieces together, then others would, too.

Alex thought back to his courtship with Penny. She truly was unlike any of his exes. He could've divorced her before it went this far. He could've found some other way to deal with the kids, but he brought them home for her.

Maybe he loved her after all. The thought was foreign to him and came as a monumental revelation.

She deserved to hear the truth. From him and not the police. And he had to make sure she wasn't implicated. Somehow, he had to make her understand why he'd done what he had and why he hadn't told her. He might not have been good at loving her, but he could spare her any repercussions of what he'd done.

Alex stared out the window and thought back to the day the girls disappeared.

⸺◦⸺

The Day the Nightmare Began

Alex arrived home to what he thought was an empty house. Penny's car was not in the garage, and the house was quiet. He headed to his office to check his answering machine. Standing in front of his desk, he pushed the button on the machine as he unbuttoned his suit jacket and laid it over the leather couch. The mayor's voice followed the machine's beep.

"Alex, we've got problems. Reynolds just called me, and he's gone nuts. He's on his way over to your place. His wife is leaving him, and he's blaming us. He says he's not covering for us anymore. Says he's going to the press with what he knows about Cassie and Ellie and about the company. All the money in the world won't keep them from running with this story, Alex. If he talks, nobody can stop this, not even your people."

The message ended. Alex stood in disbelief, staring at the machine. That kid had been trouble from the start. He was such a goodie-two-shoes, and Alex should've known that promoting him to human resources would be a problem. Well, Alex could deal with Eddie.

Alex walked around the desk and reached for the phone. He stopped when he heard pounding on the front door.

"Open up, Mr. Moore," Reynolds yelled, his voice shrill. "If you don't let me in, I'll blow the door handle off."

Alex stared through the open door to the foyer. Did Eddie really have a gun, or was he bluffing? He wasn't about to let in a crazy man with a gun. But the only way out of the office was to go through the front hall. If he was quick—and lucky—he could get to the pantry and get to the garage where his Mercedes was parked. He'd call Denny from the car. Alex started toward the front hall when a shot was fired, and the door flew open.

"Don't move, Mr. Moore," Eddie Reynolds said from the doorway. "Or I'll blow your head off."

Alex was sure he meant it and held up his hands. "Okay, Eddie, take it easy. We can talk about this."

Eddie was sweating profusely and crying. "She's leaving me, you S.O.B. She found one of the checks you've been sending for the past few months. I've never cashed a single one. But she says she always knew going to work for you was a mistake. Someone sent her a letter saying I was having an affair. How could she believe that?" Eddie choked, taking a breath before continuing.

"Now she says it's unsafe for her and the kids to be around me, that if you're trying to pay me off, I must know something big. I tried to tell her I've never taken the money. I ripped up every check, but she doesn't care. She said I should've told her, should've gone to the police with whatever it is, and she's right! She and the boys are my life, and because of you, they're gone, along with everything I ever had that meant anything!"

"Slow down Eddie, you're being irrational. Let's call Kayla and ask her to come over. We'll all talk this out."

"We're not talking it out. She won't have anything to do with you, or with me anymore." Eddie wiped his brow with his empty hand. "I never wanted to be part of this. Now I want you out of my life. I never want to see or hear from you again. I don't care anymore about Simpson or you or anything, except figuring out how to get my family back."

Eddie's voice became higher pitched. "I'm going to the police with everything I know about Harbor Supply and Distribution and about the girls. Why did you involve me in that situation anyway? You could've sent anybody to get them after the accident. Why did it have to be me?" Sweat poured from his forehead, and he wiped it away with his sleeve. "You can't stop me. It may be the only way to get Kayla to see that we can be free of you."

"You don't want to do this, Eddie," Alex said, never taking his eyes off the gun. "You know everything. You'll implicate yourself as well. Then what'll your wife do when you're sitting in jail?"

"Shut up!" Eddie yelled, waving the gun at Alex. "Don't you ever talk about my wife!" His eyes widened, blazing with madness.

Alex saw his chance when Eddie wiped his brow for the third time. Alex grabbed for the gun, and it went off, spraying sheetrock all over them. They struggled, but Alex overpowered Eddie. He fell to the ground and Alex landed on top of him. The gun went off again. Alex felt the warm flow of blood on his mid-section. He looked down at Eddie, felt his pulse.

Eddie wasn't dead, but Alex guessed he would be soon. There was a lot of blood. Alex hoisted the man onto his shoulders and took him out to Eddie's own car. He drove the car way out of town to an old, seldom used, fishing pier. He put the car in neutral and held his foot on the brake as he used his handkerchief to wipe down anything he might have touched. He jumped out, wiped the door handle, and pushed the car into the lake. Eddie would never be talking again.

Several hours later, Alex returned. Penny was hysterical. There was blood all over the front hall, and the girls were gone.

"Someone must have taken them!" she screamed. "They might be dead!"

"Calm down, Penny. Why are you holding that bear?"

"It's Ellie's. I found it under your desk."

CHAPTER TWENTY-FIVE

After

By late afternoon, Ida, Patrick, Cassie, and Ellie arrived at the beach house. Patrick checked the outside of the house, as well as the inside, to make sure nobody had been there. He waved from the door for them to come in.

They had stopped at Walmart to get food, clothes, and toiletries. Ida ran into the store while Patrick and the girls hid in the car around back. He told Ida they'd be back in front in exactly twenty minutes, and she hurried through the store, running out just as Patrick slid into the loading lane.

When they arrived at the cottage, Patrick called Susan on her cell phone.

"Dad," she answered. "Are you okay?"

"We're fine, Princess," he said. "Did you get my note?"

"Yes, we got it. We'll be there soon. And the girls?"

"They're fine. They don't know anything. They didn't see the man outside, and we told them we're taking another trip and that you and Jim are on the way."

"Thank heaven you're all okay. Are the doors locked, and is the car out of sight?"

"Of course, of course. We parked out back." He checked the window for the third time in the past ten minutes.

"Okay. We'll be there as soon as we can," Susan told him. "Don't let anyone in."

Clint took it slow as he neared Salisbury on the lower Eastern Shore of Maryland. The last thing he wanted was to get pulled over for speeding.

"Why does this road have to run through so many small towns? Haven't people out here ever heard of an interstate?" he asked his sometime-partner, Sam.

He was tired of seeing cornfields, pickup trucks, and the bumper sticker, *There's no life west of the Bay*. He couldn't wait to be back to the city.

"Don't ask me. I just got here."

The car fell silent as both men concentrated on the task at hand. Clint hated working with someone else, but he didn't always make the rules.

Patrick and Ida O'Neil owned a beach house a little under four hours from Lakespring. They had enough of a head start to be there by now. That would work to his advantage. He'd be able to surprise them in their sleep.

He wondered about the daughter and her boyfriend. Had they gone into hiding, or were they on their way to the beach house, too? He could get rid of the old man and his wife, but what about the cop? For what he was getting paid, he would take out the entire Army National Guard if he needed to.

Morelli looked over the contents of the safe deposit box for about the twentieth time. There were so many papers to go through, it would take all night to come up with something comprehensive. There were copies of bank slips, campaign finance reports, and receipts for the actual cost of the things in the reports. There were receipts for hotels, restaurants, and airfare, most of them in or to the Caribbean and, surprisingly, Las Vegas.

What excited Morelli most were the papers dealing with Harbor Supply and Distribution and the letter that went with them. The company had quite a side business going on, and the papers contained the smoking gun Jim had been looking for.

Penny Moore had been quite busy these last few years, gathering evidence to put her husband and the mayor away. Her letter didn't shed any light on where the girls came from, or why she was initially suspicious of her husband. It did, however, confirm that Alex had something to do with the disappearance of Eddie Reynolds.

Dear Detective Russell,

I can't apologize enough for allowing Alex to put Cassie and Ellie in danger. I love them so much. I was willing to do and promise anything to have children, and Alex knew that. Somewhere along the line, I lost myself to him and my dreams of being the perfect parent. Alex has a way of manipulating people into becoming whatever he wants them to be. I wish I had realized that sooner.

Two years ago, I became suspicious that Alex and Denny Simpson were involved in something illegal. I started sneaking into Alex's home office and copying his files, anything I believed might be significant. Everything I copied is in this box. I hope these help you put Alex away for good. It took too long for me to realize he wasn't the man I thought I married, and

I was too afraid to leave him, but I'm not letting him hurt me anymore. Protect those girls. I know what he's capable of.

When you listen to the tape I'm enclosing with this letter, you'll know as much as I do about what happened the day the girls ran away. Alex never knew I switched tapes after hearing the message on that old answering machine he used. He never told me what happened to Eddie Reynolds, but judging by the amount of blood he cleaned up when he returned, I don't think you'll find Eddie alive, and I believe the girls saw what happened. I thank God they're alive. I know this admission makes me an accomplice, but I hope you'll see I did everything within my power to lead you to the truth.

Everything Alex has ever done was in cahoots with the mayor, but Alex was the force behind it all. Please forgive me for not trying to stop him sooner.

Penny Adams Moore

Also in the box were papers showing an alliance between Harbor Supply and Metropolitan Trade and Investments. Morelli called one of his colleagues in the New York office who confirmed his suspicions. MTI was long thought to be a cover for the Lambinis' human trafficking enterprise. This might just explain the crime statistics. If the Lambinis were working with Moore and Simpson to bring domestic workers into the country, they were likely to be getting more than money out of the deal.

While the New York Feds and SVU were coming close to blowing the lid off the New York syndicate of the Lambini operation, it seemed Morelli and Jim had just discovered a Baltimore component as well. This explained why Jim was never able to get a clear line between the port deliveries and Harbor Supply. The Lambinis were, no doubt, controlling the cops and getting a cut of the action. That way, Moore and Simpson remained shielded by Baltimore's finest.

As Morelli and the other agents drove up Moore's driveway, he wondered where Reynolds' body was and exactly what he'd known about the girls. Morelli had a lot of questions for Alex Moore. He hoped he could persuade him to talk. Morelli was in no mood to sit in an interrogation room all night trying to extract the rest of the story.

Moore's car was parked outside, and Morelli could hear a television playing somewhere in the house. He knocked on the door and waited for someone to open it.

"FBI, open up."

After the third knock, he tried the door; it was unlocked. Morelli pushed open the door, pulled his Glock, and sidestepped into the house.

"Alexander Moore, this is Agent Morelli with the FBI. I'm coming in." Ross followed him in, and he motioned to the other agents to head around back.

He swept his gaze across the first room, Moore's office apparently. It looked like it had been hit by a tornado.

They made their way down the hall toward the sound of the television. As they drew closer, Morelli saw someone sitting on the couch. He backed against the wall and peered around the corner. The lights were off, but Morelli could see everything clearly as sunlight streamed into the room. An empty brandy bottle was on the bar. There was no movement from the couch when he called out.

"Alex Moore. This is Agent Anthony Morelli of the FBI. You're under arrest."

Alex didn't move or respond. Morelli walked around the couch to confront him face to face, his gun still drawn. What he saw made him recoil. The pistol was still in Alex's grasp, an empty glass in the other hand. Morelli turned away and swallowed hard. Alex Moore was dead.

———⋅◦⋅———

It was well after midnight when Clint pulled up to the beach house. He parked down the street and walked silently toward the cottage, able to hide easily under the cloud cover. The house was dark, but O'Neil's car was in the driveway. There was no sign of the detective's car anywhere.

Clint peered through the windows. The living room was empty.

"Psst." Sam jerked his head toward the second window. Clint crept over and peeked in, spotting the old couple in bed. The girls were in sleeping bags on the floor. That would make it easy, he mused.

Clint checked the other windows, but he didn't see anyone else. Where were the cop and the woman? Had something kept them back in Lakespring? He looked up and down the road, but everything was quiet, and Russell's car was nowhere to be seen. He motioned for Sam to go to the back.

Clint jimmied the front door and paused to listen. When nothing stirred, he headed toward the bedroom, gun drawn. He entered the room as quietly as a snake slithering silently through the grass. He decided to take out the old man first, not that he would be much of a threat. Clint aimed his gun with the attached silencer and shot the man twice. Without waiting for the woman to awake, he again shot twice. He started toward the girls.

"I wouldn't do that if I were you," came a voice from behind him. He heard the soft click of a gun and felt the muzzle on the back of his head.

Clint spun around and fired. Detective Russell jumped out of the way and rammed into him. Clint was slammed against the wall but steadied himself. Sam appeared out of nowhere, and he and Clint both fired at Russell who ran down the hall, jumped over the couch, and rolled toward the door. He fired before making his way outside.

"Follow him!" shouted Clint. He switched on the light and yanked the covers off the bed. He cursed at the pillows and kicked the sleeping bags stuffed with blankets.

Sam ran after the cop, but as Clint ran out of the house, he jumped into the old man's car and sped off.

"It was a trap! They're not here," Clint roared in anger.

⸺⸻◆⸻⸺

In nearby Ocean City, Susan was sandwiched in bed between Cassie and Ellie, pretending to be asleep. Ida and Patrick were in the other bed, their backs to each other. Susan was sure they were awake, too. When Jim and Susan reached the beach house, they shuffled everyone back in the car. No explanation was given, but they all knew they still weren't safe.

From where she lay, Susan could see the alarm clock on the nightstand. It was three in the morning. The plan was to stay at the hotel through the night and head to Mattie Harris' house in Florida at first light. Susan hadn't been this grateful to her mother's best friend since the woman decided to move to Florida and sell Susan her house. If Jim didn't show up by 5:30, they were to leave without him and call the local police as well as Lank and Agent Morelli. Susan prayed, pleading with God and all the saints, they wouldn't have to leave him. As the minutes ticked by, she became increasingly concerned.

At four in the morning, her mother climbed out of bed. "This is ridiculous," she whispered. "I'm not sleeping, and I know you're not either." She prodded Patrick, "Let's just get up and get ready."

"Mom, please quiet down. You'll wake the girls."

Ida took one look at Susan and asked, "Have you slept at all, honey?"

"No more than you did. How can I sleep knowing Jim was setting a trap for that man, by himself no less?"

"I know it's hard, honey. Jim's a good detective, and he'll be fine."

"I just wish we'd hear from him." She closed her eyes and took a deep breath. "Okay, let's get ready, but quietly." Susan scooted around Ellie and started to stand up but was overcome with a sudden and violent dizzy spell. She grabbed her mother as the room spun around her.

"Susan!" Ida stifled a scream and reached to steady her daughter. Cassie and Ellie awoke with a start.

Patrick sat up. "Susan, are you okay? What's wrong?"

Ida scolded him angrily. "What's not wrong? Everything is wrong. And she's not up to driving seventeen hours and hiding out again."

"Mom, I'm fine," Susan said shakily. "I'm just a little dizzy."

Just then, they heard a rattling at the door. Jim hurried in and shut the door quickly behind him. He took one look at Susan, ran to her, and knelt by the side of the bed.

"What's wrong?" he asked, his voice frantic.

"Nothing," Susan insisted. "We need to go."

"She never should've gotten out of bed yesterday," Ida said. "She probably never should've left the hospital. She'd be safe there, healing, not running all over the East Coast."

"Mom, enough," Susan said with annoyance. "It's a little dizzy spell, not uncommon with a concussion. Now, let's go." She tried to stand but had to grab the bed to steady herself again.

Jim stood and picked her up. "I've got you. You get the girls," he said to Patrick. "We need to leave."

The girls were fully awake, watching the scene with wide, fear-filled eyes.

"It's okay, girls," Jim assured them as he carried Susan toward the door. "We're just going to see a friend of Grandma Ida's, and it's a long drive. We need to go quickly."

They left the hotel room and drove away, leaving Ocean City and, they hoped, the hit man far behind.

⚬

They left their cars at a shopping mall in Virginia, and everyone piled into the police-issued SUV. Jim and Patrick tossed their meager bags into the hatch.

"What's going on, Jim?" Ida asked before she climbed in. "I've been a nervous wreck, waiting to hear what happened. When this is all over, I'm going to insist that Patrick and I get a couple of those darned cell phones. I hate not being in contact with Susan."

"Don't worry. Everything is going to be okay." Jim started to open the car, but Ida put her hand on his arm to stop him.

"James Russell, I've known you since the day you were born, and I have a feeling you're finally going to be part of the family, so let's get one thing straight. I will not be patronized, and you will not keep secrets from me. Am I clear?"

Jim smiled. There was the principal he remembered. "Okay. You asked, so here's the truth. There was more than one guy at the house. They had me cornered, but I managed to get away. They were firing at me as I ran to the car. They would've killed all of you had you been there. Now get in, so we can get out of here."

Ida's face paled. "Do you think they're following us now?" Her gaze panned the parking lot.

"I drove around for hours, trying to make sure I didn't lead them to you. I almost didn't come back, but I couldn't leave you all." He turned toward Susan in the back seat. "I need to make sure you're all okay."

Ida nodded. "You've done well, Jim. We're all safe because of you."

Jim felt himself blush. Ida was the closest thing to a mother he had, and her approval meant the world to him.

—◆—

Lank, Morelli, and Agent Ross met at a coffee shop at six the next morning. After receiving Jim's call during the night, they needed to plan their next move. Morelli had been at Moore's house all night.

He took a drink of coffee before speaking. "Moore is dead, shot himself sometime yesterday evening after his wife had left him. His home office had been gone through, possibly by Penny, but maybe someone else. I just left there, and forensics is still at work, going through the office and checking the rest of the house for any sign of Reynolds." Morelli took another sip of coffee.

"You're sure it was self-inflicted?" Agent Ross asked.

Morelli shrugged. "Looks that way. Forensics will verify one way or the other." He took a bite of a doughnut. "What have you got for me, Lankton?"

Lank looked at his notes as he spoke. "Okay, here goes. The girls showed up at Susan's sometime around early April, but the exact date is a little sketchy. Susan found them on the fourteenth. They weren't sure how long they'd been hiding there. On April fifteen, Eddie Reynolds' parents reported him missing. We know, of course, that Reynolds worked for Moore at Harbor Supply and had been approached about assisting the FBI. He tried to feed them what he could, but he wasn't as forthcoming as hoped."

Morelli nodded, and Lank continued.

"After Jim went to Social Services about Cassie and Ellie, their social worker, Lynette White, was killed, but there were no files on them or anything to indicate how White came to know about them. We know Penny Moore also visited White, but we don't know what was said between them. Two days later, someone broke into Jim's house and went through his files. As far as we can tell, only the information about the girls was taken, so the perp didn't care about Harbor Supply or Simpson."

"Or already knew everything Jim knew," Agent Ross interjected.

"Good point." Lank made a note in his notepad. Nodding to Ross, he continued, "You discovered Jim's landlines and office were bugged."

Morelli swallowed the rest of his doughnut and held up his hand for Lank to stop.

"Based on what you just said, we can't assume the house was broken into by someone in Moore's office. The person didn't care about the illegal stuff, just the whereabouts of the girls. In addition, the equipment was too technologically advanced for an amateur. We have to figure out whether Simpson or Moore have any contacts in the tech world who could provide them with that kind of equipment." He then indicated for Lank to continue.

"What about Simpson's son? I saw somewhere he's some kind of computer programmer." Lank began shuffling through his notes.

"Aren't they estranged?" Ross asked.

"Yeah, but blood, right?"

"Let's get somebody to check him out," Morelli told Agent Ross.

Lank made a note in the margin of his paper and continued. "I talked to Jim a little while ago. Here's the situation there. A few days after you guys found the bugs, someone smashed in the door at Ida and Patrick O'Neil's house. They ran with the kids. Jim and Susan caught up with them in Fenwick and took them to a hotel in Ocean City. Jim went back to catch the guy we assume is after the girls. It turns out there are at least two men working together, and they're out for blood." Lank looked up from his notes. "That's all I've got. Jim left me information on various bank accounts, and we have similar information from Penny."

"Which all matches the stuff we found in Moore's office."

Lank nodded and went on. "Between Jim and Penny, we have…" He held up his fingers for each point. "Penny and Alex Moore's accounts, joint and separate; info on Moore's side business, partly a front to give and get more political money, but most definitely a human trafficking scheme that was bringing in big bucks; and Reynolds' bank statements.

"According to Moore's accounts, he wrote Reynolds a number of $10,000 checks over the last several months, but Reynolds doesn't seem to have cashed or deposited any of them."

"We're looking into offshore accounts, but so far, we can't find any evidence Reynolds cashed them. We're also waiting for a warrant to get into Moore's files at City Hall and at the corporation," supplied Morelli.

"That's good. Maybe we can find out how much Reynolds knew about the trafficking and where the people are being kept. Jim was just getting started on that when all hell broke loose."

"You've done an excellent job, Lank," Morelli complimented him. "Now, here's what I can add: The two little girls weren't foster kids after all. There's no record of Cassie and Ellie or Alex Moore in the Social Services computer system. Penny is listed as a foster parent under her former name, Adams, but she hasn't officially taken in any kids. Lynette White's purse and keys were found in a dumpster near Social Services, so the killer paid a visit to the office sometime after the murder. I suppose it's possible he got into the system and deleted the file, if one ever existed. If he's the same person connected with the bugs in Jim's house, he may have enough computer knowledge to have expunged the records." Morelli stopped to finish his coffee.

"I have no idea whose kids they are, but someone wants them back, or dead, maybe a little of both, depending upon how many different people we're dealing with. We still don't know what their connection to Moore is."

"Do you think he's the father?" Lank asked.

"Could be. We can conduct a DNA test. I'll ask Jim to obtain samples from the girls."

"What about Penny Moore? Could she be their mother?"

"Not according to the information the girls told Jim and Susan. Cassie mentioned a mother more than once."

"What else do we know about Penny?"

"This was her second marriage. First husband, Joe Adams, died of heart problems. Penny spent a lot of time and energy keeping track of her husband's business and personal dealings. There are receipts for flowers, hotel rooms, airfare to and from Vegas and Little St. James, even a house in Pennsylvania. I guess she found out he was running around on her, and from the number of receipts, he'd been doing so for a long time, quite often. I have someone looking into the Pennsylvania house."

"So, he *could* be their father," Lank said.

"A definite possibility." Morelli agreed. "Moore, or somebody, racked up thousands of dollars in expenses in the islands and Vegas. Coincidentally, the city of Baltimore was billed by Harbor Supply and Distribution for event supplies in the same amount spent on each one of these trips. Obviously, this money was being used to fund Moore's, or someone else's, dalliances in Vegas and the

Caribbean, and the city was paying for it." Morelli paused to make sure Lank was following him.

"That's one way to party on the taxpayer's dime," Lank observed.

"My men have done some digging into Harbor Supply. Moore started the business years ago, probably as a front from the beginning. Harbor sold various supplies, like paper goods, safety equipment, linens, and janitorial supplies to various businesses around the Port of Baltimore. That gave Moore the ability to connect with businesses looking for cheap labor.

"In his first campaign for the city council, Simpson and Moore used funds from the business to provide money for Simpson's campaign. The money was given to the campaign through direct donations as well as overblown payments for event supplies. In addition, the company worked as a funnel for campaign contributions from other sources." Morelli paused and motioned for more coffee.

"This scheme allowed Simpson's supporters to make larger political donations than the law allows and take illegal tax deductions for the phony expenses. Simpson and his people returned the favors by rigging city procurement contracts and manipulating the activities of the city liquor board and zoning office to help his benefactors. These same benefactors were open to employing illegal workers while the city police and comptroller's office looked the other way. The scheme runs deep and wide and involves some of the best-known businessmen in Baltimore."

The waitress refilled his cup, and Morelli continued.

"Once Simpson was mayor, Harbor started doing no-bid business with the city directly. Pretty brazen, huh? The city auditor just happens to be married to Simpson's brother, and she looks the other way at the city's dealings with Harbor. Anyway, although the company still does some legitimate business around the Port, it's mostly a front for Simpson's and Moore's escapades. Moore has been making money off human trafficking for years, and the city has pleaded ignorance from Simpson's earliest days on the council.

"We believe, at some point, Moore started doing business with the Lambinis. They own bars, restaurants, and hotels from Baltimore to New York. Instead of taking part of the money, they may have been getting special treatment in the crime arena. Once Simpson became mayor, crime statistics usually linked with organized crime dropped dramatically."

Lank shook his head in disbelief. "I assume you knew this, and that's what you were hoping Jim would be able to prove?"

"We always suspected something like this. The mob connection was obvious, and human trafficking in the hospitality area is the perfect way to make big money in a tourist city. Moore keeps the domestics totally off the record, so a paper trail is impossible. With all the purchase slips Penny left us that include the 'uniform orders', we're beginning to understand how it all worked. With the FBI now officially involved, business owners are starting to speak up. It helps that some of the Lakespring businesses were approached by Moore and Simpson themselves in the beginning, and Officer Mike Russell has it all documented. Furthermore, his friends, the businessmen of Lakespring, are willing to talk."

"Jim's dad?" Lank said in surprise. "When did this happen?"

"Last night," Morelli informed him. "Jim doesn't even know yet. And the rest of that story is going to blow his mind."

"So, what do we do now?" Lank asked.

"We continue digging. We have enough to put Simpson away, but we don't know who else, if anyone, was involved. We need to find out who was in Vegas and why. The human trafficking thing doesn't connect with that, so that may be the link between Simpson, Moore, and the girls. The time frame seems right, anyway. We need to know where the girls came from and who their real parents are. We seem to have answered every question except for those, presuming they ran because they know what happened to Reynolds. Until we figure out who is after them, nobody is safe," Morelli declared.

CHAPTER TWENTY-SIX

After

Penny was walking along the beach in the Outer Banks when her phone rang. She gasped and hesitated before answering.

"Yes?"

"Hello, Penny." Denny's voice reached across the miles, sending a chill down her spine, like a skeletal hand from the grave. "I've been trying to reach you. Where are you?"

She swallowed. "What do you want, Denny?"

"I have some terrible news for you."

Denny told Penny about the tragic death of her husband. Despite the fear and hatred that had built up in her over the past few years, Penny began to cry.

"I am truly sorry, Penny. Alex was my best friend."

"Yes, I know he was, Denny. Thank you."

"Penny," Denny said, "do you need help with the arrangements? My secretary would be happy to assist you. You can come by any time. If you tell me where you are, I'll send a car for you."

"No, Denny, I won't need help. In fact, I don't plan on making arrangements. I've left Maryland and don't plan on going back. Your office can handle it if you like. I don't care anymore."

"I understand, Penny. I know what he must have put you through."

"I'm sure you do, Denny."

Penny hung up and stood calmly by the ocean. She closed her eyes and thought about her husbands, about the hopes and dreams she'd had when she married Joe, the uncertainty when she married Alex, but that glimmer of hope that she could be happy again. She opened her eyes and watched a seagull swoop down to the water and grab a fish before rocketing back to the sky and flying out of sight. She waded into the surf, her phone in her hand. When she was knee deep, shivering in the freezing cold water, she held her hand over her head and threw the phone as far as she could into the waves. She felt that glimmer again, a voice inside whispering, *you're finally free.*

⋯⋯⋯❖⋯⋯⋯

The mayor quietly placed the phone on the table. He turned to the window, glad Penny was gone. Now that the tables had been turned, he didn't relish having to clean up Alex's mess.

Yes, Penny. I know exactly what he put you through, and you're better off without him. I hope you're far from here, and I hope you stay away.

⋯⋯⋯❖⋯⋯⋯

Lank was the first one on the team—he liked being part of a 'team' again—to discover an important discrepancy. Among the many receipts saved by Moore's wife, was a Vegas hotel receipt from June 12, 1999. The last four digits of the card number matched the one that had been used dozens of times to pay for flowers, hotels, and flights to and from Vegas.

In cross-checking all Alex's accounts, Lank found a charge on another card. That account contained many run-of-the-mill charges, including a charge for flight to Little St. James for the same date. How could Alex have been in two hotels in two cities on opposite sides of the world at the same time?

That prompted the men to start comparing more receipts from the different accounts. Many times, when Alex was in the Caribbean, somebody else was using Alex's account in Vegas.

Someone other than Alex had spent a lot of time in Vegas. Who was it, and why?

***

Clint and Sam gave up their search of the Maryland and Delaware beach resorts when there was no trace of the girls or the adults with them. He picked up his cell and called his employer to check in. Telling him the girls were once again out of reach was not going to be easy, and he prepared for the backlash.

The phone rang several times before a strange voice answered. Clint quickly disconnected.

"What's up?" Sam asked.

"Don't know. Let's just get on with it. I'll try again later." Concerned they may have been compromised, Clint was eager to finish the job and disappear.

"What's his beef with the girls? They're just kids."

"Sam, you need to learn not to ask too many questions. The less you know, the better. You go poking your nose into the whys and what-fors, and suddenly you're as expendable as your subjects are. There are two very important questions you should never ask and never try to find out: why you were hired, and who hired you. One gets you killed, and the other gets you indicted."

Lank and the other men on Morelli's team continued to dig through the copies Penny made as well as whatever else they could find in Alex's office. They still had to determine whether it was Moore or Simpson leading a double life.

One thing they knew for sure. Moore was not the girls' father. The preliminary tests indicated his DNA didn't match the DNA on the toothbrushes they'd collected at Susan's house. And they confirmed his presence in the Caribbean on all the dates in question. Now they just needed to confirm it was Simpson who was living it up in Vegas.

It took several rings before Mike Russell made it to the kitchen to answer the phone.

"Where is your son?" asked the voice on the other end.

"Who is this?"

"I think you know who this is," the voice on the phone told him. "Your son has something that belongs to me, and it's putting him in grave danger. I want to help bring them all to safety. Where are they?"

"Don't try feeding me that line of bull. You and your henchmen have been threatening me and my son for years. Well, not anymore," Mike told the caller. "I've had enough of your threats and enough of keeping your secrets from Jim. Goodbye and good riddance."

"Don't hang up on me, you son-of-a—"

Mike hung up the phone. He was seething with anger, but he didn't dwell on the call. He knew fear when he heard it.

Good, be afraid. It just proves we're getting closer to exposing you and everything you've ever done.

Mike went back to his work. He still had a few more people to track down. He'd been letting Jim and everyone else down for years. It was time for the good guys to start winning some rounds in this fight.

Late that night, Mattie Harris stood on her front porch as Jim pulled into the driveway. Patrick helped Susan out of the car. Cassie and Ellie jumped out and ran to Ida's best friend, about whom they had heard many stories on the way there. Jim extricated himself from the driver's seat, where he'd been since they entered South Carolina, and stretched his arms and neck.

"Jim Russell, you're even better looking than your dad was at your age." Mattie laughed as Jim blushed.

"I can't tell you how grateful we are that you're helping us," Ida told Mattie with tears in her eyes when she hugged her friend. "I just hope we don't bring trouble to your doorstep."

"Oh, come on, in this neighborhood? These people are longing for some excitement."

Lank looked at the copies of the document he held in his hand, his mouth wide open. He couldn't believe what he was reading.

"I think we've got something here," he called to Morelli.

The agent rushed to Lank's side and took the papers. They consisted of a hospital bill, a couple doctor's bills, and a release form, all dated October 20, 2008.

"Ellie's birthday?" Lank asked.

"Looks about right," Morelli answered. "Let's get Susan on the line and find out."

Morelli read through the rest of the papers while Lank dialed Jim's cell. All the names and medical services rendered had been blacked out, including the name and location of the hospital. However, one word was still visible. Cesarean.

"Well, this answers one question," Morelli said out loud. "The girls were definitely not foster children, and Moore knew at least one of them from birth."

Jim hung up the phone and turned toward the three pairs of eyes imploring him to share what he'd heard.

"The safe deposit box was opened by a woman named Penny Adams, aka Penny Moore. According to the bank, the box once belonged to Penny and her deceased husband, Joe Adams. She hadn't been to that bank very often over the past five years, but she started accessing the box frequently a few months back. Two years ago, according to her letter, she started sneaking into her husband's office and copying his files. The files deal with Moore's business ventures with Denny Simpson, travel expenses, political funds, and certain hospital records." He leaned forward to make sure Cassie and Ellie were still coloring with Mattie before he proceeded.

"According to Lank, there are files dealing with a cesarean section which took place five years ago."

"That's why you just asked Cassie when Ellie's birthday is," Susan said in understanding.

"Yep. They had the date and needed to verify that it referred to Ellie."

"Do the papers give the names of any relatives?" Susan asked.

"Unfortunately, no." Jim handed her the notes he had taken during the call. "Here's what we've got. Do you think you can find out anything with any of this information?"

Susan frowned as she read over the pages. "It may take me a while to go through it, but I'm sure we can pull up something."

"Look at this one," Jim pointed to the paper on top. "It's from the hospital. Unfortunately, all the important information has been blacked out. Morelli's asking for a warrant, but because of HIPPA, that's going to take time and will likely be denied since we can't directly connect the records to a crime."

"I think I may know someone who can find out what the missing information is," Susan said with a smile. "That is, if you'll let me speak to him without getting all bent out of shape again."

Jim wrinkled his brow.

"Seth, my colleague you met last week. He's a computer genius who can hack into anything."

"In this case, I think I'll allow it. It won't be admissible in court, but let's get the info we need and let the guys at Quantico worry about the rest."

<hr>

"Susan, thank heaven you're all okay," Ed Tyler said from Seattle when his secretary put the call through. "I've been trying to call you for days. I can't get an answer at your parents' house either. When I couldn't reach any of you, Seth told me about the police watching the house. What on earth is going on?"

"Ed, I'm so sorry you've been worried. I'm fine. Mom and Dad are fine, too. They're here with me, but forgive me if I don't tell you where we are. I don't have any reason to believe anything would happen to you, but I'd rather be safe than sorry. At least two people are dead already."

"Susan! You're telling me people are being killed?"

"Ed, please. Everything is going to be fine. I can't tell you any details, but we're getting closer to catching whoever is behind all this. That's why I'm calling."

"Do you need my help? What can I do? Just say the word and—"

"Ed, slow down," Susan said calmly. "I need Seth's help with something. Is he there? It's very important."

"Seth? What do you need with Seth?"

"I need his expertise," she said, tired of dancing around with him. "Please, Ed, I really need to talk to him, and I don't have my old phone with his number. It's a matter of life and death."

"Fine, fine, hold on. He's on vacation, but I've got his cell number."

"Thanks, Ed. I'll fill you in on everything later."

Seth picked up after a few rings, and Susan apologized for the early call before cutting right to the chase.

"Seth, I was wondering if you could do something for me." Susan told him what she needed and hoped he would agree to help. "I realize what I'm asking is illegal, but lives may depend upon it, and I hear you're pretty good at this."

"Illegality aside, what you're asking for is no easy task. Do you know how many hospitals there are in this country, and how many probably had patients who had cesarean sections on that date?"

"I know, Seth, and I wish I had more to give you. I can tell you the hospital was either in the Baltimore or the Las Vegas area, and the baby was a girl. The name on the birth certificate will be Ellie, Elizabeth, Eleanor, or something close."

"So, what's this about? Those girls I met at your house?"

"Seth, I really can't say any more. Can you help?"

After a pause, Seth answered. "I'll do what I can. It's been a while since I tried to hack into something that secure, but I think I can do it."

"Really?" Susan nodded to Jim. "That's wonderful. I wasn't sure you'd want to get involved."

"Susan, I care about you. I'll do what I can." She turned away as though Jim could hear Seth's admission. She listened to the tap-tap-tap of Seth's keyboard. "Okay, I'm in."

"Wow, you are good at this."

There was a long pause on the other end.

"Yeah, well, it's been a long time, but I guess old habits die hard. It will take some time to comb through the site. How can I get the info to you? I've tried calling your cell a few times, but it doesn't seem to be working, and this number isn't showing up on my phone."

"I'll give it to you." She gave him Jim's number as well, just in case.

"Are you still in Maryland?"

"No. We're with a friend of my mom's, but we're fine." Jim gave her a signal to cut the call.

"Seth, I've to go. Thank you."

"That was fast," Jim commented.

Susan shrugged. "I told you he was good."

Jim frowned.

"What?"

He shook his head. "Nothing. I just remembered something I meant to do and never got around to. It's not important now. Let's get working. We need to find out what was going on in Vegas on the dates of all these charges, some kind of common bond—meetings, conventions, events the same people would return to. And let's see if we can find out what kind of place this Club Nine is. There are several charges there for the years 2004 and 2005."

Susan explained to Jim what she was doing as she searched. It wasn't as easy as typing in names of hotels. They'd have to determine which businesses had hosted conventions during that time period, which required knowing the names of professional associations, political organizations, and the like. Coming up with that information would take time.

After hours of searching, with only a short break for lunch, Jim was restless. He paced back and forth across the room while Susan read her findings out loud. As she read a list of government-sponsored conferences which took place at one Vegas hotel, Jim placed his hands on the back of her chair and leaned over her shoulder to see the monitor.

His warm breath tickled her ear, and the mere scent of him made Susan lose her concentration. She suddenly felt hot and wondered if Jim could sense the tingling sensation running through her. She shook her head and threw her arms into the air.

"I can't look at these lists any longer. My eyes are about to come out of my head from staring at this screen. Let's go over the conventions and events that meet there several times a year."

"I'll do that. Why don't you look up that club?" Jim suggested. "At least you'll see something different on the screen, and you're better at that than I am."

Susan located the website and began browsing through the pages, scanning the shows it offered. She came across a photo gallery with pictures from shows that had played there from the time the club was opened.

Susan rubbed her throbbing temple and closed her eyes, unable to look at the monitor any longer. Neither she nor Jim noticed Ellie come into the room, but they both heard her.

"Mommy," Ellie whispered, transfixed by the computer screen.

Cassie had never heard of Club Nine, but she did know Mommy was a dancer before she was born. Cassie only remembered her fixing people's hair, but she talked about dancing, and the woman in the picture was definitely Mommy. It felt so good to be able to tell someone about Mommy, Cassie couldn't stop talking once she started.

"Mommy was the most beautiful person in the world," Cassie began. "She had the prettiest voice and always sang to us before bed." She smiled, remembering her mother tucking her in and singing to her at night. It had been a long time since Cassie thought or spoke of Mommy without being angry with her for leaving them.

"She always looked pretty, but she was especially pretty when that man visited." Cassie wrinkled her nose. "Ellie and I didn't like him very much, but Mommy said we should be nice to him. She said we had to call him Uncle..." Cassie caught herself before she said his name.

"Was your uncle nice to you?" Susan asked.

"He wasn't our uncle," she said, angry at him for taking Mommy away. "Mommy didn't have any brothers or sisters, but she said we should call him that because it showed we loved and respected him." She rolled her eyes again and took a bite of the cookie Mattie handed her.

With crumbs spilling from her mouth, she continued. "We were nice to him because Mommy wanted us to be nice, but we never liked him, did we Ellie?"

Ellie shook her head. "I don't remember him, but Cassie says he didn't like us," she said quietly, reaching for her own glass of milk, and Cassie wanted to hug her sister again each time she heard her voice.

"Why would you think that, Cassie?"

Cassie shrugged. "He only wanted to be with Mommy. They always went places together and left us home. They didn't care if we wanted to go, too, or if we cried for them to stay." She scowled. "And it was his fault Mommy went to Heaven."

"What do you mean, Cassie?" Jim asked.

"Because Mommy went out to see him even though we asked her not to," she said quietly, her gaze going down to her hands.

"What happened, Cassie? Can you tell us?" Cassie let Susan take her hand and missed Mommy even more.

The room was quiet for a few minutes. Cassie felt a teardrop run down her cheek as she lifted her eyes.

"Cassandra," she whispered.

"What, Honey?" Susan said.

Cassie took a deep breath. "Mommy called me Cassandra. She called Ellie, Elizabeth. Nobody ever called us Cassie and Ellie until we went to live with Mr. Moore and Miss Penny. Mr. Moore said we should change our names, but Miss Penny said our names were beautiful and we could just shorten them. She wanted Ellie to be called Lizzie, but I said no. I wanted her to have Mommy's name."

Miss Susan gasped. "Ellie was named after your mother?"

Cassie shrugged. "I don't know. Maybe. I just know Mommy's name was Ellie."

"Girls, what would you like to be called?" Grandma Ida asked, and Cassie locked eyes with the only Grandma she'd ever known.

"Cassie and Ellie are good. I don't think I want anyone but Mommy to call us our real names."

"We understand, Sweetie," Grandma Ida told her. "Do you want to tell us what happened that night, or would you rather wait?"

"I, I think I want to tell."

"Okay, Cassie, just take your time." Grandma Ida said in a comforting voice.

"We were home at our house in the mountains. Me and Elizabeth, I mean Ellie, were playing, and Mommy was on her computer." She cast her gaze at Susan. "He gave Mommy a computer so they could talk to each other."

"What mountains did you live near, Cassie?" Jim asked.

"I don't remember," she said.

"That's okay," Grandma Ida said. "Did your mommy get a message from your uncle on the computer?"

Cassie shook her head. "She got a text and said he needed to see her, so she was going to call Mrs. Johnson next door and ask her to come stay with us. I asked Mommy not to go. It was raining really bad that night, like the night of the plane crash. I was scared, and Ellie was crying because she's scared of the thunder and lightning. But Mommy said she had to go because Uncle Dennis needed her. We needed her, too, but she went anyway." Cassie's voice cracked and she blinked away a tear. She broke a cookie and tossed it onto the plate. She took a deep breath and tried to control her tears.

"Mrs. Johnson came over, but I don't think she was happy about it. I remember she kept saying nobody should be going out on a night like that, and Mommy should be home with her babies. I tried not to listen to her say those things because it made me feel bad that she was saying things about Mommy."

"Of course, it did, Sweetie," said Susan.

"Mrs. Johnson read me and Ellie a story and tucked us in bed. I don't remember what the story was, but I do remember I just laid there and cried. I guess I fell asleep." Cassie scrunched up her nose and tried to recall what happened next. "Something woke me up. I think I heard the phone. I got up and saw Mrs. Johnson hanging it up. I asked her if Mommy was home, and she told me to come sit by her. When I did, she told me...she told me that Mommy...Mommy went to Heaven." Cassie sniffed and wiped her eyes with her sleeve, feeling her bottom lip tremble.

"Do you remember what happened to your mommy?" Jim asked.

Cassie nodded and wiped her eyes again. Mattie handed her a tissue, and she wiped her nose.

"Mommy's car crashed in the rain." She lifted her gaze to them, hoping they might be able to tell her why that had to happen. Nobody answered.

Jim cleared his throat. "What happened after that?"

"I don't remember what happened next. I remember going to say goodbye to Mommy at the church. She looked so beautiful. I kept watching for Uncle Dennis, but he never came. I guess he knew it was his fault, and I hated him for it. I was glad he wasn't there."

"He didn't go to the funeral at all?" Susan sounded surprised.

"No, but he was at Mr. Moore's the night we left home."

"The night you left the Moore's home?" Jim asked.

"No," said Cassie, "our home in the mountains." She took a sip of milk. "Mrs. Johnson stayed with us for a few days. Then one day, a man showed up. He said his name was Eddie, and he said Mommy wanted us to live with Mr. Moore. He made us pack a suitcase with some of our favorite things."

"I took Mr. Bear," Ellie interrupted.

"When we finally got to the house, Uncle Dennis was there. He was crying." She took another cookie and stared out into the backyard. She tried to picture what happened next.

"I remember Mr. Moore called Uncle Dennis a fool and told him to stop crying. Mommy said to never call people names, so I knew Mr. Moore was bad. Uncle Dennis kept saying he loved Mommy and missed her. I remember Mr. Moore told him to forget her. Even though I hated Uncle Dennis, that made me sad."

"Cassie, was Uncle Dennis at the house the day you ran away?" Jim asked.

Cassie shook her head. "I didn't see his face, but I think it was the man who took us to Mr. Moore's house."

"You mean Eddie?" he asked.

"Yeah. I recognized his voice, and I heard Mr. Moore say his name." She turned to Jim. "There was so much blood. I'd never seen so much blood before. Ellie fainted when she saw it." Cassie closed her eyes, afraid to tell the rest. She addressed Susan. "I'm so sorry."

"For what, Sweetheart?"

"It was our fault he got hurt."

"It wasn't your fault, Honey. You didn't do anything wrong."

"But Eddie said he was coming over because he knew about me and Ellie. That means we did something bad. I don't know what we did, but he got hurt because he knew we did something."

"No, Sweetie," Grandma Ida told her. "It was Mr. Moore who did something bad. You and Ellie didn't do anything wrong."

"I need to call Tony," Jim said before turning back to Cassie. "You did a really good job today, Cassie. Thank you for telling us the truth."

Cassie wiped away her tears and looked up at Susan. "Can we go home now? To your house?"

CHAPTER TWENTY-SEVEN

After

Jim and Susan boarded a red eye to Vegas that evening with the pictures they'd printed from the club's website. Cassie identified one of the dancers as her mother's friend, Dixie, but she was unable to tell them Dixie's last name. She remembered her mother and Dixie often talking online, but Cassie had never met her in person.

Cassie knew her mother worked as a dancer before Cassie was born, but she didn't know where. Her mother told stories about her years on the stage in a city "way out west" and her childhood dreams of dancing on Broadway. With that in mind, along with the information from Morelli, Vegas seemed like the best place to start.

"How are you feeling?" Jim asked Susan as he held her hand on the plane.

"Nervous. I'm not crazy about getting back on a plane. I don't know if I ever want to fly again." In fact, she felt sick to her stomach, and before he took her hand, she'd had a hard time keeping them from shaking.

"Don't you fly all the time for work?"

"Yeah, but I'm thinking of changing that. In fact, I'm thinking of changing my whole business model."

Jim leaned over and kissed her. "I'm sorry we have to do this. I knew all along Reynolds was the key to why Cassie and Ellie ran. If only I'd been able to get Cassie to talk sooner, we might have Moore in custody right now instead of at the morgue."

"It's not your fault." She offered him a sympathetic smile. "I hope we get some answers about Eddie soon. My heart breaks for his poor parents."

"Lank and Morelli have been looking into it since before we left," Jim said. "They'll come up with something."

After a minute, Susan changed gears. "Do you really think he's their father?"

"Simpson? I'd say it's a pretty good bet."

"Then why didn't he acknowledge them, take them to live with him, do something to see they were okay?"

"I guess that's what he thought he was doing by letting the Moores take them. Cassie said Penny really loved them and took good care of them."

"I know, but it just doesn't make sense to me. Why didn't he take them in himself? Were his political aspirations that important to him?"

"He's not like us, Susan," Jim replied. "Haven't you ever heard about men leading double lives? He has a wife, other kids. He has everything to lose, personally and professionally, if news of his illegitimate daughters gets out. He had bigger political plans. He couldn't let anything interfere with them."

"I know you're right, but I can't imagine anyone not wanting Cassie and Ellie." She thought for a moment. "Jim, do you think I..." Susan let her words trail off.

"Don't go there, Susan," Jim said, looking her in the eye.

"I don't want him to have them," Susan said quietly, looking down at their entwined hands. "I want them."

"I know you do, Honey, but we may not have a say in that. We have no idea how this will play out with Simpson once the news is out. His wife may step in and claim them. Stranger things have happened, especially in politics."

"Do you think I have any chance?" Susan asked him.

"You're single. That's a strike against you, but maybe we can change that." Jim leaned over and kissed her again, rekindling feelings she hadn't had in years and stirring new ones.

When Jim pulled away, Susan said, "Is that a proposal?"

"Not yet." He tucked a stray hair behind her ear. "Let's get through this first."

Susan's heart leaped, and she smiled. Maybe something good could come out of all this mess.

⊷◆⊶

He'd hit pay dirt and could almost taste the sweetness of it. Instead of dealing with the urgent business he was supposed to be working on, he'd done a little research into where the O'Neils might have gone. With this new GPS technology, anybody could be located with the right information.

Within minutes, he knew where they were—Florida. He hadn't pinpointed the exact location, but he knew it was somewhere in Clearwater. It was only a matter of time before he knew where. Then he could finish this thing once and for all.

⊷◆⊶

Clint and Sam stood in line at the airport. "We have just enough time to get through security and get to the gate. They're getting ready to board," Clint said.

"Any word from your employer?"

"No, but we've got the address of the friend."

Sam had stood guard while Clint searched the O'Neil house. The house was roped off with crime scene tape, but the cops were no longer there, and even if they were doing drive-bys, there didn't appear to be round-the-clock surveillance. Finding Ida's address book was easy. Determining where they may have gone wasn't.

"You really think they're in Florida?" Sam asked.

"It's a hunch, but I think it's a good one. It's easily a day's drive with that many drivers, but it's far enough for them to feel safe. If we get there and there's no sign of them, we check out the other possibilities." He held up the address book and then tucked it back into his bag as the TSA agent asked for his boarding pass and ID.

They'd get their guns at baggage claim in St. Petersburg. It wasn't a big deal to declare them, and Florida was a concealed weapon state. Once they retrieved their guns and got a car, it was just three miles to Clearwater, and to the girls.

***

Jim and Susan's plane arrived in Las Vegas under cloudy skies. It was 9:25 at night when they hailed a taxi outside the airport. They gave the driver the address of Club Nine. They hoped to catch the late show at the club. Susan had napped in Jim's arms on the non-stop flight, and assured him she was feeling more like herself.

When they arrived at the club, Jim flashed his FBI badge and asked to see someone in charge. While they waited, they took in the place. If there were any pictures of past shows on the wall at one time, they were gone now. The clientele looked decent, mostly men in business suits having a drink and watching the show. The door to the office opened, and a man in a grey suit came toward them.

"I'm Richard Morgan, the owner. How may I help you?" Morgan was short and overweight with a mustache and balding head.

"Mr. Morgan, thank you for giving us your time."

"I'm not sure I had a choice," he said with a glower.

"We're not here for you or anything to do with your business," Jim assured him. "We're just trying to locate somebody we believe worked here at one time. Her name was Ellie, or maybe Elizabeth. She was killed in an accident, and we need to find out if she had any relatives. She left two young children behind, and we're looking for the rest of her family."

Morgan noticeably relaxed. "In that case, I'm happy to cooperate. However, I don't keep track of every person who has ever worked here. In fact, I've only been the owner for the past three years."

Jim exchanged a look with Susan.

"Is there anyone who worked here about nine or ten years ago?" Jim asked.

"Not that I know of..." The man scratched his head in thought. "Girls don't usually last too long in this business. You know, men like 'em young and trim. The wait staff comes and goes as often as the dancers do." He continued to mull over the possibilities. He suddenly raised his head and snapped his fingers. "Wait a minute. Charlie's the janitor. He's been here for as long as the place has been open."

"We'd like to speak with him," Jim said.

"I'm sorry," he said, shaking his head. "He doesn't come in until morning. We stay open until three a.m. He comes in at eleven and cleans before we re-open at five."

"Is there any way we can get his address or phone number?" Susan pleaded. "It truly is urgent."

"I don't give out that information to anyone, unless you have a warrant," he challenged Jim. When Jim said nothing, but made no attempt to leave, Morgan replied, "Will there be anything else?"

"Please, Mr. Morgan. Would you call and ask him if he'd meet with us?" Jim watched Susan turn on her feminine charm. She caressed the man's arm. "It would mean the world to us."

He frowned but said, "I'll see what I can do."

"Nice going," Jim said when the owner disappeared into the back of the club.

"Thank you." Susan smiled.

When Morgan returned ten minutes later, the show was beginning to start. Beautiful showgirls lined the stage in elaborate costumes. Jim stared at them before turning to Susan. He didn't think any of them compared to her.

"He has agreed to see you." Mr. Morgan said to them. "If you will just follow me, I'll show you where he lives."

Jim sent Susan a questioning look before following the club's owner.

Morgan led them to the back of the club near the stage. He exited through a side door leading to a dark alley. "Just follow the alley to the staircase. Charlie's room is at the top." He abruptly turned and walked away.

"Well, how do you like that?" Jim said. "He lives here."

"At least he was easy to find," Susan commented dryly.

"Just in case, let me go first and knock on the door."

"In case what?" Susan asked, peering down the dark alley.

"In case there is no Charlie, or Richard Morgan knows more than he's letting on and has a surprise in store for us."

Jim climbed the steps, praying he wasn't putting Susan in danger by leaving her. When he knocked on the door, an elderly black man opened it a crack and looked out.

"You wanted to see me?" he asked, squinting at Jim.

"Yes, please." Jim held up his badge. "Detective Jim Russell. I'm working with the FBI, and we need to ask you some questions about a former showgirl if you don't mind."

Charlie leaned very close to the badge and looked at it for a moment

"We?" Charlie asked when he looked up. Jim moved aside and gestured to Susan at the bottom of the steps. Charlie leaned his head farther out and stared into the darkness.

If he wondered who Susan was, he didn't ask. He just nodded and opened the door to let them in. Jim waited for Susan to make it up the steps.

"You okay?" he asked, hoping this wasn't too much for her.

"Fine," she said, but he heard her breath catch with the word.

Jim poked his head in and took a quick look around before entering.

Charlie lived in what Jim guessed could be called an efficiency. He had a small sitting room with a black and white TV, the sound turned down. Jim hadn't seen a television like that since he was a kid. There was a small lamp on an end table by the couch and a well-worn recliner with a TV tray next to it. Behind that was a tiny kitchen, not big enough for even a small table and chair.

There was a door to the left of the sitting room that must have led to the bedroom or perhaps just the bathroom if the couch was a foldout. Everything was neat and tidy. There were no knick-knacks or other collectibles anywhere, but there were quaint little touches that made the place homey—a lace doily under the lamp, a crocheted afghan on the back of the couch, and a single framed picture on the wall of a stunning, twenty-something woman with large, dark brown eyes.

Once inside, Charlie motioned for Susan and Jim to have a seat. They sat on the couch, and Charlie sat in the recliner. The television flashed across the room as Susan pulled the picture of the girls' mother from her purse.

"Do you know this girl?" she asked him. Charlie took the picture and held it very close to his face. He stared at it for a few minutes.

"Why, that's December Rose," Charlie said with wonder, his eyes widening. "I haven't seen her in years, probably not since shortly after this picture was taken. She was a nice girl, never shoulda been workin' in a place like this. She coulda sang and danced on Broadway. All the men liked her, one in particular. He got her pregnant and never did come back."

"Are you sure about that?" Jim said.

"Well, I always assumed it was him and that he never came back. December Rose had to quit when she started to show. Bad for business, you know. I never seen her again after that. He sure didn't come 'round here after he got her pregnant.

"She came in one night in tears, real hysterical like. Said her boyfriend wouldn't leave his wife 'n' kids. You hear that all the time with these girls. Some nice-lookin' man starts payin' attention to her, buys her a drink, sends her flowers or gifts, finally gets her hooked, but then the jerk confesses he's married." Charlie handed the picture back to Susan and leaned back in the chair.

"She was different though. She never gave in to any of 'em. It took her a long time to give in to this 'un. He musta spent a bundle on flowers...sent her a bunch a day—started lookin' like a funeral home 'round here. I believe she really loved 'em. But like I said, she came in cryin' that he'd broken things off.

"A couple weeks later I hear the girls talkin' 'bout December Rose being with child, 'knocked up' they said. I felt sorry for her, but she seemed okay with it. Said she was gonna have the baby of the man she loved whether he wanted her or not. A few months later, she was gone. I don' know whatever happened to her after that."

When Charlie finished, everyone was quiet for a moment. Then Jim said, "Charlie? May I call you that?" Charlie nodded. "Do you know December Rose's real name? Ellie or Elizabeth?"

"No, Sir. Them girls only went by stage names."

Jim asked, "Do you remember what the man looked like? Do you happen to remember who any of December

Rose's friends were, maybe one named Dixie, and where they might be?"

"Well..." He thought about it. "There was a girl named Dixie who was real good friends with December Rose." He paused and frowned. "Last I heard, she was dancin' at Balley's. Not sure whatever happened to her after that, but her real name was Tina. All I remember about the boyfriend was that he was too old for December Rose."

Jim looked at Susan.

"He wasn't just your normal businessman," Charlie continued. "He was somebody big, maybe a politician. What was odd is that he was never alone at first. He was always with another guy, the same one every time. You notice somethin' like that in a place like this because, beg your pardon ma'am, it's not that kinda place, if you get my meaning." He looked Jim in the eye, and Jim nodded.

"Then when he and December Rose got real serious, he started comin' alone and more often. He'd sit in the back and watch the show, then wait for her to be done her shift. He always had flowers for her when she came off the stage. I thought he might be a decent guy, at the time."

Charlie was quiet for a minute. He stared at the silent television and seemed to have forgotten they were there, then he shook his head. "I can't think of nothin' else."

"Would you be able to identify him if you saw a picture?" Jim asked.

Charlie thought about it for what seemed an eternity and shook his head. "No sir, I don' believe I could. You see, my eyesight was never too good, but I always got by. Now I can hardly see to walk down the street. That's why Mr. Morgan lets me live here. That picture you got there of December Rose, that's easy for me. I knowed her for a long time. And I remember what she wore in the shows. But a man's face who I only saw in the dark theater? Naw, I wouldn' even be able to tell you if I saw him yesterday."

"Mr. Morgan, one more thing," Jim said. "You said Dixie's real name is Tina. Do you know December Rose's name?"

Charlie shook his head. "I'm sorry. Tina's the only name I know, and I only know that cause she came back here once, to see one o' the other girls. She told me I could call her Tina."

Jim and Susan stood up to leave. Susan reached for Charlie's hand and held it tight. "I can't thank you enough for your help, Charlie."

"Aw, it's my pleasure, ma'am. I hope you find what you're looking for. December Rose was a real special gal. We all loved her."

⸻ ❦ ⸻

As Jim and Susan were hailing a taxi in Vegas, Seth was checking the records of Gettysburg Hospital in Carroll Valley, Pennsylvania. It was there that he found what he'd been looking for—a woman had given birth to a baby girl by cesarean section on October 20, 2008. Her bills to the hospital were paid in full, in cash. Her name and address and the doctor's name were in the file.

⸻ ❦ ⸻

The plane landed in St. Petersburg five minutes earlier than scheduled. Clint and Sam hurried to baggage claim to wait for their guns to be cleared.

"Thank you, officers," the baggage attendant said as he handed them the bag.

"No. Thank *you*," Clint said as he took the bag and put away his fraudulent badge. "Could you please tell us where the car rentals are?"

After getting the car and consulting a map, they headed toward Clearwater.

CHAPTER TWENTY-EIGHT

After

In the cab, on the way to Bally's, Susan's phone rang. She pulled out her iPad and took notes while she listened. Jim leaned toward her and read what she was typing. When she hung up, she smiled triumphantly at Jim.

"He did it. Seth has the name of the hospital and the doctor. The mother's name was Tina Smith. Not much to go on there."

"That's great news," Jim said. "Now we know where December Rose went when she left Vegas.

"And used her best friend's name at the hospital. I'm betting Tina knew exactly what was going on and who the father is."

They arrived at Bally's and inquired about a dancer named Dixie.

"There's no dancer named Dixie here," a young waiter answered when Jim showed him his badge and began to ask questions.

"We were told Dixie was a dancer here." The waiter started to walk away, but Jim hurried to catch him. "Wait, what about Tina? Is there a dancer here by that name?"

The waiter laughed in surprise. "Tina? You mean Ms. Marshall? Maybe she was a dancer in her younger days," he laughed at the absurdity of it. "Over there." He nodded to the stage wing, his hands busy with a tray of drinks in one hand and a breadbasket in the other.

Jim and Susan exchanged a look. They located the door to the wing, and Jim showed his badge to the bodyguard at the entrance to the backstage area.

"Is Ms. Marshall back here? We just need to ask her a few questions," Jim said with authority.

The man—at least 200 pounds of solid muscle with several gold chains and a large hoop earring adorning his shaved head—let them through the door.

"Excuse me, nobody is allowed back here but performers." The voice came from a beautiful woman in her late thirties. She had an air of confidence and self-assuredness that only comes with years of being on stage. She had shoulder length, wavy brown hair, expensive clothes, and lots of jewelry.

"Are you Tina?" Susan asked.

"Who wants to know?" she asked, not with attitude but with genuine curiosity, her right eyebrow arching. Jim held up his badge.

"Jim Russell, FBI. We'd like to talk to you in private about a friend of yours, December Rose, maybe Ellie or Elizabeth something."

"Elaine? Is she... It's been so long. Has something..."

"Elaine? Cassie said her name was Ellie, short for Elizabeth."

Tina shook her head. "Her name was Elaine. Though I think she went by Ellie after she left town."

"I'm sorry, Ms. Marshall," Jim said. "Elaine is dead."

Tina put her hand to her chest and sat on an old, wooden bench in the hallway. "I knew something must've happened. I just knew it." She leaned her head back onto the wall and began to cry, her tears mapping trails through her foundation. Jim and Susan gave her a moment. She shook her head and dabbed her cheeks with a tissue Jim magically produced from his pocket. "After she left town, we kept in touch for a long time, but one day she just disappeared." She sniffled and let out a shaky breath. She closed her eyes and continued to speak.

"I kept trying for a long time, but she was just gone." She looked at Susan. "I tried calling her, but the number was disconnected. I always knew something happened to her." Susan sat next to Tina on the bench and put her arm around her. "She was my best friend. She would never, ever just stop writing or answering my calls." Tina took a deep breath. "What happened?"

Tina looked up at Jim. Her mascara ran through her tear tracks, and her lipstick was slightly smudged, but Susan thought she was still beautiful. Her heart broke for this woman.

"A car accident," Jim told her. "About two years ago."

Tina nodded. "That would've been about the time she disappeared. I'd just started working here. But...why are you here? What does this have to do with me?" Tina looked confused, but Jim didn't provide any information.

"Can you tell us anything about the man who fathered her child?'

"Children, you mean. She had two of them, girls, Cassandra and Elizabeth." A look of horror crossed Tina's face. "Are they okay?" She started ringing her hands.

Showgirls pranced off the stage and looked at the trio, but Tina ignored them. A stage manager ushered them away.

"Yes, they're fine," Jim said, focused only on Tina. "Did the same man father both girls?"

"Ab-so-lutely." She drew out the syllable and bobbed her head a few times. "Elaine was head over heels in love with him. There was no other man for her, ever."

"We had the impression he was married or something." Jim baited her, and she took the hook.

"Oh, he was, but he took very good care of Elaine. He showered her with gifts, took her to the best places, made her feel like a queen. When he broke it off with her, I told her she was too good for him. She didn't want to hear it. She cried for a day or two, but she was always sure he was going to come back to her. Several months later, he did. When he saw that she was pregnant, he took her to a little town in Pennsylvania, near Gettysburg. That's where she was living when she had the girls." Tina confirmed what Seth had found.

"So, she was pregnant with Cassie, not Ellie," Susan said.

"Not yet," Tina confirmed.

"Tina, this is very important," Jim said. "Do you know the name of the man she was in love with?"

"Of course, I do. We had no secrets from each other."

Susan felt gooseflesh run up and down her arms. This was the moment they'd been waiting for.

Susan thought Tina would continue, but she didn't.

"Tina," Jim said, "could you please tell us his name or identify his picture?"

"I promised her I'd never tell anyone." Tina looked around nervously. "But I guess since she's dead..."

Once Susan confirmed the girls were from Pennsylvania, Lank looked up the address of a home in that state owned by Moore. He then used a national database to pull up the names of the other people on the street. A Mrs. Dorothy Johnson lived next door. Lank easily found her number.

He dialed the number and counted six rings. It appeared Mrs. Johnson might not be home, but she picked up on the seventh ring.

"Hello?" she said in an elderly voice.

"Mrs. Dorothy Johnson?"

"Yes. May I help you?"

"I hope so Ma'am. My name is Abe Lankton, and I'm with the Lakespring Police Department in Maryland. Do you know two little girls by the names of Cassie and Ellie, or Cassandra and Elizabeth?"

"Why, yes, I do, or I used to." She answered without hesitation. "They used to live next door, but I haven't seen them in a couple years. Are they all right? Has something happened to them?"

"Yes, they're fine, Ma'am. But there's been a problem with their foster family, and the children believe they may have a relative who could take them in, an uncle perhaps."

"Humph." Mrs. Johnson didn't sound pleased. "He's no uncle, I guarantee that. I'd bet my bingo money what he and Elaine were doing together wasn't what sisters and brothers do. Not decent ones anyway."

"So, you don't think he's related to Cassie and Ellie?"

"I didn't say that," she retorted. "I'm sure he's their relative, but he's no uncle."

"Are you saying you believe the man to be their father?" Lank confirmed.

"You bet that's what I'm saying. That no good politician. They're all the same. Take what they want without caring about—" Lank cut her off.

"Mrs. Johnson, do you know who the man is?"

"Of course, I do. We get Baltimore news here. I see him on TV all the time."

<hr>

A completely sober Mike Russell burst into Agent Morelli's office. Russell was dressed in clothes resembling a police uniform and looked ready to report to work. He informed Morelli there were a dozen men willing to testify that Moore and Simpson spoke to them about hiring domestic workers.

The Maryland U.S. Attorney's Office, the Department of Justice, and the Maryland Port Authority were brought in on the case. A relative newcomer to the office, the Attorney General was shocked by the extent to which domestic workers were being trafficked into the country through the Baltimore Harbor. His office was working with the State Legislature to pass laws dealing with sex trafficking, and he was anxious to use Moore and Simpson as examples of why the laws needed to include all forms of trafficking.

Mike couldn't wait to see those guys in handcuffs. It was what Officer Russell had been working toward for years.

Susan called her mother from the tarmac. It was shortly before three in the morning in Florida. "Where are you?"

"We're at a hotel in South Carolina," her mother answered. "Is it still safe to head home?"

"I think so. We're on the plane, getting ready to take off. We'll be in Baltimore in a few hours. He's going to be arrested when we get there, but hold tight until we know whoever is after the girls is in custody."

"Will do," her mother said. "I love you, Honey. Please, be careful."

Susan turned off the phone as the flight attendant made the announcement to prepare for takeoff. She and Jim were both excited and apprehensive at the same time. He wrapped his arms around her and pulled her close. Her head was pounding, but she felt hopeful for the first time in days. Shortly after takeoff, she closed her eyes and started to nod off for one more restless nap amid several days of little sleep.

"We'll all be home soon." She heard Jim whisper as he kissed the top of her head. "You, me, Cassie, and Ellie will be together. It's almost over."

Susan nodded sleepily.

"I love you," Jim said into her hair.

Susan smiled and nestled closer to Jim.

⚬

Jim's knee bounced nervously as they neared Baltimore. He felt guilty for keeping information from Susan, but he reasoned with himself that he didn't actually have anything to tell her. It was more of a gut instinct, something that had been bothering him, but he was worried Susan wouldn't agree with him.

Even Lank questioned his motives when Jim asked him to look into Seth Winfield. There was something off about that guy, but Jim couldn't put his finger on it. When Lank asked Jim if this had to do with his feelings for Susan, Jim balked at the idea, but he had to wonder about that himself.

Was he jealous? Well, of course he was. Was he over-thinking their relationship? Probably. Did that mean he was wrong about Winfield. Not at all. Whatever it was that bothered Jim about the guy was going to have to wait until they got back to Maryland.

Before

When Simpson was elected Mayor of Baltimore, easily defeating his opponent, he hadn't been to Vegas for eight months. The election was over, and the holidays were approaching. He was longing to see Elaine and told Alex to arrange a short getaway. Alex was not happy.

Denny flew out to Vegas and was surprised to discover Elaine was no longer performing at Club Nine. He drove to her condo. When a very pregnant Elaine opened the door, Denny encircled her with his arms. She had never looked more beautiful or more desirable.

Denny hatched a plan to keep Elaine's whereabouts a secret from everyone—Alex, Denny's wife, June, and their other children. He moved Elaine from Nevada to Pennsylvania. He loved to ski, but June did not. He settled Elaine in a small house he owned near a ski resort and found her a job in a salon. The house was in the company's name as a tax write-off, and Denny took his kids there to go skiing when they were young.

Elaine had no desire to return to the stage, especially after she gave birth to Cassie. Denny and the baby became her life, and she ached for a full-time husband and father for her daughter. By the time Simpson was running for his second term as mayor, he had two small daughters with Elaine and two grown sons by June.

A distraught Denny went to Alex, just before the election, with the news that Elaine had been killed in an automobile accident, and he had two small daughters who were dependent upon him.

"You have to help me, Alex. You're my best friend. I loved her, really loved her. I don't know how I can go on without her. I don't really know the girls. I visited them, and I gave them presents, but it was really Elaine I loved. They don't even know I'm their father. I want to provide for them, but I can't take care of them, and I can't look at them without seeing her. And June will go ballistic. And my sons, I don't know what this would do to them." Simpson collapsed into a chair sobbing.

After the yelling and accusations, Alex came up with a plan. "We'll take the girls. Penny will love having them around, and you'll have to see them all the time, and think of your precious showgirl." Alex laughed as he walked out and slammed the door, ending a thirty-year friendship.

A once confident and powerful mayor sank to his knees and cried like a baby. For the first time, he resented the girls he once loved.

CHAPTER TWENTY-NINE

After

Clint and Sam found Mattie's house within twenty minutes of leaving the airport. They could almost smell the money they were about to make.

Unfortunately for them, the house was empty. There was no sign anyone had been there in a long time. The rooms were clean, the refrigerator was empty, and the power had been shut off at the main box.

If they had checked the garage any closer, they would have seen a fresh oil spot from Mattie's car. If they had looked in the trashcans, they would've found the evidence of meals that had been eaten in Mattie's house over the past two days. If they had gone to the house next door, they might have gotten a glimpse of Mattie, sitting with her friends in their kitchen—the very friends who had spent the night helping Ida, Patrick, and Mattie pull off the set-up.

But they were in a hurry and going on days of no sleep and endless frustration and only saw what they wanted to see. Their prey was not there and, they supposed, never had been. Clint's instincts weren't as good as he thought they were.

The local FBI agents closed in on the house. They had the men in their sights. It was only a short time before the pair of hit men was in custody.

Just after dawn, the Lakespring authorities pulled Eddie Reynolds' car from Liberty Lake on the Baltimore and Carroll County border. Eddie's body was in the back seat, a bullet hole in his gut. His wound was bad, and would have required extensive surgery, but may not have been life-threatening. Eddie's gun was in the car with him.

Inside the glove box was a Ziploc bag which held a list of every transgression Eddie knew Moore and Simpson had committed. With it, was a letter to his wife, Kayla, saying if anything happened to him, he hoped she knew how much he loved her.

Morelli and his men waited for the signal outside Baltimore City Hall. They were ready to go in but promised Jim they would wait for him. They weren't in a hurry. The girls were safe. Agents in Florida had the hitmen in custody, though the men weren't talking. Jim and Susan were on the way from the airport. And the mayor sat in his office, still thinking he owned and ruled the world.

Nobody notified the Baltimore City police, knowing word would get back to the mayor before they were even in the door. They didn't have agents surrounding the building. As far as everyone outside the investigation was concerned, Moore died of a heart attack while his wife was out of town. The mayor was working, despite his friend's death, and presumably had no reason to fear his world was about to come crashing down.

When Lank pulled up behind Morelli, after picking up Jim and Susan from the airport, the agent got out of his idling car, and the men went into position. On the way over, Lank filled Jim and Susan in on everything they'd discovered, including Reynolds' car. Lank told them of the coroner's assessment that Reynolds might have lived if he'd been taken to the hospital. Toss up another ruined life, and untimely death, to Simpson and Moore.

"Oh, and that other thing you asked me about," Lank began.

"You can fill me in later," Jim said as the came to a stop in front of the building."

"I really think you need to know—"

"Later," Jim said before opening the car door.

Lank shrugged, stepped out of the car, and walked over to Morelli.

"Wait for us out here," Jim told Susan. "I love you." He kissed her before opening the door.

"I love you, too, Jim. Be careful in there."

Susan watched as Jim joined Lank and Morelli on the sidewalk. They were ready to go in.

When they entered the mayor's office, his secretary told them she needed to announce them. They assured her they could announce themselves.

"You're under arrest, Dennis Simpson," Jim said, opening the door to the Baltimore City mayor's office, "for the attempted murders of Cassandra and Elizabeth Simpson, conspiracy to commit murder, accessory to murder, falsifying documents, illegal use of campaign funds, human trafficking, and tax fraud, to start."

Mayor Simpson held up his hands and smiled. "Welcome, gentlemen. I've been expecting you."

Susan did as Jim said and waited in the car. A couple minutes after the team went into City Hall, a knock on the window startled her.

She was shocked to see Seth standing on the sidewalk. She rolled down the window, a smile replacing her surprised expression. "Seth! What are you doing here?"

"I didn't want to miss the excitement," he told her. "I flew out as soon as I could. Come on, you don't want to miss the big finale, do you?"

"I don't understand," she said, opening the door. "You hardly know any of us. Why would you come here?"

"I've gotten to know you all pretty well," Seth said. "I feel like I've known Cassie and Ellie their whole lives. Come on. It's time to go in."

"I'm not supposed to go in," Susan protested. "Only the agents went in. I was told to stay here."

"Come on, Susan. Jim called. They've got him. He said for us to go up."

"Jim called you? Why didn't he call me? I don't understand."

Something's wrong. Why would Seth care about this?

A chill ran down her spine. What did she know about Seth anyway?

The man Susan now realized was a complete stranger grabbed her arm and pulled her from the car.

"Seth, let go." Susan tried to break his grip, but he was stronger than he appeared.

"We have to hurry. Come on."

Seth pulled Susan into City Hall through a back door.

"Where are we going? Don't all visitors have to go in through security at the main entrance?" Susan's unease was growing by the minute.

"Usually, but Jim told me to go this way."

Susan's senses heightened. She was certain Jim would not call Seth before he called her. He didn't know the man at all, and how would he have gotten Seth's number?

Susan pulled her arm. "Seth, stop. I'm waiting here. I don't want Jim upset with me." Seth yanked her arm.

"No, you're not," Seth insisted. "I need you to come with me."

"Seth, please let go of me. You're hurting me."

Seth didn't answer. He kept a steel grip on her arm as he pushed the button on the elevator. Susan tried again to wrestle her arm away, but his grasp was too strong. His fingers dug into her flesh.

They stepped into the elevator, and Susan watched, speechless, as they approached the floor on which the mayor was being arrested.

How does he know right where to go? A knot formed in the pit of her stomach.

She suddenly remembered her first impression of Seth—Spider-Man's alter ego, Peter Parker. Who was Seth's alter ego?

"Seth, I thought we were going to stay out of the way," Susan said, her voice shaking. Seth still didn't answer. He was staring straight ahead as the doors opened. He led Susan down the hall and into the outer office of the mayor.

"Mr. Simpson!" The mayor's secretary jumped from her seat, her eyes wide with alarm. "I don't think you should go in there."

"Mr. Simpson?" Susan repeated. "What...?"

"It's Mr. Winfield to you." He sneered at the secretary. "I told you to never call me by that name."

"Seth, what is going on?" Susan was fighting hysteria as Seth pushed their way into the mayor's office.

When the door opened, Jim spun around. "Susan!" The handcuffs he was about to put on the mayor dangled from his hand. "What on earth are you doing here? And why are you with him?"

"Thank you for your visit, gentlemen." Simpson smiled as he reached for the handle of a second door just behind his desk. "Why don't I meet you later to get this straightened out?"

"Not so fast, *Dad*," Seth said, his words dripping with disgust. He slammed the door behind him, still holding onto Susan's arm. He tightened his hold and pulled a gun out of his coat. Holding it to her head, he ordered the men to toss their weapons toward him.

An astonished Jim dropped his gun to the ground and kicked it toward Seth. Morelli and Lank did the same.

"Take it easy, Seth," Jim said. "You don't want to do anything foolish."

"Foolish? You don't want me to do anything foolish?" A sinister laugh escaped Seth's lips. "I've been doing something foolish my entire life, actually looking up to my father, while *he...*" Seth motioned to the mayor with his head, the gun never moving from Susan's cheek, "was making fools of our entire family, especially my mother."

"Now Seth, you don't really mean that." Denny walked around the desk toward his son.

Seth pulled Susan even closer, pressing the gun farther into her temple.

"Stay back, Dad. If you come any closer, I'll kill her and then you."

"Seth, I don't think you really want to kill anyone," Jim said, his eyes never leaving Susan.

"Wanna bet?" Seth roared. "Though I would be awfully sorry to see Susan go. It's *him* I want dead."

"Then why bring her in here at all?" Jim asked as Susan felt the gun press harder into her throbbing head.

"Because she got involved, that's why. She got in the way, so it was only fitting she be here to see how it all plays out. I didn't have any intention of hurting her, but she didn't want to come, so I had to use alternate persuasion techniques."

"Seth, if you wanted me dead, then why did you call to warn me they were coming? Why lead me to believe you were going to come up with a plan for my escape?" Denny asked his son.

"Because I wanted to be the one to expose you, to show you what it feels like to be betrayed by someone you love and trust. I wanted to let all these people know what kind of man you are, how you screwed around on my mother throughout your entire marriage, how you brought your own illegitimate daughters to live not sixty miles from your real family. You never even tried to hide your affairs from us; it was only your precious public image you were concerned with. Well, how's your image going to fare now, Dad?"

"Seth, was it you after Cassie and Ellie this whole time?" Susan asked, recoiling at the thought of Seth eating at their table.

"Of course, it was. And you led me right to them without either of us even knowing it. Imagine my surprise when I found your phone number on Supercop's caller ID." Susan saw Jim flinch. "When I first discovered his notes, I figured it was a coincidence. There had to be several Susans in Lakespring. Then I saw your name in his files and your number on the call list. How stupid is that? He didn't even clear the calls, and in trying to play the big hero, he led me right to you."

The anguish on Jim's face made Susan's heart wrench. *It's not your fault*, she tried to tell him telepathically.

"I even called you on my cell from his house then and there to ask if we could get together the following night. I had to see for myself if you really had my so-called sisters. I would've taken care of them that night, but there was always a cop around. If it weren't for that stupid kid who showed up at your house and tackled me, I could've killed both of 'em before that FBI wanna-be was out of his car. Of course, they're dead now. They were killed early this morning."

Simpson gasped, "No, Seth. What have you done?"

Seth laughed maniacally. "Nothing," he replied. "I didn't have to do a thing. Your *best friend* put out a hit on his own foster children. Imagine my glee when I discovered that little tidbit."

"Alex?"

"Moore?"

In unison, Denny and Jim exclaimed their disbelief.

"You're all such amateurs!" Seth's laugh deepened. "Your surveillance equipment was a day late and a dollar short. *Uncle Alex* hired the hit after he dumped Eddie's body. He wanted the death to look like an accident, but when he got home, the girls were gone, and he knew what happened. I lost my best friend, Eddie, to you and Alex years ago, and then I lost you to that woman and all those other women, including my *secret* sisters. Now your best friend is dead, and your daughters, and next it will be you."

"How do you know all this?" Jim asked.

"I've had my father's phones bugged ever since he took in the brats."

"But you're wrong, Seth," Morelli said. "We apprehended the men this morning. Everyone was safe by then."

Seth turned to him, the look on his face revealed both shock and dismay that his plan hadn't worked.

"What have you done?" he yelled. "They were supposed to go first!" Seth faltered for just a moment before regaining his composure and pressing the gun harder against Susan's flesh. "Forget them. If they inherit anything, I'll fight it. They have no right to what's mine." He took the gun away and used his shirtsleeve to wipe beads of sweat from his forehead. "Truthfully, it was never about them. It was always about you," he yelled at his father, his hand erratically swinging the gun in the air.

"Seth, what is it you want to happen here?" Morelli addressed him from the other side of the room. Seth looked his way again.

"I. Want. Him. Dead." In an instant, Seth pushed Susan away and turned the gun toward his father.

Jim gave Lank a signal. Lank dove for his gun, and Jim lunged across the desk at Seth, shoving his arm into the air. The gun went off, sending plaster falling from the ceiling. As Susan crumpled to the ground, she glimpsed Simpson reaching for the knob to the conference room door. Morelli jumped across the desk to stop him, but the door slammed in his face. The agent retrieved his gun, threw open the door, and ran after Simpson.

"Freeze!" Lank commanded Seth as the mayor's son struggled to loosen the grip of Jim's hands around his neck. Jim seemed to have no intention of letting go.

"Jim, stop!" Susan screamed, and just before Seth passed out, Jim let go and shoved him to the floor.

"You're lucky *I* don't kill *you* for what you've done to Susan and what you would've allowed Moore to do to Cassie and Ellie." Jim dropped down beside Susan. "Are you all right?" he asked, caressing her face with his hand.

"I'm fine," she said through deep breaths. "I'd just like to get out of here."

Lank read Seth his rights as Jim and Susan headed into the outer office where a great crowd of people had gathered. They held each other close in the staff elevator, avoiding the crowds in the main lobby of the building. When they reached the street, they were accosted by a throng of reporters already on the scene. Jim held up his badge.

"We have no comment at this time." Jim kept walking. "The Lakespring Police Department, in conjunction with the Justice Department and the FBI, will issue a statement when our case is completely wrapped up."

Morelli came toward them from around the side of the building, shaking his head. Simpson had gotten away.

CHAPTER THIRTY

Hours later...

"Let's start at the beginning." Jim sat across the table from Seth in the small, grey interrogation room. His digital recorder sat in the center of the table. He'd had to calm himself down before entering the room. He was enraged at how close this guy was able to get to Susan, and he was even more angry with himself for not investigating Seth as soon as he showed up at Susan's house.

"Did you have anything to do with the death of Elaine Rose Parker?" Jim asked.

"You don't have to answer that," Seth was advised by his family attorney.

"I'll answer anything. I'm glad I did what I did. That woman deserved it."

"Seth, answer the question," Jim said. Lank stood in the corner, observing the exchange.

"Yes, I had something to do with her death. I only wish I'd done it sooner. I should've taken care of her when I first saw her and my father together."

"When was that, Seth?"

"Six years ago, in Gettysburg, Pennsylvania. Eddie and I were there with friends. Eddie had this thing about leaving

Kayla alone with the kids, but we talked him into going skiing. We were on our way to a bar when I looked across the street and saw my father and that floozy coming out of a ritzy restaurant. I was so enamored with my father, I actually believed it was an innocent business dinner. I started to call out to him, but then he put his hand on the small of her back, and she looked at him with such..." Seth's words dripped with revulsion.

"What did you do next, Seth?"

"I started following him when he went out of town. They always met at some restaurant, or bar, or..." His face contorted with anger. "Or hotel. If I had done something sooner, he wouldn't have knocked her up again."

"Did Eddie see them, too?"

"I didn't think so, but yeah, he did. He didn't tell me, the jerk. His precious job was more important to him than telling me what my own father was doing behind my mother's back." He shook his head, and his eyes flashed with hatred. Whether the hatred was directed at Reynolds or Simpson, Jim didn't know. He suspected it was aimed at both.

"You know what kills me the most?" Seth said suddenly. "I spent my whole life looking up to that man. All I ever wanted was to make him see me, who I really was, appreciate what I could become. He thought computers were for nerds, for unpopular geeks who hid behind monitors because they couldn't make friends. He never understood the amount of power you can obtain from the computer. He didn't even get it when I hacked into the high school computer."

"Seth," his attorney spoke up. "Stop talking."

"Don't tell me what to do. I didn't hire you. You're only here because my mother wants you here." Seth tried to stand, redirecting his anger at the lawyer, but the leg irons prevented him from getting up. He shook the table with his leg, attempting to break free. Lank jumped and looked at Jim for direction.

Jim held up his hand, letting Lank know everything was under control.

"Sit down," Jim commanded.

Seth glared at Jim but took his seat. "What do you want to know now?" he growled.

"Why did you kill Elaine? Was it just petty jealousy?"

"Jealousy?" He laughed an evil laugh. "I did it for my mother, for our family. My father..." He spat as though the word left a bad taste in his mouth. "My father wanted the best of both worlds. He had to be taught that life doesn't work like that. I had to show him he couldn't have it both ways."

"Did you tamper with Elaine's brakes yourself?"

"No. I paid someone to do it. Then I hacked into Dad's email and sent a message to her that he wanted to see her. I told her to bring the girls with her, that he missed them." His face contorted with rage. "But the floozy went alone. They should've all been in that car."

"You said you hacked into your father's email. Did you do that often?" Jim asked.

"All the time." Seth smiled. "I read every dirty, disgusting thing they wrote to each other. I bugged their phones, too. I could've killed them all so many times, but I wanted it to look like an accident."

"You broke into Elaine's house?"

"It was my house! I was supposed to be living there! It was his way of bribing me to live close to home—close enough for him to control me but far enough for me to think I wasn't being controlled. I'm not stupid." He was yelling. "I knew what he was trying to do! He bought that for me when I graduated from college, but I told him I didn't want his house. He thought I'd never be successful working with computers, but I knew I could prove him wrong, that computers are the way of the world."

Jim was becoming uncomfortable being in the room with Seth, but he refused to let it show. *He's as crazy as they come, and he needs psychiatric help badly.* Jim wanted the questioning to end.

"Let's get back to recent events. When did you decide to get rid of Elaine and the girls?"

"As soon as I discovered there was another brat on the way. I'd left Maryland, for good as far as I was concerned. I moved as far away as I could, so I'd never have to see my father again. I stopped spying on him, stopped listening in on their calls. I was good at what I did, but I wanted more. I wanted to start my own company. I asked Dad for the money, but he told me no." Seth shook his head in astonishment. "Can you believe it? He told me no. He said if I wanted his money, I'd have to move back here. So he could control me."

"What happened next?"

"I was angry, no furious. I knew he was giving lavish gifts to that woman and her child, their child. He was giving my money to them! I hacked into his financial records and saw the monthly doctor bills to an OB/GYN. I knew that meant one thing. He had another kid on the way."

"So, you decided to end the affair on your own terms."

He yelled an affirmative answer laced with obscenities. "I knew I needed to end it, or he'd give away everything that belonged to us—my mother, my brother, and me. When the girls ended up being alive and went to live with the Moores, I knew my father had come through for them again. I decided getting rid of them wasn't the answer. I had to expose my father to the world." Seth sat back with a smug expression on his face, his breaths coming hard.

"But your plan didn't work, did it?" Jim goaded. "Your father got away."

Instantly, Seth's face changed. His control was gone again. "It's her fault my plan failed, hers and yours."

"Who's?" Jim asked.

"Susan, you idiot." Seth's hands held the edges of the table, his knuckles turning white. "I tried to get Eddie to expose my father's secrets, but he refused. So, I sent a message to his wife telling her he was having an affair. I started researching computer-consulting companies in the Baltimore area. My goal was to get a job with one of them as an excuse to come back here. You can't imagine my joy when I discovered Susan lived right here in Lakespring and was a consultant to Blue Sky Communications in Seattle where I was living. If I could get a job with Blue Sky, I wouldn't even have to move home. I just had to get Susan to fall in love with me so I could come and go as I pleased. And I would have, if you hadn't gotten in the way."

It was all Jim could do not to jump over the desk and strangle Seth with his bare hands. He reminded himself that Seth could never get close to Susan again.

"What happened with Eddie's wife? You said you sent her a letter."

"I led her to the blackmail checks the idiot never cashed and convinced her he was having an affair. She threatened to leave him, and he went after Moore. He knew my father was a yes man, that he only did what Moore instructed him. I never thought Eddie would get killed. That's my only regret." Seth almost looked remorseful.

"How did you know Cassie and Ellie would go to Susan's?" Jim asked the one question he couldn't come up with an answer to.

Seth laughed. "I didn't. I never imagined that in my wildest dreams. It was like divine providence when I found your files and Susan's name on your caller ID. It was better than anything I could've planned."

"Susan found the girls, and Moore's hit man sent them running. You didn't expect that."

"He hired an idiot," Seth hissed. "The man couldn't find his way out of a paper bag. I tracked down Susan and the girls by accident, and he couldn't find them with everything Moore gave him. All I needed to do was follow Moore's sloppy trail which led me to Lynette and to you." He sneered at Jim. "We dated, you know, briefly. She remembered me."

"Did you kill her?"

Seth's attorney began, "Seth don't—"

"She deserved it for helping to cover up the truth about those brats. Pity though. She still looked good after all these years."

Jim was sickened by the thought that Seth had been in Susan's home, but he was even more repulsed by the way Seth referred to her. Jim fought his anger and maintained his demeanor.

"So, you admit to killing her?" Jim asked calmly.

"That will be two counts of murder you've admitted to, Seth. You're digging your own grave," his attorney cautioned.

"Go to hell," Seth told the attorney. "Yes, I admit it. I only wish I'd gotten to those brats."

"But you admitted that tried to kill them the same night you killed their mother. Is that true?"

"Yes, I admit it!"

Seth's lawyer put his hand on his client's shoulder, but Seth shrugged it off.

"Why did you help Susan track down the girls' father?" Jim asked, already knowing the answer.

"Simple," Seth said. "It led you right to my father and all his dirty little secrets. I couldn't wait to see him go down."

Jim ended the questions there. He took his digital recorder straight to the District Attorney, who was watching behind the two-way mirror.

"Good work, Jim," the D.A. told him.

"Thank Susan. We'd never have gotten half of the information if not for her."

Jim took several calming breaths as he left the station. His case was closed, and he couldn't wait to go home to Susan, Cassie, and Ellie and start the rest of his life.

Nine Months Later

Cassie and Ellie cheered as Jim hung the trapeze on the swing set in the backyard. Susan clapped, the sunlight dancing off the ring on her left hand.

"Mommy gets to try it first," Jim called and waved for her to join them.

"Oh no, let the girls go first," Susan protested.

"Come on Mommy," Cassie pleaded. "We want you to go first."

"Yes, Mommy, please go first," Ellie begged as she clapped her hands. As usual, Susan couldn't resist giving in to Ellie's beautiful words.

Susan smiled as she sat on the swing. Jim wrapped his arms around her and pulled her toward him. He nuzzled against Susan's cheek and kissed her before releasing the swing. Susan went flying into the air, laughing as she glided back and forth. She felt as though she could touch the clouds, which made sense because, despite everything she'd been through, Susan had been living on cloud nine since the day Jim asked her to marry him. Once the adoption was finalized, she'd have everything she ever wanted.

EPILOGUE

Mayor Denny (Dennis) Simpson's resignation was received by a Baltimore news station the day after he disappeared through the conference room door. It was sent from Baltimore, but Simpson hadn't been seen in or near the city since the day of his son's arrest. Rumor had it the letter was found in a sealed envelope on his desk within minutes of his escape from the FBI.

Simpson may have been no more than a figurehead, but he isn't stupid. He knows nothing is certain in life, and he planned his escape for a long time. After losing Elaine, Denny knew he'd never spend time in the mountains again, so he chose to live out the rest of his days in the sun. Instead of giving orders to campaign workers, he now gives orders to pretty waitresses in bikinis. He doesn't know it yet, but today, the waitress has something special for him—an invitation to a one-of-a-kind resort, compliments of the FBI.

Seth Winfield Simpson was found to be mentally unstable and is a resident at St. Elizabeth's Mental Hospital outside of Washington, D.C. His mother and brother visit him daily. After petitioning for a court-ordered divorce, Mrs. Simpson moved from Baltimore to the District of

Columbia to be closer to her son. She still blames her ex-husband for her son's breakdown.

Penny Moore moved to New Mexico where she finds the climate more to her liking. She rediscovered God and started volunteering at the church-operated day care where she loves helping the small children. She is enormously happy with her beau, Fred, a widowed grandfather to seven children. She still thinks about her former life, but her faith helps her move past her mistakes. She's happy Cassie and Ellie are in a loving home. She misses them but realizes Susan and Jim can give them so much more than she ever could.

The Hernandez Family remains close to Susan and Jim. Teresa became an American citizen after being released from the hotel room she called home for two years. All the other workers who were brought into the country by Harbor Supply and Distribution were reunited with their families. Gina's cancer remains in remission. Mannie still works in construction, but on a much larger scale. He expanded his own construction company and is working on a big contract with the town of Lakespring.

Officer Abraham Lankton was promoted to detective. He mostly solves small crimes, but he works hard and shows a lot of promise. He transferred to Baltimore City, and recently, he was persuaded to travel to Colorado to investigate a case out there. You can read about Lank's adventures out west in *Summer's Squall*.

Officer Mike Russell was given the distinguished Medal of Valor in honor of his years of service to the town and the department. He hasn't had a drink in two years. But he has been known to spin some mighty incredible yarns when asked by his grandchildren to tell them stories of his glory days. Mike learned that his wife, Jim's mother, died of cancer just a few years after Mike kicked her out of their lives. He rekindled an old friendship with his high school classmate, Mattie Harris, and they correspond on email these days. He often talks about taking a vacation in Clearwater, Florida.

Kayla Reynolds, widow of Eddie Reynolds, returned to her hometown to start over. Her story is told in the Chincoteague Island Trilogy, beginning with *Island of Miracles*.

Ida and Patrick O'Neil never moved to the beach although they continue to vacation there with their family. They keep themselves busy with their four grandchildren.

Susan and Jim married that fall and took a quick honeymoon to Lewes Beach, Delaware. They adopted Cassie and Ellie, and a year later, Susan gave birth to twin boys. Jim was offered and accepted a position at the FBI, teaching state and federal governments how to spot and bring down human trafficking rings. His name pops up in other stories from time to time. Susan uses her computer skills to assist police departments in tracking down missing children. In her spare time, she raises money to help children in the foster care program. Jim and Susan are firm believers everyone needs *a place to call home*.

Amy Schisler is an bestselling novelist author, spiritual writer, blogger, speaker, reader, and avid traveler. She's published three children's books and numerous novels, including the award-winning *Chincoteague Island Trilogy* (where Kayla Reynolds and her sons can be found) and *Summer's Squall* (featuring Abe Lankton). Born in Southern Maryland, Amy holds a master of Library and Information Science. A former librarian, she lives a busy life on the Eastern Shore of Maryland with her husband, Ken. She can typically be found on a boat, hiking, or spending time with her daughters and grandchildren.

The recipient of numerous national literary awards, including the Illumination, Independent Publisher Book, International Digital, Eric Hoffer, and the Golden Quill Awards and honors from the Catholic Press Association, Amy's writing has been hailed "a verbal masterpiece of art" and "Everything you want in a book." Amy's books are available internationally, wherever books are sold, in print and eBook formats.

Visit Amy's Website:

Keep up with Amy and her writing by subscribing to her newsletter:

Follow Amy on social media:

Also by Amy...

Spiritual Books and Bible Studies

Stations of the Cross Meditations for Moms (with Anne Kennedy, Susan Anthony, Chandi Owen, and Wendy Clark)
A Devotional Alphabet
Meet the Saints from A-Z, A Children's Introduction to the Saints
Clothed With Strength and Dignity: Women of the Bible
Sowing the Seeds of Faith: Inspiration from the Garden of Saints
Meditating on the Mysteries of the Rosaries

Praise for Amy's Books

Praise for the Award-Winning, *Chincoteague Island Trilogy*

"A beautiful account of the love and healing support of community!" *Chandi Owen, Author*

"[Amy] draws you in to the lives of her characters...she paints the picture so eloquently it's almost like you are there. *Cindy, Amazon*

"I love Amy Schisler's books. I cried tears of both sadness and joy while reading this. I read this book in a day!" *Mitzi Mead, Goodreads*

"A joy to read...The author makes the book come to life." *Ann, Amazon*

Praise for *The Buffalo Springs Series*

"Another one of Schisler's books that I just couldn't put down. I don't want to give anything away but from the very beginning you find yourself holding your breath." *Elizabeth, Amazon*

"Schisler's ability to write complex flawed characters, and the deeper themes of grief, depression, the search for a home–both physical and spiritual–make this a much more poignant and satisfying experience than you might expect." *A.R.K Watson, Catholic Reads*

Praise for Award-Winning, *Whispering Vines*

"The heartbreaking, endearing, charming, and romantic scenes will surely inveigle you to keep reading." *Serious Reading Book Review*

"Schisler's writing is a verbal masterpiece of art." *Alexa Jacobs, Author & Past President of Maryland Romance Writers*

1. What are your thoughts about the title of the book? What would you have named the book?

2. Susan O'Neil displays both confidence and insecurity. What qualities most endear her to the reader? How do we identify with her?

3. Rekindling a high school romance is a fantasy of many gown women. Why do you believe Susan and Jim's rekindled romance works, both as literature and realistically?

4. What scene was the most pivotal of the book? How do you believe the book would have been different if this scene had not taken place?

5. What surprised you the most about the story?

6. Were there any moments where you disagreed with the characters' choices? What would you have done differently?

7. How do you think the issue of human trafficking was handled in the book?

8. Did you think the ending was appropriate? How would you have liked the ending to go?

9. How have the characters changed by the end of the book?

10. Are there any books that you would compare this one to? How does this book hold up to them?